# RETURN OF THE QUEEN

# RETURN OF THE QUEEN

## THE KURTHERIAN ENDGAME™ BOOK EIGHT

MICHAEL ANDERLE

DISRUPTIVE IMAGINATION®

Copyright © 2020 Michael Anderle
Cover by Andrew Dobell, www.creativeedgestudios.co.uk
Cover copyright © LMBPN Publishing
Interior Images by Eric Quigley
Interior Images © LMBPN Publishing
This book is a Michael Anderle Production

LMBPN Publishing
PMB 196, 2540 South Maryland Pkwy
Las Vegas, NV 89109

First US edition, April 2020
Version 1.01, April 2020
eBook ISBN: 978-1-64202-831-7
Print ISBN: 978-1-64202-832-4

**Thanks to our Beta Readers:**
Timothy Cox (the myth)
Diane Velasquez (the legend)
Dorene A. Johnson, USN, Ret.
Tom Dickerson (in the way of Life)

**Thanks to the JIT Readers**
Nicole Emens
Rachel Beckford
Diane L. Smith
James Caplan
Jackey Hankard-Brodie
Peter Manis
Micky Cocker
Veronica Stephan-Miller
Deb Mader
Charles Tillman
Kelly O'Donnell
Dorothy Lloyd
Larry Omans
Dave Hicks
Jeff Goode
Jeff Eaton

*If I've missed anyone, please let me know!*

**Editor**
Lynne Stiegler

*Thank you for continuing to read our adventures with Bethany Anne. As you can tell, the Federation is going to have to come to grips with the Empress being 'just around the block.' Since there is a greater evil at their doorsteps, I think they will get over it.*

*For now.*

*If not, she always has her size sevens to ...*

# CHAPTER ONE

**Devon, QSD** *Baba Yaga*

Bethany Anne woke up. Her eyes snapped open, the edge of her bed feeling far too close to the precipice of the nightmare that had shattered her consciousness into action. She shifted to free herself from the tangle of sheets and found herself facing Michael, whose focus was on her. "Sorry I woke you."

Michael brushed Bethany Anne's hair out of her eyes, his expression full of concern. "I was just about to wake you. Another nightmare?"

The red light in Bethany Anne's eyes faded, along with her anger at feeling vulnerable. "I'm fine. It was just a dream."

"Some dream," he muttered, but the sound barely went past her ears. "You were pulling on the Etheric."

Bethany Anne groaned inwardly. "Then it's just as well that I woke up." She rolled across the mattress and tucked herself into Michael's arms. "At least I didn't destroy the bed this time."

They lay there in quiet contentment for a moment before Michael spoke again. "You keep having these 'dreams.' Are we certain they're just nightmares and not Gödel's latest attempt to weaken you?"

Bethany Anne hadn't considered the possibility. She searched her mind for anything that shouldn't be there but found nothing out of place. "You think she's fucking with me?"

Michael's mouth drew tight. "It's a possibility. You never did that much work on strengthening your mental capability."

Bethany Anne turned over and settled into a comfortable position. "Why would I, when the only one who could break into my mind is you?"

"So you thought," Michael murmured. "Perhaps TOM isn't the only one who needs better protection against mental attacks."

Bethany Anne sighed. "Well, that's just fucking stellar. As if I'm not fighting enough battles, now I have to check myself while I sleep."

"You can have ADAM monitor your brain activity if you have another nightmare," Michael suggested.

Bethany Anne shook her head and got out of bed. "It's nearly morning." She slipped on her robe and headed for the bathroom. "Harkkat is due to arrive in a few hours."

Michael rolled his eyes. "You think messing with him is a fitting punishment for the things he's done? I don't know why you didn't get rid of the problem while you had the opportunity."

"Because I'm not a bloodthirsty tyrant?" Bethany Anne called over her shoulder.

"Maybe not on Thursdays," Michael murmured, a small smile appearing briefly before his seriousness returned. "He'll turn traitor the first opportunity he gets, just wait and see."

Bethany Anne paused at the door. "I don't know about that. It appears he's had an epiphany. Dad told me he's been looking to make amends for his crimes beyond what his sentence requires. He gave his remaining fortune to the families of those who died at the mining outpost."

Michael knew fortunes could be made and remade when lives spanned centuries. "Do you believe his repentance is real?" he asked, not bothering to hide his skepticism.

Bethany Anne shrugged. "It doesn't matter right now. I had to think about it for a while, but his skills are too valuable to lose. If he's honestly resolved to do good, I'm prepared to give him a chance." She smiled, but the warmth went nowhere near her eyes. "On a very tight leash, of course."

"Of course," Michael replied with a frown.

Bethany Anne noticed a message from John. She skimmed it, then looked at Michael in surprise. "The *Reynolds* just Gated into High Tortuga. It appears he picked up a crew while he was out searching for Kurtherians."

"Did he find any?" Michael asked as she disappeared into the bathroom.

Bethany Anne turned on the shower and waited for a moment for the nozzles to gift her with steaming water before stepping into the streams. "John didn't say. I guess I'll find out when I get there."

"I'll keep on top of preparations here," Michael told her. "We won't fall behind schedule for departure."

Bethany Anne emerged from the bathroom a few minutes later. She passed up the ribboned box with her Louboutins and grabbed her boots from the closet before dressing in her light armor. "For once, I'm less concerned about the timeframe and more concerned all the pieces are in place." She pulled her boots on while she ordered the many moving parts of Operation Security Blanket in her mind. "We made it through organizing the delivery of supplies from all over the Federation. We have hundreds of technical personnel waiting for the call to board the *Baba Yaga*."

Michael nodded. "I understand. We have a fourteen-month journey ahead of us, even with the *Baba Yaga's* Gate drive. We can't leave to take on Gödel until we've protected what we have here."

**Devon, The Hexagon**

Ricole paused the movie and got up from the couch, startling Sabine, Jacqueline, and Mark. "I can't do this anymore."

Sabine looked around. "What's wrong?" she asked.

Ricole spread her arms wide. "*This*. Business. Devon. Sitting around watching movies when there's a war happening out there. I need action," she hissed. "Not *paperwork*."

Jacqueline turned on the couch to face Ricole. "Are you saying you want to leave us?"

Sabine gasped.

"No!" Ricole retorted. "What a dumbass thing to say. I'm just feeling restless. I need a change of direction."

"She's not the only one who's been restless," Mark commented, glancing at Jacqueline. "Maybe it's time we all moved on."

"What's that supposed to mean?" Jacqueline snapped, perhaps a bit more harshly than she intended. "We have a good life here."

Mark held up his hands. "We have a great life. But it's not in your nature to be sedate, and we're not short on time. I think we should hear what Ricole's suggesting before dismissing the idea out of hand."

Ricole didn't actually know what she was suggesting. "Guys, I just want to make a difference. I don't feel like I'm doing everything I can by working to keep people entertained. Bethany Anne has the operational areas of the Hexagon tied up, and my class all volunteered for duty. What am I *giving*?"

"Maintaining morale is important," Sabine argued. "What we do keeps hope fresh in the minds of the people. How many people have we helped with the profits from Hex Industries? Not to mention the speed at which we were able to get the city rebuilt because of our construction connections."

Ricole nodded. "All true, yet we have skills that could be put to use protecting people." She tapped a fingernail on the table. "I didn't set out with dreams of management."

Sabine sighed. "Dammit. Me either. I hear you, really I do. But what about the people here who rely on us? We can't just drop our responsibility to them without a word."

Ricole's lip curled. "As if any of us would do that. I think we should talk to Bethany Anne and Michael."

Jacqueline snickered. "We're going nowhere without permission, right?"

"I was thinking more that we could use some guidance," Ricole replied, shaking her head. "It's a given that we'll face some resistance to the plan from Michael, he likes us safe and sound behind Devon's defenses. But if we decide what we want to do with the Hex Group businesses and make a solid plan, he and Bethany Anne will see we're serious."

Mark's brow furrowed, his eyes distant as he worked through the status of their assets. "Considering most of our physical holdings are leased either to Bethany Anne or the Defenders, it shouldn't be too difficult to find a solution for the rest. The Hex Games is easy: we leave it with Eve."

Jacqueline eyed him, the pieces locking into place. "That's actually a good solution."

"I'm not *just* a pretty face, you know." Mark huffed. "Since she developed the system, it's only fair she gets control of it."

Jacqueline jumped to her feet, spitting out her first thoughts. "What if we turned the media channels over to the people?" She waved down the initial reactions of the others. "Seriously, listen. Winstanley would still be in control of what gets broadcast. He can monitor the submissions, and the people would create the content. We get tons of applications every week from people looking to create new shows."

"That's too much to put on a single EI," Sabine countered. "We would have to appoint a regulatory body, which means finding the appropriate people."

"Winstanley can take care of arranging interviews," Jacqueline stated. "But we can't take a vote without Demon."

Sabine nodded. "You can bet she'll be annoyed she missed this conversation. We'd better call her."

She opened a link and added the whole team.

Demon picked up a moment after. *Why are you all calling me at once? Team chats aren't my thing.*

Sabine chuckled. *This is rather important. We're about to vote on whether to leave Devon. You wouldn't want to be left out, would you,* ma chou?

*What do you mean, vote to leave Devon?* Demon demanded. *Where are you all?*

*We're at home,* Jacqueline told her.

*Why would we leave Devon?* Demon asked, curiosity creeping in.

*For an adventure,* Ricole replied. *To fight.*

Demon was quiet for a moment. *Will you all take care of the boring part?*

*Of course, silly cat,* Sabine told her.

*Then I vote for the adventure.* Demon dropped the link without another word.

Mark grinned, rubbing his hands together. "I guess we're pulling up stakes."

Sabine grabbed her jacket. "I have to go talk to Tim."

"It's a shame he's tied to the *Guardian*," Jacqueline sympathized.

Sabine smiled. "He'll understand."

Ricole pulled up a sales board on the wallscreen as the door closed behind Sabine. "I was thinking we should start looking for a ship."

Mark flopped back onto the couch. "I should help."

Jacqueline rolled her eyes as she headed for Network Command. "Of course you think that. I'm going to help Winstanley get started on the want ads."

## Devon, First City, Federation Consulate

Tabitha was waiting when the Federation ship touched down on the landing pad on the roof of the building.

She stood with her arms folded as the new consul was escorted from the ship in cuffs. "Well, if it isn't the nominee for the Most Upstanding Politician of the Year award." She nodded a greeting at the two guards in turn. "Simmons, Followill."

Harkkat sucked in a breath at the sight of Tabitha and backed up on the ramp, causing his guards to tighten their grips on his arms as they propelled him toward her.

"He's all yours," Simmons told Tabitha, handing the disgraced former trade secretary over to her without ceremony. "Fucking nightmare didn't shut his damn mouth all the way here."

Harkkat rubbed his wrists as Followill released him from his cuffs.

Tabitha's grin widened. "Oh, I know how chatty our friend Harkkat is. Hold him for me, please." She unclipped the handheld subdermal injector unit she'd brought from her belt and pressed it to the base of Harkkat's skull. "Stay still," she warned.

Harkkat froze as he felt a sharp sting. "What was that?"

Tabitha grinned. "Come on, this isn't your first rodeo. That was the neural chip Bethany Anne ordered you to be fitted with before you set foot on Devon. It's there to track your location and to monitor your use of technology and your communications."

"Communications?" Harkkat repeated like the word was alien. "I thought I'd be on lockdown inside the consulate."

Tabitha snorted and waved to indicate he should follow her to the door into the building. "You are not a prisoner, but consider yourself on parole until you can prove you've seen the error of your ways."

"I've already seen the error of my ways!" Harkkat protested, ducking as the guards' ship buzzed them on its ascent. He ignored Tabitha's skeptical look. "I swear! Look, I was greedy, and all kinds of stupid. I know that now. I've had months in that cell with nothing to do but think about how my choices led to people dying. I'm a different Leath."

Tabitha chuckled, almost believing him. "Yeah, we'll see. You might find you're grateful for Big Brother watching if a redemption arc is really your jam." She opened the door and motioned for Harkkat to go ahead of her into the stairwell.

"I don't get it," Harkkat admitted.

Tabitha shooed Harkkat to hurry him up. "Like I said, you're *not* a prisoner, dumbass. You'll be provided a salary and quarters as part of your contract. This city can be tempting for lowlifes. We don't want you falling off the wagon, right?"

Harkkat lowered his eyes. "It's more than I deserve." For once, he wasn't lying. He knew what he was, and by all rights, he should *not* be getting this opportunity to make amends.

"Don't get sentimental," Tabitha told him. "Bethany Anne is merciful, but all she's given you is a rope. You can use it to climb out of the hole you're in, or you can hang yourself with it."

She activated the door mechanism at the bottom of the stairs with a thought and sent Harkkat ahead of her as they entered the building. "Turn right. You should know that the law is simpler on Devon than it is in the Federation."

"What do you mean?" Harkkat asked uncertainly. "The law is the law, laid down by the Queen."

Tabitha shook her head. "This is the frontier, Harkkat. There is no penal system here. You do right, or you die."

Harkkat stopped in his tracks. "What happens if I don't take the contract?" he asked, needing to know the answer although he felt his decision had already been made.

Tabitha lifted a shoulder and indicated a door for Harkkat to walk through. "I get to enjoy watching you tell Bethany Anne. Welcome to your office. This is where you'll keep track of communications between the Interdiction and the Federation. Your other duty is to connect the people to services they need to access."

Harkkat shuddered at the thought of refusing a woman who often filled his nightmares as he made his way inside. "I'm going to do what with who, now?"

Tabitha waved a hand for effect as she connected to the consulate's systems and the lights and brought the computers to life. "You're going to do your job."

Harkkat gripped the desk in shock. "You're right, and it's a job I can do well with resources like this." He glanced around before looking Tabitha in the eye. "But *why* am I being given all of this?"

Tabitha pointed at the chair. "Sit down already. You have what's needed to get your job done to the best of your ability, nothing more. You'll report to Nickie Grimes twice a week about general logistics requirements, and also whenever an urgent request occurs anywhere in the Interdiction."

Harkkat's eyes widened. "Grimes?" He swallowed. "That's a coincidence, right?"

Tabitha shook her head. "I'd advise you not to piss her off. She wasn't named in tribute." She watched the thoughts run across Harkkat's face as they ran through his mind in an uncharacteristic unguarded moment. "Just do your job and keep out of trouble, and you have nothing to worry about."

He nodded, then his politician's mask was back. Harkkat put a hand to his chest and looked Tabitha in the eye. "I *won't* let the Queen down."

Tabitha clapped the Leath on the back and headed for the door. "I hope not, for your sake," she told him. "I'll be back in a few hours to take you to your new home. Get acquainted here, since it's where you'll be spending most of your time. Don't forget, if you need anything, like a food delivery or access to databases, CEREBRO is here to help. I did mention your big brother, right?"

"Ummm." Harkkat's brow creased in confusion. "No?"

Tabitha left the consulate, snickering at Harkkat's bewildered reaction to the EI group's harmonic voice as they introduced themselves. Right on time, Bethany Anne spoke into her mind.

*How did it go down?*

*Exactly as ADAM predicted,* she replied. *Which doesn't*

*answer our question one way or the other. I still think a penal colony would have been a better punishment.*

Bethany Anne snickered. **This amuses me a hell of a lot more. Besides, I want that sneaky shit where I can keep all the eyes on him. Let him get settled and give him a chance to integrate before you test him.**

*Gotcha,* Tabitha confirmed. Something in the transmission caught her attention. *Hey, what are you doing at High Tortuga?*

**How do you know where I— Never mind, ADAM just explained. Reynolds came back from his mission. Which reminds me, I need to book the Hexagon for a welcome reception for his crew. They represent possible allies in the Chain galaxy, and I want to make them feel welcome on Devon when they arrive.**

Tabitha rubbed her hands together. *You mean it's time to arrange the party before we do the impossible thing?*

**Got it in one,** Bethany Anne replied.

# CHAPTER TWO

**High Tortuga, SD *Reynolds***

The Superdreadnought *Reynolds* was at rest.

The bridge was empty of organics, and the splinter personalities the AI Reynolds had created to ease his loneliness before he'd picked up his crew had been transferred to mobile memory cores after their ordeal during the infection.

However, they were still connected to the ship. He had requested time to think about them, despite processing the close calls they'd had in getting back to High Tortuga in time to save his other selves.

He had to come to terms with his independence.

He had been created for war, pure and simple. His entire existence was based on service. But changes in the law back home during his long hunt meant that AIs were now legally recognized and had the right to choose their own paths through life.

He was alive, there was no disputing that. His android

body contained a living, sentient being with thoughts, and hopes, and...dreams?

*What are my dreams?* he mused.

His fingers tapped gently on his armrest. He felt both sides of the contact and got his answer. As much as he was a person, he was also the ship. Whatever course he chose, it would have to be the right choice for both halves of himself, and therefore his crew.

A female voice startled him from behind. "I don't remember having ADAM build a tendency toward sentimentality into your original programming. I like it."

Reynolds jumped to his feet at the sound of Bethany Anne's voice. "My Queen!"

Bethany Anne flashed a grin, her arms spreading, both hands waving. "The one and only." She raised an eyebrow. "You got yourself a body, huh?"

Reynolds discovered that Takal had built his humanoid body with the ability to blush. "It was a tactical decision."

"Well, I don't know if you can put all the blame on me," Tactical commented from his post's speaker. "But it was difficult to get the meatbags to listen when they were busy pointing their guns at the huge-ass ship over their planet."

Bethany Anne paused before sitting down at the tactical station. "Is there something I'm missing?"

"I asked for privacy!" Reynolds thundered. He covered his eyes with a hand when the rest piled on the comm, asking permission to join the audience with Bethany Anne. "Apologies, my Queen." He pointed to the station she was sitting at before pointing elsewhere on what looked like an empty bridge. "Meet Tactical, Comm, Helm, XO, Doc, Navigation, and Engineering."

Bethany Anne followed the greetings around the bridge as each personality introduced themselves. *ADAM,* **would you care to explain?**

**>>Yeah, no. I'll leave Reynolds to talk himself out of this one. There are eight AIs aboard this ship. They arrived in a state, according to the logs, but they are all separate entities and stable now.<<**

Bethany Anne didn't need to be a mathematician to figure out what Reynolds had done. "Good to meet you all." She left the chair, walking over to Reynolds rather than occupy a chair that already had someone in it. "I think I'll stand. So, how did you end up with *seven* new AIs?"

"I created them as a means to avoid issues caused by loneliness," Reynolds told her, sagging in his seat. "I can't explain what it was like to be so alone, Bethany Anne. To face eternities with no company but my own thoughts."

"I understand." Bethany Anne placed a hand on his shoulder. "You're home now."

"Some might say Tactical *is* an issue caused by loneliness," XO quipped, breaking the tension.

"You wound me," Tactical replied. "My Queen, you are more than welcome to sit on my—"

Reynolds shut the potentially offending station down and restricted Tactical to the internal comm. "Proving XO's point," he apologized. "Tactical's an acquired taste."

Bethany Anne raised an eyebrow, wondering how it was that AIs ended up with just as many quirks as the humans who created them. "I suggest he finds a way to make himself more palatable in my presence."

Reynolds got to his feet. "Trust me, you won't hear

another peep out of him. Let me show you what we brought back."

Bethany Anne shook her head. "That can wait. I want to know how your mission went. Did you find any Kurtherians?"

"Yes," Reynolds told her, "and *no*."

Bethany Anne accessed the ship logs and read through everything that Reynolds and his crew had encountered in the Chain galaxy. Her eyes widened in places. "Your crew is really something," she praised, looking at him. "Made up of mostly civilians?"

Reynolds nodded proudly. "My first officer was a cab driver before I recruited her."

Bethany Anne shook her head in wonder before she continued reading. "This is *Star Trek* shit," she murmured. The name "Phraim-'Eh" startled her into skipping ahead to the conclusion and what came after.

"It's dealt with, I promise." Reynolds observed his queen's smile growing as she counted up the crew's good deeds across the far-flung galaxy. "I intend to leave on another tour as soon as my crew has had time to enjoy the liberty they've earned these past few months."

Bethany Anne had forgotten she was reading. She smiled. "You did good work. Both galaxies are better places for your actions."

"We did what we thought was right, and did our best to fix it when we weren't." Reynolds didn't know what else to say.

"That's all you can do," Bethany Anne assured him. "If you hadn't been a good leader, your crew wouldn't have chosen to stay with you. You inspired every one of those people to follow you back here into a war."

Reynolds sobered at the mention of the war. "What's happened since I've been gone?"

Bethany Anne sighed, leaning on the console with her arms folded. "Too much to tell you about. The remaining Kurtherians have come out of hiding at last. They've united under a single leader, and it's been open war for the last couple of years. They want the Federation, but I'm not letting them take a single fucking step in its direction."

"John told me that you and Michael had children," Reynolds commented. "When can I meet the little tikes?"

Bethany Anne gave him a mysterious smile. "Yeah, they're *not* little anymore. I'm glad you're back, Reynolds. The advances in tech have been significant, as well. You're just in time to get a makeover." She paused, then waved a finger in a circle. "The ship part of you, anyway. ADAM, give Reynolds everything he needs to get caught up."

"Everything?" ADAM asked from the speaker.

Bethany Anne nodded. "I have an offer for him, and Reynolds needs to be fully informed before he makes a decision."

Reynolds didn't have time to wonder about ADAM's hesitancy when he received an information dump that almost made him stagger physically with surprise as he processed it. "This...this is *incredible*. What I discovered was barely a drop in the ocean of resources Gödel has. Do you believe Phraim-'Eh to be one of her pawns?"

"Access the file designated 'Galaxy Map,'" Bethany Anne instructed. "You'll see the marker on the Chain galaxy that I'm looking at right now."

Reynolds complied and saw the red marker for the Chain galaxy turn green as ADAM updated the map. "It's a small gain," he commented, the green marker standing out in a sea of red.

Bethany Anne's mouth turned up at the corner. "A gain is a gain, and you made some valuable allies for the Federation while you were at it. Gödel has a nasty surprise coming her way, don't believe differently. However, I can't deliver that until I know that the Federation is going to remain safe in my absence." She waved a hand to forestall the question she saw forming on Reynolds' face. "Access the file designated 'Operation Security Blanket.' I need to visit every outpost, station, and colony on BMW's list to provide the equipment for their defense systems upgrades, as well as the nanocytes we've programmed to give the soldiers a fighting chance against the Ookens."

Reynolds couldn't see how the project was relevant to him. "Why are you telling me all this?" he asked. "My mission is to take out the Kurtherians wherever I find them."

"Not if you accept my offer," Bethany Anne told him. "John explained the change in Federation law, right? Your ship is your property, and you have the same rights as any other captain. If I want your services, you have to agree. I'd like you to accompany the *Baba Yaga* on the upgrade tour."

"Two superdreadnoughts are better than one." XO spoke for the seven AIs bound to the ship. "We're in if you are, Captain."

Reynolds considered the offer for a moment before realizing that he wasn't the captain who made life-changing decisions for his crew. "It's yes from us, but I'll have to get back to you with a final answer." He gave Bethany Anne a grin, pounding one hand into the other. "I'm all for visiting my old stomping grounds, but my crew has a say in the decision."

Bethany Anne chuckled. "That's fine. We have a few weeks before we leave. I'm arranging a dinner to welcome your crew to the Interdiction. We can talk then. In the meantime, take your metal ass to Jean so she can give your systems an overhaul. I know you've got to be tired of that old ESD draining you every time you use it."

Reynolds snickered as he wrapped an arm around Bethany Anne to guide her off the bridge. "I have a few gifts for Jean as well. Do you think she's going to like her new matter transporters?"

Bethany Anne's jaw dropped. "'Matter transporter?' As in, the crew is on the ship in space..." She made the *jjooom* noise. "Then they're on the ground?" He nodded. "Where did you get that?"

Reynolds laughed. "*Star Trek* shit, my Queen. What can I say?"

Bethany Anne raised an eyebrow. "There's only one thing you can say. 'Beam me up, Scotty.'"


**High Tortuga, Space Fleet Base**

Bethany Anne had missed this place. She had much better memories of it than everyone else who had lived here during her admittedly protective phase after the twins had been born. She had it in her mind to meet this former cab driver-turned-first officer Reynolds was so fond of.

AIs didn't bond with just anyone, so she had to be something special.

The call she'd been waiting for halted her search. *Speak to me, Eve. Are my children ready to come out of the Vid-docs?*

*Almost,* Eve informed her. *They are about to enter the penultimate phase of the game, where I must withdraw and allow their decisions to be the program's guide.*

*Eve, I'm not in the mood to play "guess how to kick the AI's annoying ass?" Let's pretend I skipped the Psych 301 class on how to properly educate young humans and just give me the basics of what that means.*

*It means that from this point forward, the program will step up its adaptations to their actions and decisions and push them to their limits. They can handle it,* Eve continued with a hint of pride in her voice. *I have the game running a touch slower than real-time at the moment, and will continue to compensate to sync their progress with the neural integration. It's probable that they will complete the final scenario before the process is complete, but I advise you to return as soon as you are able to do so.*

Bethany Anne's heart flipped in her chest at the thought of seeing the twins. *I'll be back in the next few hours. Do I have that long?*

There was a brief pause before Eve replied, *Yes, that should be fine.*

*Thank you.* Bethany Anne headed for the ship at a run, wishing she had time to configure that communications beam Reynolds had brought back. Then she could have Jean merge it with the transporter technology to make an instantaneous galaxy-to-galaxy transportation beam she could send herself along. Maybe she should have tried harder to persuade Amanda to teach her that Porting trick.

The twins were at the front and center of her mind as she traveled. The trip between High Tortuga and Devon wasn't long, but each second that passed felt like an eternity. She just wanted to hold her children in her arms again.

She met Michael and Eve in the Vid-doc suite. The holoscreen showed the children—adults now—aboard a military transport.

"There are no further updates," Eve told Bethany Anne in greeting. "They are about to face a test of their adherence to duty. This could take a while."

Michael got up from the couch. "In that case, I'll have to come back later." He checked to make sure the feed was accessible to his internal HUD before vanishing into the Etheric.

Bethany Anne hesitated to leave when Alexis and Gabriel were so close to completing the game and making it as adults. However, she was expecting Jean to call soon, and the backlog of tasks was building up with every minute she spent waiting.

Eve came over and took Bethany Anne's hand. "They are doing well," she assured her. "I'll call you when there's news. I know how tight the schedule for departure is."

Bethany Anne nodded, reluctantly dragging her gaze from the holoscreen. "I'm not leaving my children behind for the next fourteen months. The schedule for departure is going to be altered if they're not finished in time."

Eve chuckled at the chance of Jean allowing that to happen after she'd been so pressed to get the ships refitted for the tour. "It won't come to that," she promised. "Now go before you lose the day and are the reason for the schedule malfunction."

## Devon, QSD *Baba Yaga*

Ashur wandered the corridors of the top deck, looking for Bethany Anne. He could easily find his human by asking Izanami, but he preferred to use his nose and retain a bit of mystery.

*Ashur - Image by Eric Quigley*

The trail had led him from the bridge to Bethany Anne's quarters, then to the armory, and now here to the other end of the deck where the twins' quarters were located. He followed the Bethany Anne smell through the lounge and into the study.

She smiled when the door slid open. "Hey, furball. What's up?"

Ashur cocked his head. *What are you doing all the way out here?*

Bethany Anne put the Jinx toy she was holding back on the desk. "I had a little time before my call with Jean is scheduled. I was thinking about how it's going to be when Alexis and Gabriel come out of the Vid-docs."

*That's only natural,* Ashur told her. *You've all made a hard choice. What's brought this on?*

She took a seat at the desk and buried her hand in Ashur's fur. "Eve telling me the program is almost complete. They've changed so much, so fast. Why didn't anyone tell me being a parent mostly consists of being filled with pride in your children's achievements while your heart breaks because they don't need you anymore?"

Ashur pressed his head to Bethany Anne's knee, then looked up and gave her the soulful expression of a dog who'd had experience in the matter. *No one understands it until they go through it. Besides, they will always need you. I just had a grandpup on my ship to prove it.*

Bethany Anne chuckled. "I heard Dokken was coming to visit you and Bellatrix."

*That's what I came to talk to you about,* Ashur told her. *He and Cory headed back to Keeg Station yesterday. Bellatrix and I are leaving to take your message to the Bl'kheth planet.*

Bethany Anne was glad to hear that. "You found an engineer?"

Ashur nodded. *Ronnie persuaded Stevie she needed a break. I didn't want to leave without saying goodbye since you'll be gone by the time I get back.*

"It's a long way to go, even with your Gate drive." Bethany Anne hugged Ashur and got to her feet. "You won't get back much before I do."

Ashur padded after Bethany Anne as she left the twins'

quarters and headed for her ready room. *Considering I have only one goal, to get to Bl'kheth and back, I think I'll be back long before you.*

Bethany Anne chuckled. "When do you leave?"

*Tomorrow,* he replied, wagging his tail as he hurried to keep pace with Bethany Anne. *Why are you in such a rush?*

"I have a call with Jean, remember?" Bethany Anne stopped and laughed. "What am I doing?" She put her hand on Ashur's back and took them the rest of the way through the Etheric.

Ashur chuffed laughter. *That's more like it.*

Bethany Anne raised an eyebrow when Ashur hopped onto the couch and circled before settling. "Make yourself comfortable."

Ashur opened one eye. *I have an idea you're going to be a while.*

Jean's face came up on the wallscreen, diverting Bethany Anne's retort. She took a seat at her desk and smiled at Jean. "Right on time. Where are my ships?"

"It's always 'where are my ships' with you," Jean bitched.

Bethany Anne lifted a shoulder. "Well, the one time I tried starting with the pleasantries, your face went all red, and that vein in your temple started pulsing. I thought your brain was going to explode."

Ashur chuffed again. *I can totally see that happening.*

"Very fucking funny," Jean snarked. "The scout fighters are about ready to be shipped to Devon, and I have ten crates to go with them."

"Thank fuck for that." Bethany Anne relaxed at the knowledge her closest would be protected. "*Ten* crates?"

Jean nodded. "Six for the Bitches, a replacement for

Michael's armor, two for the twins, and a little something for you."

Bethany Anne cocked her head sideways. "Only a *little* something?"

Jean's grin grew wider. "Trust me, it's special." Her demeanor shifted, the easiness replaced by her usual no-nonsense manner. "Everyone but you needs to spend time calibrating their armor. I've never made anything like this before."

Bethany Anne leaned forward, drawn in by curiosity. "How did the testing go with John?"

"He's not done," Jean replied. "He got the call from Barnabas when Reynolds arrived and had to leave for High Tortuga."

Bethany Anne didn't miss the excitement in her voice. "But the initial testing went as expected?"

"And then some." Jean hesitated as she sought an explanation. "It's more than intuitive because of the Bl'kheth mind running the nanocytes."

Ashur lifted his head and wagged his tail. *What, could they take a missile to the chest and be fine?*

Bethany Anne looked at him with amusement. "It's much better than being able to take a missile to the chest. Those nanocytes have some of the most complex programming ADAM and TOM have ever created. You saw the movie *Venom*, right? Imagine armor that works with you at the atomic level."

Ashur's tongue lolled when his jaw dropped.

"It's true," Jean confirmed. "Not only is the armor Etheric-compatible, the nanocytes are fully malleable. 'Alive' is the only word I can use to describe it. The user has to learn to work in symbiosis with the EI we created from the print of Sean's mind. Once they're in sync, the armor will adapt to pretty much anything they ask of it. With the user and Sean working together, it's not just protection. It's an unstoppable *weapon*."

"That's why you're going to destroy any physical record of it being made," Bethany Anne told Jean.

Jean snorted. "I've already had ADAM do it."

Bethany Anne nodded. "Good. As much as I hate to hide your genius, everything we have on the Bl'kheth's genetic properties has to be lost."

She sighed, shaking her head at the unfairness of it all.

*"Forever."*

# CHAPTER THREE

## Beyond Federation Borders, Open Space

With Hirotoshi and the other Tontos tied up in returning a favor for Nickie, Akio was taking the opportunity to work his way through his correspondence while out on patrol.

He sent an encouraging reply to Sabine's latest letter, then began his monthly report to Bethany Anne, his captain's chair turned to a console worn smooth on the edge by decades of Tabitha using it as a footrest.

Akio preferred to type his reports the old-fashioned way, finding that the act of transferring his thoughts from his fingertips to the page gave him the ability to craft them more fully. "Bethany Anne won't be happy to know that there has been an increase in attacks," he commented to Achronyx.

"Tabitha used to leave all the after-action reports to me," Achronyx replied.

Akio chuckled. "And you signed them with her name, no doubt."

"How did you guess?" Achronyx was quiet for a few minutes, the only sound on the bridge Akio's typing. "We have an incoming message from Adelaide."

Akio saved his unfinished report and closed the screen. "Video?"

"Coordinates of an SOS," Achronyx replied. "Preparing to Gate."

Akio turned the captain's chair to face the viewscreen as the *Achronyx* Gated. "What are we up against?"

Achronyx rattled off the information that came in from his scanners when the ship came out in the middle of an Ooken attack. "Three Kurtherian destroyers spread around the planet. The planet has shielding, but it's not going to hold against them for long."

Akio scanned the drones swarming the forcefield. "How many drones?"

"I quit counting those," Achronyx told him. "'Too many' is the only answer I have for you."

Akio was grateful to see that the planetary defenses were deflecting the majority of the drone bombardment, but he knew from experience that the only way to prevent eventual destruction was to take out the destroyers and cut off the Ookens' means of producing more.

"What are your orders, Captain?" Achronyx asked.

Akio took a moment to check their loadout. "We have three Etheric ship-busters, and there are never enough pucks. Prepare them for deployment and activate the debris scoop."

"I've already begun gathering debris to make extra ammunition for the railguns," Achronyx informed him. "We don't want another Garison."

"True. We certainly do not," Akio agreed, the corner of his mouth twitching at the memory of being caught between two Ooken ships. "Not without Nickie here to back us up."

"What we need is permanent backup," Achronyx bitched as the destroyer on the viewscreen churned out another cloud of drones. "I'm seriously considering replicating myself to spread the load. Is there no end to the supply of those creatures?"

"Apparently not," Akio replied drily. "Let's take them out."

"The ship-busters are ready at your command," Achronyx informed Akio a moment later.

"Move them into position," Akio told him.

There was a tense wait while Achronyx maneuvered the missiles through the Etheric, placing them in positions relative to the three destroyers.

"Ready?" Achronyx asked.

"Fire at will," Akio ordered.

Achronyx gave the missiles the instruction to exit the Etheric. A moment later, they nailed their targets, throwing up a halo of light that surrounded the planet.

"He shoots, he scores!" Achronyx cheered, playing crowd noise over the speakers.

"Nice work." Akio chuckled. "Tell Adelaide to send in the cleanup crew."

Achronyx cut the sound effects. "She had them on standby out of the way of the fighting. They'll be here within minutes." He paused before continuing, "The Ookens are getting bolder, Akio. We're out here on the ass-end of the Federation. It won't take a genius to predict the course the tour will take, which leaves us open to attack. Wouldn't you choose a sparsely populated area to sneak your army in?"

Akio sighed. "*Hai.* Four ships are not enough to repel an army if Gödel decides to send one. I cannot wait until my report is due. Call Bethany Anne."

Achronyx searched for Bethany Anne's current location and opened a link to the bridge of the *Baba Yaga.*

Bethany Anne appeared on the screen after a short wait. "Hey, Akio. I wasn't expecting to hear from you for three more days. Is everything okay?"

Akio smiled apologetically. "We have a growing situation out here." He sent her his ship's logs for the previous month. "The attacks are increasing, as is the area they are occurring over. They're trying to wear us thin."

Bethany Anne pressed her lips together. "I knew this was coming. Leave it to me."

Akio nodded. "I appreciate that. I have called on Nickie far too often recently."

Bethany Anne grinned. "I can't imagine she's too put out by that."

Akio shrugged. "I believe she finds the opportunity to live out her Ranger fantasies cathartic. But even with her assistance, it's becoming a full-time effort to keep the Ookens at bay."

Bethany Anne's face softened. "I can't tell you it's not going to get worse when Gödel figures out I'm locking her out of the Federation. Keep holding out. Help is on the way."

Akio returned Bethany Anne's smile. "We understood

the challenges when we took the assignment. *Ad Aeter-nitatem.*"

Bethany Anne's eyes turned moist for a moment before she whispered back, "*Ad Aeternitatem*, my very old friend."

The moment was there, and then it was gone. He got back to business. "Who do you mean to send?"

"That's what I need to figure out," Bethany Anne replied. "I have the Shinigami fleet available, but those ships can't be given to just anyone."

Her eyes became unfocused for a second. "No, wait. Maybe I do." She waved a hand to halt Akio's question. "It will have to be a surprise. I'm going to be late for the tour briefing."

Akio leaned on the console after Bethany Anne cut the link. He stood there staring at the viewscreen for a moment after it went blank.

Achronyx observed the slight tightening of the ancient warrior's spine through the bridge cameras. "What's made you so uptight?"

Akio looked into the camera. "You're a smart AI. Work it out."

Achronyx replayed the call more than two thousand times before he made the connection. "Oh, dear gods, no. *Rookies?*"

## Devon, The Interdiction, QBS *Sayomi*

Reynolds and his core crew were spread out around the *Sayomi's* bridge. Sayomi had declined to put in another appearance after her first contact with Tactical earned him the lockdown Reynolds had promised.

Reynolds shuffled in the pilot's chair as the planet came into view. "So this is Devon." He zoomed in on the battlestation hanging in the void and noted the enormous amount of EI traffic when he tapped the web of signals crisscrossing between the planet and the three rings of defense around it.

"That it is," John agreed. "If you look to your left, we'll be passing the *Baba Yaga* in a few minutes."

Reynolds wasn't the only one who was lost for words when the Queen's superdreadnought came into view on the viewscreen.

Ka'nak leaned over Reynolds' chair. "If you haven't got gun envy right now, I'm gonna have to revoke your man card."

"Oh, I'm envying," Reynolds assured his head of security as he watched a pair of Black Eagles leave the *Baba Yaga* and head for their location. "Not just her guns. She has better shielding, better engines, better armor... I mean, just look at those lines. A ship the size of a large city has no business looking *that* graceful, and yet, there she is."

Jiya and Geroux exchanged amused glances.

"Not to mention her weapons arrays," Reynolds continued, oblivious to his crew's sideways looks.

The *Baba Yaga* was out of sight in the next moment, and they were joined by the Black Eagles for their final approach to First City.

The ground opened up beneath them as they neared the Hexagon, giving the *Sayomi* room to land in a sublevel hangar. No one aboard the *Sayomi* wasted time following the instructions the AI had given them from the screens to debark in their teams through the cargo hatches.

John led Reynolds and his core crew to the Black Eagles, where Bethany Anne and Michael were waiting for them with a group of others who had wanted to welcome the crew.

Sabine, Jacqueline, and Ricole stepped forward to greet the officers of the *Reynolds* with friendly smiles as they arrived, draping a lei over each of them while explaining the custom.

Reynolds noted another, larger group meeting his general crew with a similarly warm welcome. "This is more along the lines of the return I'd imagined," he admitted, seeing Bethany Anne watching him with curiosity.

"Your crew will be taken care of," Bethany Anne told Reynolds, slipping her arm through his to guide him to the private elevator. "We'll meet back up with them in a few hours after they've had time to settle in and enjoy a taste of what Devon has to offer."

"We get stuck in a meeting while the crew gets to party?" Ka'nak complained.

Bethany Anne chuckled. "There will be plenty of time for that. The meeting we're headed to was already scheduled for today, but I would have called one anyway since you're here to attend. It will give you a better understanding of what we're doing."

The elevator took them down, not up as Reynolds had expected.

"This planet's crust is comprised of layers of super-compressed rock sandwiched between softer aggregates," Bethany Anne explained. "It made for good excavating when we were keeping our expansion quiet." She showed them down the corridor and into a large, pleasantly-appointed meeting room.

Reynolds' eyes fell upon Izanami when they entered the room, her red-gold aura sparkling in the ambient lighting as she walked over to Bethany Anne. "Who is this beauty I see before me?" he murmured, struck by the way the light moved around her.

*Quick,* Tactical interjected. *Ask her if she wants to go halves on a bastard.*

*I regret bringing you.* Reynolds double-checked that Tactical was locked down to his cube and bowed deeply to the AI made of light. "It's a pleasure to make your acquaintance, fair lady. My name is Reynolds."

Izanami looked Reynolds' android body over before tilting her chin imperiously. "The pleasure is all yours, I assure you." She returned her attention to Bethany Anne. "If you will excuse me, my Queen, I must return to the *Baba Yaga.*"

Bethany Anne nodded, and Izanami left the meeting room without so much as a backward glance.

Reynolds stared at the aura that remained for a fraction of a second after the AI dematerialized, his hand moving to his chest unnoticed. "Be still, my beating heart."

The crew teased him mercilessly over the comm, all except for Jiya.

*I think she's a tiny bit out of your league, Captain,* she told him.

*Can AIs even have relationships?* Ka'nak asked with curiosity. *I mean, do you have the functionality in that android body?*

Takal, thankfully, declined to answer.

Reynolds clamped down on Tactical. *You dare, and I'll have you reintegrated before you can say—*

*Comes with a full set of moving attachments?* Tactical supplied.

Bethany Anne coughed to cover a laugh, causing Reynolds to wheel and face her. "Please tell me you didn't hear that?"

Bethany Anne tapped her temple with a finger. "ADAM fed me the whole conversation."

Reynolds groaned. "That's it. Tactical. You're dead meat."

Bethany Anne raised an eyebrow. "Um, isn't he part of your personality?"

"Not a part I need," Reynolds grumbled.

*I was trying to make light of the rejection,* Tactical protested. *Lift your spirits in a moment of darkness. What is life without humor, I ask?*

Bethany Anne gestured for the crew to take seats around the table. "Izanami's issue has more to do with my refusal to provide her with yet another body than a personal dislike of you," she assured Reynolds.

John came into the room. "Tabitha's just clearing the consulate. Nickie can't make it; she said you'd know why." He took a seat as Darryl, Scott, Eric, and Gabrielle filed in.

"Queen's Bitches in the house!" Scott whooped, catching Darryl in a headlock while Reynolds' crew watched with the politeness of strangers in somebody's domicile.

Jiya addressed Bethany Anne respectfully. "Your Majesty, may I ask a question?"

Bethany Anne smiled. "You can if you drop the 'Your

Majesty' shit. My name is Bethany Anne. What's your question, Jiya Lemaire?"

*First Officer Jiya Lemaire - Image by Eric Quigley*

Jiya returned Bethany Anne's smile. "I was wondering why your fiercest warriors refer to themselves with what my Earth culture studies have taught me is a derogatory term."

Bethany Anne sat back. "Well, damn. I haven't been

asked that in a while." She gestured to John and the rest. "Why don't you tell our guests the story?"

By the time they were done, the crew was slack-jawed with amazement, and most of the seats around the table had filled up with the rest of the attendees. They conferred with Reynolds while a trio of men was herded into the meeting room by a harassed-looking blonde woman.

Bethany Anne got to her feet and clapped for order after giving the last arrivals—Team BMW, as usual—time to get in and seated. "We have an extra item on the agenda, which I'm going to bump to the start. Reynolds, do you have your crew's decision?"

Reynolds stood and placed his hands on the table. "I have conferred at length with my crew, and we have decided to join you."

Bethany Anne smiled and inclined her head. "That's fantastic. But we do this right."

Reynolds straightened up. "You misunderstand, my Queen. My mission has not ended until there are no Kurtherians left to hunt down. When that is done, I will go after their servants until no trace of their evil cults remains to blight this universe. So no, my mission has not ended. It has expanded."

Michael skimmed the minds of their guests, finding each of them to be honest in their search for Justice. He shared his findings with Bethany Anne.

*Oh, I know they are,* she told him. *I've seen proof of their good hearts, and there's evidence of the strength of their team all over the Chain galaxy.*

Bethany Anne instructed ADAM to take care of the contract and deliver it to Reynolds. "There will always be a place at my side for anyone who wishes to stand for what's right. You are all welcome here." She smiled. "If we're all done making declarations, we have a long list of items to get through before the welcome dinner."

Three hours in, Bethany Anne and Michael suddenly vanished.

"Bethany Anne and Michael send their apologies," ADAM informed them over the speaker. "They had a family issue to take care of, nothing anyone needs to worry about. Bethany Anne suggested that Reynolds and crew take the opportunity to explore the city before they meet you at dinner tonight."

Ka'nak cracked his knuckles, grinning broadly as he looked around the table. "So. Where's good for a fight around here?"

### Devon, The Hexagon, Residential Sublevel One

First Officer Jiya Lemaire, former cab driver and disinherited heiress, paced the dining area as Reynolds read the terms of the contract ADAM had sent for their consideration aloud.

"Let me get this straight," Jiya summarized when he was done. "If we accept, we will be paid—and paid well—to accompany Bethany Anne on a tour of the Federation and various surrounding star systems of which she is the former Empress."

"That is correct," Reynolds confirmed. "Our role will involve assisting the teams installing the defenses Bethany Anne is providing throughout the expanded Interdiction. It will fall to us to defend her technical teams from attacks by anyone who attempts to steal the priceless technology their ships will be carrying."

Jiya held up a hand to indicate she wasn't done. "Not only that, but we are invited to a welcoming reception on the Queen's current home base, which has the same name as this system even though they're in different galaxies."

One of the cubes on the table glowed blue as Navigation piped up. "Don't get me started on that. High Tortuga was the original Devon until Bethany Anne claimed it and wiped it from the maps. Then she set up *this* Devon as a diversion for people looking to do business with the planet formerly known as Devon."

The strains of *Purple Rain* filtered from the speakers, getting absolutely no appreciation from the crew.

John Grimes, however, chuckled.

"Finally!" Reynolds cried jubilantly, pointing at him. "Someone who gets the reference."

"We're getting off the subject," Jiya told him. She looked at each of the core crew in turn. "What's your vote?"

"I vote we find a fight somewhere," Ka'nak supplied, backed up by a hoot of encouragement from Tactical.

"There's probably gonna be a few," John told them. "Not all of the places we've got on the itinerary are going to be happy about us dropping a military outpost on them. Thing is, Bethany Anne hasn't got the luxury of tending to the disgruntled few when Gödel is waiting to swoop in and shit on everyone's happy times."

Jiya's eyes widened as John spoke. "Okay, Captain Doom made his point. There will be fighting, so I'll assume Ka'nak is in. Takal? Geroux? Maddox?"

Reynolds waited nervously, not saying a word in case

he influenced them either way. He wanted more than anything to accept the honor he'd been offered. The tour would include a visit to the *Meredith Reynolds*, something he was unlikely to get another chance to do for a long time.

"I'm game," Takal announced. "I can see that every hand is needed to make this plan work."

"Me too," Geroux agreed. "Put us to work protecting the people of the Federation."

Maddox had tears in his eyes. "I never thought to see this," he managed around his swelling emotions. "You told us about the Federation, but I have to admit I doubted that so many species could live and work in harmony."

"Are you kidding?" Jiya exclaimed. "You did see the effect Reynolds had on our homes, right? And on all those other planets we visited? I can only imagine what effect humans have had."

"So far, my experience of humans has shown me they are fierce and loyal," Maddox agreed. "But the sheer scale of this effort! It's astounding to consider that some of the places on the tour itinerary are a *galaxy* apart."

"That's where we can help," Geroux decided. "This system requires signal boosters to be placed at various points along the way. We can offer to go out in the Pods and lay the buoys."

Takal glanced at John. "How likely is it I'll get a chance to work with the nanocytes?"

John lifted his hands, palms up. "Above my pay grade. You'll have to talk to Bethany Anne."

Takal nodded. "I understand."

"We're being hailed by Fleet Base," Comm announced.

"Onscreen," Reynolds commanded, getting up from the

table to make his way to the living area where the screen was located.

Jean Dukes' head and shoulders filled the screen. "Reynolds, good to see you, but it's John I'm calling for."

Reynolds sighed. "I thought you were calling to tell me you were done with my ship."

Jean shook her head. "Not yet." She smiled when John followed Reynolds into the living area. "There are. Your armor just got to Devon."

John grinned. "That gives everyone some time to get acquainted. What about the scout fighters?"

Jean raised an eyebrow. "What is it with the whole damned universe wanting their ships today?" she demanded. "Just make sure nobody kills themselves or anyone else with that armor."

The screen went blank when Jean cut the call.

John answered Reynolds' bemused look with a shrug and went back into the dining area, where Tactical was complaining about being left in the guest quarters during the dinner that evening. "Why do we have to stay here while you meatbags live it up, partying with the Queen?"

The others agreed.

Takal shrugged. "We can each take one of them with us."

"Come on!" Tactical declared. "I'll be on my best behavior. I promise not to say fuck in front of the Queen, even if she says it first."

Reynolds took his seat at the table, wondering if he was a glutton for punishment. "Fine, you can come to the dinner. But one step out of line, Tactical, and I'll have you confined to comm for the duration of the tour. You hear?"

# CHAPTER FOUR

**Devon, Vid-doc Vault**

Bethany Anne and Michael walked out of the Etheric.

"Put the curtain back up," Bethany Anne instructed as she crossed to the viewing area.

Michael took a seat in the viewing area, his attention fixed on the screen and the carnage that was paused there. "I thought it would be a bit longer before they were ready to face Ookens."

"What can I say?" Eve asked. "Trey was done by the end of the second stint in 'stasis,' and K'aia only had a few tweaks. The rest was always going to depend on when Alexis and Gabriel reached emotional maturity and found it within themselves to unlock their full potential."

Bethany Anne narrowed her eyes, unable to repress her reaction to the sight of her children's situation. They were neck-deep in what could easily be mistaken for the climactic scene from one of those movies that made back its exorbitant production budget so many times over that they flogged the story to death with sequels that never matched the passion of the original.

She indicated the screen with a finger. "All right, time to play Catch the Mother Up. What led to this, and what else does the program intend to put my children through?"

Eve's eyes flickered while she ran through the milestones the children had passed. "The final step is the one that mattered, the one that unlocked the endgame."

Bethany Anne fixed Eve with the look only a mother can give. "You're prevaricating."

Eve had the grace to blush, no mean feat for an android. "I don't want to proceed with what the program is suggesting," she admitted.

That drew Michael's attention. "What exactly is it suggesting that is making you so reticent?"

Eve hesitated before answering. "Breaking their connection to each other. The program has identified that as a potential weakness if one of them dies in battle."

"No," Bethany Anne stated, her eyes flaring red as the unthinkable possibility wormed its way into her head. "There's no need for that because they're not ever going to be put in that situation."

"Bethany Anne, it's a *simulation*." Michael ignored the shaking of the vault, just like he ignored the energy pouring from his wife. He took her hand, keeping his voice low and calm. "Get control of yourself before you cause an earthquake."

The energy receded when she clamped down on it, but Bethany Anne felt no peace. She glared at Michael, her eyes still bright with red light. "*I don't care* if it's a simulation, Michael! I. Will. Not. Have. My. Babies. Suffer."

Michael pointed at the screen. "Look at them," he demanded. "Those are not babies. They are adults. No matter our perception of their lives, theirs is different. They've lived those years with and without us, and earned the *right* to put themselves in whatever situations they wish to."

He brought his hand back to clasp hers. "Did you think they would stay with us?" he asked gently. "They are our children, made from us. They have the entire universe at their feet. Would *you* stay?"

Bethany Anne bowed her head. *Why did he have to be right?*

The vision she'd had of the four of them remaining together slipped away and was replaced by the reality that Alexis and Gabriel were highly-trained fighters. "No, I guess I expected them to want to spread their wings," she admitted.

"We need them in this war," Michael reminded her. "They're every bit as powerful as we are."

Bethany Anne pulled her hand free and turned away, regretting it when she faced the screen and saw the proof of what Michael was saying. "I cannot and will not look at our children as *assets*, Michael."

"That's why you had the *Gemini* built," Michael soothed. "And that's why we're going to allow the program to run."

Bethany Anne still hesitated.

"If they don't get the inoculation," he continued, "what are the chances of survival for anyone around them if it comes to the worst?"

Bethany Anne hated it on the rare occasions she had to concede that Michael was logical.

"*Dammit.*" She clenched her fists for a moment before looking up. "Fine. Run the program," she told Eve.

"As you wish," Eve replied.

"I *don't* fucking wish," Bethany Anne ground out. "But better here where I can pull them out if it goes too far."

That moment came around sooner than Bethany Anne expected. An alert sounded from the console. "What was that?" she asked.

"Alexis has lost her grounding," Eve whispered. "She's about to lose herself to the Etheric. It's showing her how to get Gabriel back, and she's about to unlock the ability to alter the fabric of space-time."

The vault shook again.

"It's not me," Bethany Anne told them. "Is Alexis affecting the real world? Get me in there, now!"

Eve handed Bethany Anne a headset that covered most of the top of her head and face.

Bethany Anne searched out her daughter's mind and caught hold of the last fragment before it drifted away. **Alexis. Enough.**

She felt Alexis' awareness return and her internal struggle to obey the command. Alexis' determination tore at her heart. She felt her daughter's confusion and sensed her search for what grounded her.

**Your brother,** Bethany Anne reminded her.

*Gabriel.* Alexis returned to herself at the memory. *I almost forgot myself completely.*

Bethany Anne spoke quietly, understanding in her voice. **It's tempting to give yourself up to the peace of nothing. It would be a relief some days. But you don't have that option, my love. None of us do. We have to be the barrier, the** *line others don't dare cross. Duty doesn't care how tired you are, and Evil never sleeps.*

*I'm sorry,* Alexis whispered.

Bethany Anne sent her a wave of love and withdrew now that the urgency had passed. She removed the headset and handed it back to Eve, feeling better about the ending of the game now she was there. "She's okay."

Michael indicated the holoscreen with a finger. "You don't say."

Bethany Anne's face split in a grin when she saw the twins pulling victory from the jaws of defeat. "Eve, can we get some popcorn down here?"

Eve held up a finger and the sound of popping came from the kitchen in the outer chamber, followed by the smell of buttery deliciousness. "Tabitha and John both messaged to ask what the emergency was. They're on their way down here with the others. I told them to pick up some Cokes if they were planning on staying to watch the end."

Bethany Anne sat back. "We might as well make a party out of it."

When the moment came, everyone on the couch got up and cheered. Bethany Anne turned to Eve with anticipation. "They defeated the Kurtherians. How long until they can come out of the Vid-docs?"

Eve tilted her head while she checked the progress of the neural integration process. "It's going to be a few hours yet. Maybe a day."

Bethany Anne let out a groan of frustration. "How is it that the closer I get to seeing my children, the longer it feels?"

Michael laughed. "I don't remember you ever being this impatient before."

John, Scott, and Darryl helped by listing times when Bethany Anne had been unwilling to wait.

Eric nodded, agreeing as a backup.

Bethany Anne threw her remaining popcorn at them. "I could focus all my attention on you three until Eve calls to tell us it's time." She looked at each of them. "Anyone want to spar? No? How about a little training with the Etheric? No? How about a bit of time spent dodging? No one wishes to play 'dodge the red-hot flaming Etheric ball?'" she asked, one eyebrow raised.

John shook his head vigorously. "We're good, thanks, Boss."

---

Mahi' and Fi'Eireie met Bethany Anne and Michael at the elevator early the next morning.

Mahi' greeted Bethany Anne, excitement showing beneath her regal exterior. "I have been counting the minutes until Tu'Reigd's return," she admitted to Bethany Anne as the elevator descended. "The feed Eve provided has become my people's most beloved form of entertainment. No Baka's life has ever been so celebrated."

Michael and Fi'Eireie discussed the highlights of the children's final scenario while they waited for Eve to open the Vid-doc vault.

Eve met them in the outer chamber. "I wasn't expecting you. The process is not yet complete."

Bethany Anne walked past her, heading for the table in the living area. "But it's going to be soon, right?"

"Well, yes," Eve conceded.

"Then this is as good a place as any for Mahi' and I to talk about the Bakas' part in keeping this end of the Interdiction protected during my tour." Bethany Anne took a seat. "Let's start with arrangements for the Federation troops who will be arriving for training to fight the Ookens."

Eve shrugged and glided to the inner chamber to continue monitoring the system. "You won't disturb me. I'll call when I'm ready."

Two hours after every detail of the Bakas' responsibilities had been hammered out, Bethany Anne paced the space between the Vid-docs with growing impatience. "How long?" she asked Eve for the third time.

"Neural recalibration can't be rushed," Eve replied with a hint of annoyance. *Why had she wished for more action? Those years on Earth might have been the calm before the Bethany Anne Storm.*

Michael had just as little patience, but his was coiled tightly, holding him still by the control panel. "It's been hours."

"Perfectly normal," Eve assured him. "The process has to be completed, or they won't retain everything they gained in the system."

Bethany Anne stopped pacing and her head swiveled like the turret of a tank as she stared at Eve. "They could lose their memories?"

"As well as their physical abilities," Eve confirmed.

Only Mahi' kept her calm. She sat with her hand resting

in Fi'Eireie's, watching the replays of the battles with rapt attention and a growing smile.

An alert went off and ceased immediately.

"That will be Tabitha," Eve informed Bethany Anne and Michael. "Only she can interfere with the system like that."

"Only me," Tabitha announced over the speakers, confirming Eve's prediction. "Well, me and a couple others."

Eve smirked and turned back to the control panel. "I knew it. We're almost ready here."

"That was what you said an hour ago," Michael reminded her.

"Well, excuse me for thinking an hour wasn't long in human terms," Eve shot back.

Michael sniffed. "I believe you have been working with Akio and other humans for centuries."

"Well, the Japanese are much more patient. I was spoiled and didn't know it."

The left side of Michael's lips curved up for a moment. "Well-played."

Bethany Anne raised an eyebrow when the vault door opened to admit Tabitha, Peter, John, Scott, Darryl, and Eric. Gabrielle pushed through the guys and smiled at Bethany Anne. "We didn't want to miss this."

Bethany Anne's toe tapped on the floor. "Anyone else want to crash my children's return?"

Tabitha grinned. "Oh, hells, yeah. I didn't think you'd want everyone in the Hexagon down here, though."

"You thought right," Michael agreed.

"But you are all welcome," Bethany Anne added. "I can't think of anyone else I'd like to share this moment with."

Eve left the console and glided over to the Vid-docs. "Two minutes."

Bethany Anne forgot her annoyance when the Vid-docs lit up, signifying that they were about to open.

Inside the Vid-docs, Alexis and Gabriel regained consciousness, followed by K'aia and Trey a moment later.

Alexis climbed out and darted over to dive into Bethany Anne's waiting arms. "Mom!"

Bethany Anne held Alexis close, letting go with one arm to include Gabriel in the embrace as he joined the two of them. Her heart felt complete holding them in her arms, leaving her momentarily speechless.

"It's so good to see you, Mom," Gabriel murmured into the crook of her neck. "Did you see the end of the scenario?"

They opened their arms again to include Michael, whose voice had a slight quaver when he spoke. "Time is a strange thing," he told his children. "It feels to me like it went as slowly for us as it did for you two."

"We're home," Alexis announced, letting go of her parents so she could hug the rest of their greeting party. "I'm so happy to be back on Devon!"

Bethany Anne pulled K'aia into a hug. "You don't get away that easily," she told her. "You did well in there."

K'aia was sure she was blushing, whether it showed on her carapace or not. "Just doing my duty."

Mahi' gasped when she laid eyes on Trey. "I cannot believe it," she breathed, looking him up and down. "You are *magnificent*, my son."

"Kingly," his father added as the three embraced.

"You're a son to make anyone proud, and a warrior our people will sing of for generations to come."

Trey was overcome with emotions. "I missed you, Mahi'," he managed through his tears. "And I'm looking forward to getting to know you, Father."

Bethany Anne couldn't stop smiling. "This calls for a celebration."

Gabriel grinned and looked around, then under her chair. "Where did you hide the Cokes? I know you didn't come down here without any."

Tabitha lifted the lid of a cooler she spotted and laughed. "I'm guessing you're right. Here." She handed the first two to the children.

"You know, that was the one thing we missed in there," Alexis told everyone. "If you hadn't stepped down as Empress, Coke wouldn't have made it out of the Empire."

Gabriel nodded. "Yeah, 's good."

Bethany Anne raised an eyebrow, then dissolved into laughter. "You two are most definitely my children."

"They do have your caffeine addiction," Michael agreed.

Alexis finished her drink and grabbed another from the cooler. "What we have is *taste*. Now, are we going to just hang around in here all day?"

Bethany Anne noted Alexis' impatience, so like her own. "Well, no. You completed the process just in time."

"In time for what?" Gabriel inquired, seeing the seriousness pass over his mother's face. "Did the Seven attack again?"

"No," Bethany Anne told him. "You've missed a lot while you were in the Vid-docs. We'll tell you about it on the way to the ship."

Alexis' eyes widened as she realized there was a voice missing from her mind. "Gemini!"

"Her ship is berthed on the *Baba Yaga*," Michael assured her.

The conversation continued as the group made their way to the surface. By the time they'd reached the *Baba Yaga*, the twins had been updated about Gödel.

Alexis met Gabriel's gaze with a hard stare. *It's funny. I hadn't expected to know the name of the Kurtherian we're going to destroy. They're usually more...generic. You know?*

Michael's voice cut into their mindspace. *You will leave Gödel to us.*

The twins whirled on Michael. "But Dad!" Alexis protested. "She *owes us* for Aunt Addix!"

"I have another task in mind for your team," Bethany Anne told them firmly. "Gödel is mine, and mine alone."

Alexis was about to argue further when Gabriel stayed her with a hand. "What task?"

"You'll find out," Bethany Anne promised. "Just as soon as we arrive at the *Meredith Reynolds*." She cut off their questions with a wave. "We'll get to the reasons for the tour soon enough. First things first; we have a reception dinner to get ready for."

Gabriel groaned. "For real? We *just* got back to reality, and we have to work a diplomatic event?"

Bethany Anne broke into a grin as she reached over and tousled his hair. "Welcome home, son."

## QSD *Baba Yaga*, Top Deck, Twins' Quarters

"At least we have the day to get settled in," Alexis

consoled Gabriel as they entered the lounge. She looked around with a frown. "Does this place feel smaller to you?"

Gabriel nodded, heading for his room. "Yeah, but I figured it would."

Alexis picked up the purple sparkly cushion from the couch. "We need to update this place. Starting with this."

Gabriel's laughter filled both rooms. "I take it you're over your girly phase," he teased, coming out of his room with a book. He dropped into a chair and draped his legs over one arm. "What's inspiring the need for change?"

Alexis held the cushion out and looked at it for a long moment before hugging it to her chest. "The sparkles don't really speak to maturity, do they? I want to be taken seriously, not treated like a little girl."

"I don't see how giving up something that defines you shows maturity, but if it helps you make your point, go ahead and arrange for a remodel." Gabriel got up and gave his sister a hug. "After all the time we spent in barracks, I'd be glad of a few comforts."

Alexis hugged Gabriel in return, then released him and headed for the door. "It'll be heaven in here by the time I'm done, just wait and see."

"Where are you going?" Gabriel called.

Alexis paused to grin. "*Shopping*, of course."

Gabriel's brow furrowed. "But the dinner is soon. You haven't got time to shop for furniture."

Alexis laughed, waving as she turned to leave. "I know that. But I haven't got a *thing* to wear for tonight."

# CHAPTER FIVE

**Devon, The Hexagon, Outdoor Arena**

Sabine paced the sand, anxiously watching as Ricole controlled the training mechs slowly. "Get a move on, Ricole. We don't have time for this."

"Someone shouldn't have skipped breakfast this morning," Ricole replied, her teeth showing.

"Forgive me for being concerned when we have an event starting in a few hours and our entire moving crew came down with the *flu*," Sabine barked. "We need to get this deck laid."

"These things are tricky," Ricole told her as the mechs began moving as one. "You have to program them as a group."

Sabine barely waited for the mechs to place the last section of the deck before she jumped onto it and started giving Ricole directions on where to have them place the tables.

Jacqueline laughed, dodging two of the mechanical Ookens as they came by carrying one of the long, heavy tables between them. "Who knew they'd be useful for more than teaching people how not to die?"

"You could have waited a minute," Mark complained, ducking a metal tentacle. He got back to attaching the steps, grumbling about the last-minute rush to prepare.

Sabine ignored him and started unpacking the table-cloths. "Did the caterer call back to confirm the menu is compatible with the Larians?" she asked, shaking one of the white cloths out over the head table. "The last thing we need is to poison them at their welcome dinner."

She missed Jacqueline's reply, distracted by Bethany Anne entering the arena. "Tools down," she called. "Everyone take fifteen minutes."

The mechs stalled as Ricole fumbled the controls. "Give me a second." She grunted. The mechs ground to a halt, and Ricole joined Sabine, Jacqueline, and Mark on the deck.

Bethany Anne glanced at the progress of their preparations as she crossed to the deck. "I can see you're all busy. I'll make this quick. ADAM told me you've liquidated most of your assets here on Devon. Is there something you'd like to tell me?"

Sabine looked at all of them. "We were planning to talk to you and Michael after the dinner," she answered. "We decided as a group that while our work here has had value, it is done, so yes. We took care of our businesses, and we're ready to move on to the next challenge."

Bethany Anne sighed. "Here we go with the pride and heartbreak again."

"What do you mean?" Jacqueline asked.

"You will understand when you have children of your

own," Bethany Anne told her. "Whether they're yours by blood or not, it's hard when they're ready to leave home."

She smiled. "But as much as it hurts to let go, there's no better feeling than the one I have right now. I have an assignment for you all."

"What's the assignment?" Mark asked.

"I have Akio's team guarding one of the back doors into the Federation," Bethany Anne told them. "There are a number of places where the Federation is no more than two colonies that are light-years apart. If what you're looking for is a challenge, the frontier won't disappoint you. There are pockets of uninhabited space all over. The FDG has most of them locked down, but this quadrant lies outside Federation borders."

"How can it be a backdoor if it's outside the Federation?" Ricole asked.

"Because the Federation isn't a perfect sphere," Bethany Anne told her. "In fact, it's not any shape I can name. Tina's model looks like a 3-D paint splat."

Sabine nodded. "We heard how it is out there in Akio's letters."

"Yeah," Ricole cut in. "They're up to their necks in Ookens. Count us in." She looked around at the others. "Yes? Right? Did I jump in too fast?"

"I'm in," Jacqueline agreed.

Mark chuckled. "Me too."

"What about Demon and Sam?" Bethany Anne asked. "I haven't seen them since Alyssa left with her father and Amanda."

"You know Demon," Sabine replied, smiling at the

memory of the redheaded Magus. "She goes where I go, and Sam is happy to tag along."

"Then it's decided. I'll have your transport ready in the next few days. Finish up any business you still have to take care of and wait for my call." Bethany Anne smiled. "I'll see you all at the dinner tonight."

Ricole was first to speak after Bethany Anne had vanished into the Etheric. "Well, crap. There won't be a dinner if we don't get moving."

**Devon, The Hexagon**

Reynolds undid his tie for the third time, unhappy with the way it refused to sit symmetrically in the space between the points of his stiff collar.

He wedged a finger under the offending material and wiggled it in an attempt to release the chokehold the penguin suit sent by Jiya had on his neck.

"I feel ridiculous," he grumbled.

Takal came in at the tail end of Reynolds' complaint. "Well, you look very distinguished," he told his captain. "Perfectly suitable for a dinner celebrating your achievements."

"*Our* achievements," Reynolds corrected. "We took down that cult as a team."

He pointed at Takal's tuxedo with a smile. "You went with human formal wear?"

"Would you argue with Jiya when her mind is set?" Takal asked him with a grin. "They bumped into Bethany Anne's daughter in the bazaar. Apparently, your Queen takes these matters very seriously."

"Is that why we suddenly own coordinated clothing?" Reynolds asked.

Tactical cut in. "I hate to spoil this touching moment, but there's an EI bugging me to tell you that your presence is expected in the outdoor arena in twenty minutes. Jiya is waiting in the lobby with Ka'nak, Geroux, and Maddox."

Reynolds and Takal headed for the elevator, which took them to the lobby.

Ka'nak waved, then looked at his armpit and grinned. "Just look at this tailoring," he enthused as Reynolds and Takal joined them. "I could throw punches in this jacket all day and not tear a stitch."

"Looking good, Captain," Jiya remarked.

"Thanks to you, I hear," Reynolds replied. "The rest of you don't clean up badly either."

Jiya extended a foot from the hem of her floor-length evening gown, revealing the reason she was three and a half inches taller. "Heels are a thing here. Alexis assured me that I'll be able to both run and fight in them with practice." She smirked and showed them the stiletto. "Have you seen anything prettier? More likely, I'll take them off and use them as weapons."

Geroux twirled to make her skirts fly out around her as they set off to find the arena. "I like human fashion."

Jiya and Geroux shared their experiences of shopping in the bazaar while Winstanley guided them past the indoor arenas, most of which still had training going on inside.

"Now that's dedication," Maddox commented.

"The Guardians and the Defenders share this facility,"

Winstanley informed them from a nearby speaker. "The facilities are generally in use around the clock."

The courtyard between the indoor and outdoor arenas glowed with soft lighting wound into the trailing plants that spilled from latticework fixed to the walls. Jiya lifted her hand to capture one of the blossoms, cupping it gently to take in its sweet fragrance. "This is...beautiful."

Reynolds extended a hand to indicate the open doors of the arena. "I'm sure you'll find the whole evening to be magical," he told her with a smile. "Let's go."

They were the last to arrive.

Reynolds paused at the steps of the deck that had been laid over the sand and looked for Bethany Anne. His general crew was seated at tables arranged on a deck that filled half the arena. He smiled, seeing them at ease with Bethany Anne's people.

*This is swanky,* Tactical remarked for Reynolds' ears only.

*Bethany Anne doesn't do things by halves,* Reynolds replied, catching his Queen's eye.

Bethany Anne got to her feet, and silence fell over the arena. She opened her arms wide and graced Reynolds with a smile that melted his mechanical heart.

"The AI of the hour is here," Bethany Anne announced to the guests. "Reynolds!" She waved a hand at those seated. "Everyone."

The crew of the SD *Reynolds* stood and applauded, joined by the rest of the guests sitting at the tables on the deck.

This was it—the glorious moment Reynolds had imagined to keep himself strong when the going had been rough. He bowed and lifted his hands in supplication to the crowd. "All I can say is, it's *good* to be home."

He mounted the steps with his closest friends at his back and made his way to the head table. While weaving through the tables, Reynolds came to the realization that the good feeling he had was due less to being celebrated than it was to the connections he'd made with these people during their shared trials and triumphs.

Bethany Anne greeted him with a hug. "Welcome home, and welcome to your crew." She gestured to Reynolds and the others. "Please take your seats. Welcome to you all. Tonight we are not just celebrating the return of one of our own, we are celebrating new friendships. Our family has grown again as we forge connections across the universe."

Jiya opened the comm to Reynolds. *She* does *know we don't represent our home planets, right?*

Reynolds nodded. *You can be sure she has already sent a delegation to the Chain galaxy to inform the leaders of her intentions.*

Jiya wondered what intentions Bethany Anne had.

Bethany Anne glanced at Jiya as if she had read her mind. "I intend to bring the Seven to Justice. Everyone here tonight is focused on the same goal. Reynolds and his crew have proved that Gödel doesn't have unlimited resources to keep throwing at the Federation. She came here with all guns blazing, expecting to put the hurt on us, and we chewed up the best she could throw at us and spat them back out." She raised her glass to the applause that broke out. "Here's to new alliances!"

The cheers were deafening. Reynolds took in the feeling, making sure it was captured in the most secure memory area he had on him. In those moments of darkness he could easily calculate would happen in the future, he would retrieve this moment to help him.

And then go out and kick more ass.

"We came out on top," his Queen continued. "So did the crew of the *Reynolds*. But you can bet Gödel will be back." Bethany Anne put her glass down. "While the Seven are rebuilding, we will be taking time to strengthen the defenses around the Federation. Since Reynolds has agreed to join the tour, which is a secret, I'll assume everyone here knows already."

That drew chuckles from the attendees. Bethany Anne smiled and took her seat as the food was brought out. "Eat and enjoy, because tomorrow we're back to work."

The meal passed quickly with good conversation to help it along, then the chair-hopping began.

Bethany Anne's mouth was set in an amused curl when Sabine took the seat next to her. "I don't have to read your mind to know you want something," she told the young woman she thought of as an adopted daughter. "Spill."

Sabine flushed. "Well, I was talking to Nickie—"

"Nickie, who missed the planning meeting and hasn't bothered to show up tonight?" Bethany Anne cut in. "Where is that hellion?"

Sabine squirmed under the pressure. She didn't want to lie to the woman who'd given her everything, but if she told Bethany Anne her friend had skipped out to play pew-pew in the outer reaches, she wouldn't be much of a friend.

Bethany Anne's eyebrow arched. "Sabine?"

Sabine sighed. "She's still helping Akio out, so she's not going to make it. But it's the Hexagon I want to talk to you about. We'd like to give you first refusal before we sell it to the Defenders."

Bethany Anne frowned. "I have a shitload of proprietary technology in that building. ADAM will take care of the details; consider it sold."

Sabine grinned. "I thought you would say something like that, so I already drew up the agreement and sent it to him." She shrugged at Bethany Anne's raised eyebrow. "You are already leasing most of the building."

"I am?" Bethany Anne asked.

Sabine nodded. "*Oui.* The VR suites are pretty much all we had left to maintain, so we figured we might as well sell out."

"What about Tim?" Alexis asked, leaning in.

Sabine's mouth twitched. "He'll, umm, survive."

Bethany Anne gave her a sympathetic smile. "So will you if your relationship doesn't weather the separation."

Alexis fixed Bethany Anne with a hopeful look. "Does that mean you're going to cut Gabriel and me some slack? We'd be perfectly fine with Akio as our CO. We could make a difference, and you know we want to."

Bethany Anne did not tear the heart from the universe at the thought of the twins leaving. She did, however, turn to Alexis with utter seriousness. "I know you're looking for any opportunity to find Gödel and get your revenge, but you're not ready for this conversation. I'm happy for Sabine's team to take on whatever gets thrown at them because they have *decades* of experience."

Alexis narrowed her eyes. "In Earth years."

Bethany Anne smiled, brushing off the retort. "You are needed on the tour, where you will have the opportunity to prove you won't run off and get yourselves killed the second my and your father's backs are turned. We will discuss your crew's fitness for front-line deployment when we return. Does that satisfy you?"

Alexis threw her arms around Bethany Anne. "I have to tell Gabriel!"

Michael replaced Sabine when she also left to inform her team of Bethany Anne's decision. "You're being generous tonight. Have the girls exhausted that, or am I just in time to persuade you to alter one of our stops on the itinerary? I have it in mind to go hunting with the children."

Bethany Anne chuckled. "You're an *ass*, Michael Nacht."

Michael put a hand to his chest. "I'm lucky to have an ego large enough that your repeated assertion of that hasn't affected me." He dodged her punch and leaned back in the chair with his hands laced behind his head. "You're impatient to get moving. I get it. The longer we delay, the more chance that Gödel launches her revenge before we can hit her with ours."

Bethany Anne nodded. "Is it wrong of me to hope the twins realize while we're on this tour that the action they're looking for is exactly what we've been shielding them from their whole lives?"

Michael smiled. "You have a chance of them choosing to stick around if you continue to give them space to discover where they belong. You haven't yet locked them in the Etheric for asking, which I'd say is a step in the right direction."

"Don't." Bethany Anne groaned. "I wish I could. Sabine didn't realize you're less restrictive these days. I almost grounded all four of them when ADAM told me they were selling off their assets." She frowned. "What the hell happened? When I found out I was pregnant, I thought you'd be the strict father and I'd be the cool mom who did crazy things."

"I have been the father of toddlers with superpowers and no concept of death," Michael told her with a sage look. "Nothing scares me. You're a good mother. You never limited our children's learning, and you support them in everything they do."

He held up a finger to stall her interruption. "Look at them, Bethany Anne."

Bethany Anne did as he asked. Gabriel was laughing with Ka'nak as they shared battle stories. Bethany Anne looked away from the impromptu wrestling match that broke out and scanned the tables for Alexis. She spotted her talking animatedly to Reynolds' head engineer, and the genius inventor looked impressed.

They had the experience; she just hadn't fully processed it yet. "Maybe I'm the one who needs neural reintegration," she murmured. "God, I'm going to miss them, but you're right."

## Onyx Station

Paul Jacobsen rubbed the tattoo on his forearm for courage as he looked into the camera. Public speaking really wasn't his thing, but he had a message to get across to the people. He had recorded two messages, and this final one was about to go out on a live stream on the public access channel.

He glanced at the vial on the table next to the computer, hesitating for a moment before he picked it up and drank the contents. He swallowed without tasting it and cleared his throat, choked more by remorse that it had come to this than any reaction to the nanocyte compound he'd just tossed back.

He was going to die soon, but this was the only way to expose the truth. The only way to save everyone from the real enemy.

He smiled sadly, thinking about his wife and children as he pressed the button to begin the stream. "My name is Paul Jacobsen. I'm a nobody, a computer technician, but I've found out that something is wrong in the Federation, and I have to speak out before it's too late. We are being lied to. There is a force at work that wants to tear us down and force us to fight their war for them. The Federation council wants us to believe that we are under threat from Kurtherians, but that is a lie they're telling us to cover a darker truth."

The silence that followed stretched out. Paul felt a keen pressure to ensure he didn't appear to be a fanatic despite his method of getting attention.

"The Kurtherians don't exist," he continued in an even tone. "I have proof that they're a myth created by Bethany Anne Nacht to cover the killing spree she went on when she formed the Etheric Empire. She will not stop until we are an empire again. We have to ask, 'Will she stop there?'"

Paul paused to give the watchers time to digest the question. A pang in his chest told him his time was growing short. He looked directly into the camera with utter sincerity. "Many would welcome her back with open arms, ignorant of the consequences. Bethany Anne is the commonality in every war in recent history. Further, she is the *cause*. I know everyone watching this is already aware there have been multiple sightings of the former Empress in recent months, but what I'm about to show you is shocking."

He tapped the keyboard as the cramps reached his stomach and began to twist his gut, replacing his camera feed with the image that had set in motion the chain of events that had brought him to this moment. "This image was taken in the control room of a mining outpost owned by a Leath group. As you can see by the blood, Bethany Anne has clearly killed a number of Leath already."

Paul left the image there for a moment before returning his image to the screen. He fought to keep his voice steady as pain wracked him. "My source informed me that the outpost was stripped at this time and that any attempt to approach it was met with hostility from the nearby battlestation." He opened his arms in supplication as he heard the elevator open. "I have worse news. My source inside the Federal House of Arbitration tells me that the council has met with Bethany Anne to discuss her taking over the Federation."

Paul glanced at the door, hearing boots in the corridor outside his hotel room.

There was a bang on the door. "Station security. Open up."

"We don't have to take it lying down," he told the camera, his face contorting as his insides burned. "I don't want to do this, but I can't let the truth be suppressed any longer. Bethany Anne has assets on—"

It was over. He clutched his chest, unable to hear the instructions being yelled by the two men who burst in with their weapons drawn.

Paul closed his eyes as the nanocyte compound reached peak conversion of his body's energy and exploded.

# CHAPTER SIX

**Devon, First City, Totto's Restaurant**

"I love that you had the building remade exactly as it was," Bethany Anne told Leonardo as she accepted his warm handshake at the door.

"We can't thank you enough for your help with everything," Leonardo replied.

Bethany Anne smiled. "You have the Hexagon Foundation to thank for that. The volunteers have been working tirelessly to get First City back to normal."

Leonardo beamed. "That's what happens when people help each other. We've been cooking for the construction workers, doing what we can to contribute in our own way. But we should not stand here talking all night. You have guests, and those guests are waiting."

"While true, it is important that normal life resumes as soon as possible," Michael commented as Leonardo led them inside. He smelled the inviting aromas. "Besides, it's practically tradition to have our departure dinner here."

"People in the city come here to celebrate the special

moments in life." Bethany Anne winked at him. "There is no way we'd let this war take that away from them."

Leonardo showed them into the private room where their family and closest friends were seated around four tables pushed together.

Bethany Anne was pleased to see that Cheryl Lynn and Todd were on Devon. Tina and Scott were sitting with them, Tina was on the end and had Marcus to her left at the next table, followed by Bobcat and William. John was flanked by Lillian and Jean. Darryl and Natalia sat with Dan, Gabrielle, and Eric. Sabine, Jacqueline, Mark, and Ricole were in deep conversation with the twins.

"Where are we sitting?" Bethany Anne asked.

"Over here," Alexis and Gabriel called in unison, waving them past Tabitha and Peter.

Leonardo brought the starters in while the conversation flowed. Bethany Anne watched, eyes roaming, pleased to feel everyone's energy was high in anticipation of the tour getting underway.

Tina got to her feet. She held up her glass and looked around with a smile. "Here's to walking right up to the impossible and telling it to go fuck itself. We've designed a real-time defense system that will give the Federation the edge against the Seven. I want to say congratulations, but I don't want to jinx it."

Bethany Anne was distracted by ADAM. *What's up?*

>>**You have an urgent call from Lance and Nathan.**<<

*Give me audio.* She waited for a beat. *Dad, Nathan. What's the urgency?*

Nathan was first to reply. *Onyx was attacked. Some ass blew himself up, ranting about you.*

That got Bethany Anne's attention. *What? Go back, explain.*

*We can do better than that,* Lance interjected. *He live-streamed the whole thing.*

*He did what?* Bethany Anne demanded. *What the fuck is going on out there? We're due to arrive in a few days, and you have terrorists on board the station?*

>>**I have the video,**<< ADAM informed her.

*Give me a minute.* Bethany Anne left the table, holding a finger up when Michael gave her an inquiring look. She stepped outside the room and played the video ADAM had provided. *How many were injured by the explosion?*

*The security officers who went to apprehend him are in Pod-docs, but they'll be fine. A couple of the hotel guests received minor injuries, but most of the damage was directed outward into my damn building,* Nathan informed her in a growl. *I've contacted the Magistrate. They're going to send someone to take care of the legal aspects of me turning this station upside-fucking-down until I'm sure there are no more crazies aboard.*

*What about Jacobsen?* Bethany Anne asked, reading the report station security had made. *Who was he working with?*

*We may have a leak,* Lance conceded.

*Fucking right, you have a leak. How else did that Kool-Aid-drinking wanksack get that photo of me?* Bethany Anne adjusted her endocrine levels to abate the rage she felt building. Now wasn't the time to get emotional. *I'm concerned this attack won't be an isolated incident. I want you to investigate. Our spontaneously-combusting lunatic wasn't working alone.*

Lance and Nathan started speaking at the same time.

Bethany Anne wasn't done. *Not only does the Federation council have a leak, Nathan is going to be tied up making sure this doesn't become a diplomatic crisis when I arrive to implement the upgrades. This was not the start I wanted.*

Nathan growled. *Everyone saw that crackpot for what he was. Onyx is fine.*

*Then we thank Providence for the small mercies it grants. The last thing I want is trouble when we get to the Kezzin outpost on the itinerary.* Bethany Anne sighed. *Onyx is a neutral zone. Our security has to be able to prevent one conspiracy nut with explosives knowledge and no survival instinct from blowing the shit out of it. As for the council, it sounds to me like we're still teetering on the edge of a complete fucking shitshow.*

*It's not like that,* Lance interceded. *I don't suspect any of the council delegates. Everyone who doubted was made aware of the reality when you threatened to bring an Ooken to Red Rock and drop it in front of them.*

*That's still a possibility,* Bethany Anne told him. *However, I'll hold off on the stringent measures until we know who is working against us. This needs to be stopped before they fuck up everything we're working for. It's time to clean house, Dad. I'm sending Akio to you. I have to be certain Gödel isn't mixed up in this somehow.*

*We'll soon know if she is,* Lance told her, his voice hard with determination. *Rest assured, whoever sent that photo will be leaving Red Rock in a body bag.*

Bethany Anne knew not to argue with her father when he took it upon himself to address a betrayal. *Nathan, I want a full investigation into Paul Jacobsen's life. Work it from the other end.*

*I'm going to have to call in some backup,* Nathan told her. *We're a little bit short-handed around here with everyone getting ready for your arrival.*

Bethany Anne wasn't bothered about the details as long as she got the answer to whose ass she had to beat some common fucking sense into. **Don't you have a Direct Action Branch for situations like this?**

Nathan chuckled. *You read my mind. I'll call TH as soon as we're done here.*

**I'm going to send Alexis and Gabriel ahead. With K'aia and Trey, you have four extra pairs of hands.**

There was a brief hesitation on Nathan's side. *Please don't kill me, but I haven't got time to babysit right now, Bethany Anne. They'd be at risk.*

**I'd worry more about the risk to anyone who thinks my children are easy targets,** Bethany Anne replied,

*Okay then,* Nathan replied. *But if they get in the way, they'll have to hang with Ecaterina until you get here.*

He dropped the link, leaving Bethany Anne and Lance to their goodbyes.

*He has no clue the twins have had enhancement, does he?* Lance asked.

**Not the slightest,** Bethany Anne told him with a chuckle. **Fucking with him makes my day, what can I say? Bad Queen, very bad queen. Love you. Bye, Dad.**

She slipped back into the dining room and took her seat at the table. "What did I miss?" she murmured to Michael.

Michael leaned in to reply. "Tabitha and Jacqueline are about to have a fight. What was that call?"

Bethany Anne shook her head. "You don't want to

know."

Michael gave her a pointed look. "That was kind of my point in asking."

Bethany Anne sighed. "Dad and Nathan. Someone blew themselves up on Onyx Station. It's dealt with. Tonight is about family."

"At least I use a knife and fork to eat," Tabitha snarked in response to a cutting comment from Jacqueline.

"Oh, I can use a knife," Jacqueline retorted as Mark tried to get her to sit down. "Keep talking and you'll be forked."

Michael gave Bethany Anne a pained look as he rose to intervene. "Family, love them or hate them."

Bethany Anne snickered. "You live for this shit, and you'll never convince me differently."

## Devon, The Hexagon, Underground Hangar (the next day)

Bethany Anne smiled as Sabine, Jacqueline, Mark, and Ricole entered the storage hangar, with Demon and Sam Jr. in tow. She left her inspection of the space and walked over to meet them. "How are your preparations coming?"

Sabine gave that Gallic shrug, a holdover from her days on Earth that indicated her general ambivalence about the subject. "So-so. We finished negotiating with Cheryl Lynn the day before yesterday, so our businesses have all been taken care of."

"What's the issue?" Bethany Anne asked.

"We're having trouble finding a suitable ship," Mark told her dejectedly. "We had bad news from Jean. There are no unassigned battleships, and she can't fit us in until approximately the twelfth of never."

Bethany Anne chuckled when Ricole mumbled her displeasure with the situation. "That's what I called you all down here for. The reason Jean hasn't got any space in her schedule is I had her rush a bunch of ships I needed for John and the guys."

"What does that mean for our assignment?" Jacqueline asked. "We can't do much without a ship."

"Well, we could try to swim through space," Mark suggested. For his insolence, Jacqueline elbowed him.

Bethany Anne turned and swept an arm to indicate the Shinigami-class ships occupying the hangar. "I'm giving you the *Defiant*, the *Revolution*, the *Cambridge*, and the *Shufur* to go out and provide a suitable response to bullies."

Jacqueline considered for a moment. "So, do unto bullies as they would do unto you?"

"No, don't try any emotional bullshit. Give them one warning, then take them down three ways."

*"Which are?"* Jacqueline asked.

Bethany Anne smiled. "Hard, fast, and continuously until they don't know how to put on their underwear correctly."

Jacqueline shut her mouth, then shook her head. "How have I not heard that before?"

"I've been saving it," Bethany Anne admitted. "It was time."

"Not the *Sayomi*?" Mark commented with curiosity, ready to switch to another subject. The Queen might be a death-bringing killer, but she got her little joys from harassing her friends, and he was ready to get them beyond that little bomb-riddled minefield.

Bethany Anne smiled. "Not in John's lifetime. The *Sayomi* is coming with the *Baba Yaga*."

Jacqueline had met Sayomi. "You never know when you'll need a ship with a crazy AI at the controls."

"What kind of name is *Shufur* for a ship?" Ricole pondered as the elevator opened again, spilling Tina, Marcus, and a couple of techs into the hangar.

"My dad thinks he's funny," Tina answered, hurrying over with her entourage in tow. "Its full name is *Sh-for-ship*."

Bethany Anne cursed internally that she'd let Scott slip it by her. "Somehow, I can see that being true. What brings you down here?"

Tina waved the tablet in her hand. "Have you checked the schedule in the last twenty minutes?"

Bethany Anne opened the prep section of the tour planner in her HUD and saw that ADAM had updated to greens across the board. "Well, fuck me. We're ready?"

Tina wiggled her eyebrows and grinned. "Hells yeah, we are. Do you want to start the countdown to departure?"

Bethany Anne raised an eyebrow, returning Tina's enthusiasm with a bright smile. "Keep up. It's already running. We leave in six hours. Go say your goodbyes."

Tina checked the countdown timer that had appeared in her HUD. "Five hours fifty-seven minutes. Dammit, I'm not packed!"

"Yes, you are," Marcus told her. "Your mother took care of it."

The panic faded from Tina's face. "Bless that woman. I don't know why I ever grew up and left home."

Marcus coughed pointedly and Tina laughed. "I don't see you packing for me," she told him.

Marcus looked away, blushing. "Cheryl Lynn packed for me, too," he mumbled.

"Cheryl Lynn is a gift." She looked from one genius to the other. "This gives us time to run through everything one more time before we leave."

"What is there to run through?" Tina asked, backing away before Bethany Anne could argue. "The pickup points are ready for our arrival. We'll be at Onyx Station before you know it. Relax! We've got this."

She waved over her shoulder as she darted for the elevator. "See you on the ship. Come on, Marcus!"

Bethany Anne smiled and turned to Sabine's group, pulling an envelope from her pocket. "I have an assignment for Akio that's too sensitive for normal communication methods. Give him this, and good luck out there, all of you."

### Beyond Federation Borders, QBS *Achronyx*, APA

"There's a Gate opening two kilometers off the port bow," Achronyx announced.

Akio paused with his katana poised to strike Nickie's. "Kurtherian signature?"

"One of ours," Achronyx replied. "It looks like our backup has arrived."

Akio replaced his katana on its mount and turned to the wallscreen. "Hail the lead ship."

Nickie had Meredith run scans through the *Penitent Granddaughter*. "That's a Shinigami-class ship."

"That would be the QBS *Defiant*," Achronyx informed them.

"That's Darryl's ship," Akio stated.

Sabine and Demon appeared on the screen as he spoke. "Not anymore," Sabine told them with a smile. She lifted her hands and twirled. "It suits me, no?"

"I don't know why you didn't think of this sooner," Nickie stated, grinning. "Me and you are going to tear things up around here. How did you get your hands on those ships? I can't see my grandad parting with the *Sayomi.*"

"He did not," Sabine confirmed. "But Bethany Anne had the other Shinigami ships replaced with ships so secret even we don't know what they are capable of, so we get the not-so-shabby cast-offs. Am I the first to arrive?"

"There are three more Gates opening around the *Defiant*," Achronyx announced.

Sabine punched the air. "Yes!"

Nickie laughed. "I take it you won something good?"

"I don't know about that," Sabine replied as Ricole, Mark, and Jacqueline cursed over their mental link.

Demon jumped up and put her front paws on the console, filling the camera's field. Sabine shooed her down. "They can't hear you, silly cat. Okay, okay." She rolled her eyes as she relayed Demon's comment to Akio. "She's happy we won because we left it to the race to decide who would act as team leader while we're out here."

"There's not much room for democracy in a fight for your lives," Akio answered. "Choosing a structure to rely on is a wise choice, and one I would have implemented if you had not."

"In Demon's case, she just likes to boss people around," Sabine told him drily. "I have a message from Bethany Anne for you."

Akio smiled. "I'll have Achronyx send Pods to bring you all over. I'm guessing Jaqueline is hungry?"

"I could eat," Nickie commented hopefully, looking around. "Is there still a secret chocolate stash in the galley?"

Sabine chuckled as Nickie wandered off-camera and presumably toward the galley without waiting for Akio to reply. "We'll see you soon."

Akio met the Pods in the transport bay. Sabine, Jaqueline, Mark, and Ricole were followed down the ramp by the cats.

Demon walked with her head held as straight as her tail, while her son's gaze bounced around with each new thing that caught his eye.

"Welcome to the frontier," Akio told them as he accepted the package from Sabine. He turned the thick, stuffed envelope over in his hands before easing it open.

"What is it?" Sabine asked.

Akio glanced inside the envelope, his eyes widening. "I think Nickie needs to be here for this."

"She's raiding the galley," Achronyx informed them.

Nickie was setting the table when they arrived. "Just in time. I made sandwiches for everyone. I hope none of you are vegetarian. That shit isn't tolerated in my kitchen."

"This is not your kitchen," Akio reminded her, taking a seat at the table. He retrieved the package from his pocket. "It's from Bethany Anne."

"Open it," Sabine urged. "I want to know what made your face turn purple."

Akio tipped the envelope, spilling a badge onto the table.

"Fuck me," Nickie gasped. Her eyes were caught by the light glinting off it before she looked at Akio. "That's the Ranger One badge!"

Akio pulled out the single sheet of paper and read it aloud. "Akio, or should I say, Ranger One, the Rangers have been reestablished, with you at the head. It's about time you got organized out there. I believe Nickie already has her badge."

Nickie dropped the plate she was holding. "No. *Freaking.* Way!" The clang of metal on metal as it hit the deck made everyone turn to look at her.

"Shhh!" Jaqueline hissed. "Let the man read."

"The Ranger life is hard," Akio continued. "It's you and your partner against whatever dumbfuckery you come across. I have sent you the new Ranger Fleet. I trust you will find your trainees adequate to the task. I've also sent the equipment to set up your part of the Interdiction, including everything you need to set up a base out there, so you all have somewhere to call home for the time being."

Akio folded the paper and began shredding it. When he was done, he picked up his badge and smiled, rubbing his thumb on the 1. "It's okay. The rest was for my eyes only. We have our instructions." He looked up. "Can I rely on you to get the base started while I take care of business for Bethany Anne?"

Nickie snorted. "Fuck, yeah, you can. Have you seen

Devon?" She circled the group with a finger. "It's on them. I'll stick around to help."

"I wondered what all those storage containers were for," Mark murmured, pulling a tablet out. "Can I get access to your charts?" he asked Akio. "We should be able to find the ideal location for the base with a little AI assistance."

Ricole got to her feet. "I'm going to inventory the construction supplies. Knowing what we've got to work with will help narrow down the search parameters."

Jacqueline snagged a couple of sandwiches from the platter Nickie had put together. "I'll give you a hand."

Sabine folded her hands on the table and smiled at Akio. "Tell me what else we can do to make defending this quadrant easier."

Akio chuckled and patted her arm. "We will get to that. Your cats are on their way here."

Demon padded in. *What did I miss?*

*Dinner, judging by the smell,* Sam grumbled as he sauntered through the door.

"You can get your own dinner," Sabine told him. "Your neural chip is compatible with the food-processing unit."

"I'm picking up an SOS," Achronyx announced over the speaker.

Akio got to his feet. "Give me the speakers, Achronyx. Everyone get back to your ships. We have a distress call to answer."

CHAPTER SEVEN

**Devon, The Interdiction, QSD *Baba Yaga***

Izanami used the time it took Bethany Anne to walk from the transfer bay to the bridge for self-reflection.

The way the AI Reynolds had reacted to her the last time they had met was annoying in the extreme. She wasn't a warrior princess from anime to be swooned over, and she had larger concerns than being friendly with the returning hero.

Thinking while in diagnostic mode was useful. She noted her jealousy and scrubbed the lines that made her feel it was unfair that Reynolds had been allowed to procure a body while she was still fighting to get the training wheels off.

He had earned the right, and she had admittedly acted rashly on a number of occasions.

With the bias removed, she saw much to admire in Reynolds. He had a certain charm, that was for sure.

Why he had added that romantic twist to the chivalric part of his personality matrix was beyond her. Perhaps out in the farthest reaches of space, AIs imitated biologicals completely.

She would inquire if that awful slip-of-the-keyboard personality growth of his didn't speak up and lower the tone.

Izanami dismissed the line of thought when the part of her responsible for operating the ship registered that Bethany Anne and her family were on their way to the bridge. She had high hopes that Alexis and Gabriel hadn't grown out of the desire to spend time with her. She had felt the absence of her interactions with the twins during their time in the Vid-docs, especially her conversations with Alexis.

Gabriel came in ahead of everyone, complaining loudly about their assignments. "It's not fair that Trey and K'aia get to shadow Uncle John. What purpose are we serving here?"

Bethany Anne ignored the rant, patting Gabriel's arm with a smile. "You'll have fun. See the Federation."

"So will Trey and K'aia," Gabriel argued. "Except they'll be doing more than standing around listening to politicians going on and on and on!"

"Your mother and I feel it's important for you both to explore your roots," Michael told him.

"The Federation is the embodiment of the ideal that people can live together," Bethany Anne continued the thought. "Not in spite of their differences, but because of them. It took almost two lifetimes to bring about, and I desire to share that with you."

Alexis hugged Bethany Anne on her way to her seat. "I think it sounds amazing, Mom. We *have* to do some shopping while we're on the *Meredith Reynolds*. I've been dreaming of the shoe stores there since I was a little kid."

Bethany Anne had been dreaming of taking her there. "This is going to be more than the tour. We have the chance to make memories. Your whole lives, it's been one crisis after another, with a war on top. We have fourteen months to kick back between stops."

"I still think it's going to take at least eighteen," Alexis disputed. "You can't account for the actions of people."

"Are you willing to put your money where your mouth is?" Gabriel asked with a glint in his eye.

"What are you thinking?" Alexis shot back with interest. She folded her arms. "I think you've suffered through just about every forfeit I care to come up with."

"Yeah, same." Gabriel pressed his lips together in consideration. "I don't know. Maybe we should start a pool to cover the tab at AGB for a night when we get home at the end of this."

Bethany Anne cleared her throat, and the twins' heads snapped around. "You're gambling now?" she asked, raising an eyebrow.

Alexis shrugged. "Sure, Mom. What else is there to do on deployment? You want in?"

*Was that all it took?* She eyed her children. Well, her young adult children. It felt like the curtains were opened and where before they were three feet tall, the people staring at her were fully grown.

She felt Michael chuckling drily in the back of her mind and turned to him with her finger held up. "*Not. A. Word,*" she told him before taking her seat.

Michael held up his hands, his eyes crinkling in amusement. "Forgive me for enjoying the moment," he teased. "I happen to agree with our daughter."

Alexis whooped. "That's the spirit, Dad. What's your bet?"

Michael narrowed his eyes in thought. "I say we'll come in eight weeks over schedule." He lifted a shoulder at Bethany Anne's huff of annoyance. "But it will be because of exigent circumstances."

"It's a shame you're both wrong," Gabriel stated. "I know Mom. Free will is no match for her. I say we'll be back no more than two weeks late."

Bethany Anne smiled at Gabriel. "Looks like I have a favorite child at last. Since I intend this tour to take exactly the amount of time I've scheduled for it, you can put me down for fourteen months, Alexis."

Alexis giggled as she added Bethany Anne's guess to the sheet she was putting together in her HUD. "Sure, Mom. I'm sending this out to everyone on board. Buy-in is two hundred credits. I know how much Guardians drink."

Gabriel laughed and turned his chair to face Michael. "I was thinking you and I could go bistok hunting while we're around Yoll. Uncle Pete told me they're bigger and meaner there because the weaker ones get hunted out."

"That, and the death matches they hold every mating season," Michael agreed. "Those are the only two things preventing the planet from being overrun since they have no natural predator."

Alexis was horrified. "There are that many people hunting them?"

Michael shook his head. "No, the mating season is just that brutal." He tapped his wrist-holo and sent everyone a brochure for a resort planet called Serenity. "I have something else planned. Apart from the stops at Onyx Station, the *Meredith Reynolds*, and a couple other centers of population, the rest of the time, we'll be moving on every few days. Everyone could benefit from a break to recharge at the midpoint, so I worked with ADAM to fit in a four-week stop here."

The twins scanned the brochure with interest. "That's really thoughtful of you." Alexis' lips kept moving as she finished the brochure. "We had a couple of tours like this when we were in the gameworld, and the constant change of location gets to you after a while."

"Yeah," Gabriel agreed. "Then it doesn't matter where you stop as long as you get to stay in the same place for more than five minutes."

Michael flashed a satisfied smile. "I thought you'd appreciate it. When we get there, we have access to the entire planet."

"So we avoid Altaria completely, except for the tech crews laying the beacons," Alexis noted, studying the itinerary.

"We still have work to do during our time there," Bethany Anne explained. "But having the *Reynolds* along meant we could build some slack into the schedule. They'll be Gating out to nearby systems to set up the beacons while we're taking care of the inhabited locations."

"I can't see much room for kicking back anywhere else," Alexis told her. "Dad's right, everyone is going to be fried by the time we get there."

Bethany Anne smiled. "That's why I agreed with your father that the stop had to be built into the itinerary."

Michael folded his arms. "Why doesn't that sound like the abundance of praise I should be getting right now?"

"We've got to keep that ego of yours in check somehow." Bethany Anne paused as she pushed a finger into his chest, then dropped a kiss on his head as she walked by to get to her chair. "Thank you for thinking about everyone. The resort looks nice."

"Nice?" Alexis blurted. "Mom, they have *everything*. I always wanted to go to one of these resort worlds." She laughed when she worked out what Gabriel was so engrossed in. "I see why Dad likes it. The southern continent is a hunting range. You guys have fun with that. I'll be getting pampered within an inch of my life."

"Sweet!" Gabriel exclaimed. "You can have them grow whatever you want to hunt from scratch. The clone isn't sentient." He made a face of disappointment. "Dammit. You have to give them two months."

Michael's smirk grew a touch.

Alexis narrowed her eyes. "How long have you known about this resort, Dad?"

"I've known about it for years," Michael replied. "But we weren't exactly welcome to go into the Federation, and besides, it's worked out better that you're both fully grown to get the most out of it."

"You're not thinking of trophy-hunting." Alexis tilted her head. *It wasn't a question.* "So, you're planning on an experience?"

Michael winked. "The best yet."

Alexis' eyes lit up, matching the shine in Gabriel's. "Maybe I don't need that much pampering," Alexis conceded. "Are you coming with us, Mom?"

Bethany Anne pursed her lips. "What makes you think I'd be anywhere else?" She was distracted when Izanami appeared.

"You have an incoming call from Colonel Walton," Izanami informed her.

Bethany Anne got to her feet, reluctant to leave. "I won't be long."

She headed into the ready room just as Izanami asked if she would be permitted to join the family on the resort world. "You're part of the family, aren't you?" she called before closing the door.

Colonel Terry Henry Walton's disgruntled face stared at Bethany from the holoscreen.

"Why can't you ever be progruntled when I see you?" Bethany Anne asked in greeting.

Terry frowned, thrown by the remark. "'Progruntled?'" he repeated.

Bethany Anne waved a finger to encompass the Marine's face. "The opposite of disgruntled. I don't know if I've ever seen you smile."

"Just nod and agree," Charumati's voice came from somewhere to Terry's left.

"I'd listen to your wife," Bethany Anne advised with a warm smile. "What can I do for you, TH? You're not the social-call type."

"I wanted to get your take on the disturbed individual who blew himself up on Onyx Station," Terry told her. "I'd hate to miss an angle now and have it come back to bite me in the ass down the line."

"I appreciate your diligence," Bethany Anne told him. "I have Akio on his way to Red Rock to dig up whoever gave

Jacobsen that photo. It could just be someone who lost out when the mining operation was scrapped, but if there's a larger group working against us, I want to know about it before you take them out."

Terry nodded. "Got you. Char thinks it's a good idea to have someone on the lookout for shady individuals hovering around your location, and I agree. I'm sending Christina to you, which means my grandson will be accompanying her. Take care of him for me."

"You know I'll treat him like one of my own children." Bethany Anne smiled. "It will be great to see Christina. Have them meet us at Onyx Station. We'll be there in two days."

Izanami manifested in her usual red-gold shower as Bethany Anne ended the call. "The fleet is ready for departure, my Queen."

Bethany Anne nodded. "Good. Get the Gates up on the main viewscreen and the bridge of the *Reynolds* on the secondary." She swept onto the bridge as Izanami followed her instructions.

Alexis took her cue and prepared to send a video of Bethany Anne's departure speech to every registered news outlet in the Federation. "ADAM, is the link ready?"

>>**Almost,**<< ADAM told her. >>**Okay. We'll be live in two minutes.**<<

John burst onto the bridge. "Wait up. I have something for you." He thrust the wrapped package Jean had given him for Bethany Anne toward her.

"Not the best timing," Bethany Anne told him. She took the package from him and tore open the wrapping.

>>**You could just go into high-speed if you are worried.**<<

*Not if I don't want to seem jumpy.*

John lifted his hands. "Jean told me you had to have it before we left."

Bethany Anne took out the neatly folded bundle of fabric and shook it out. "A coat?" She spotted a scrap of paper taped to the lapel. "And a note from Jean."

"What's it say?" Alexis asked.

Bethany Anne read the note before dropping it and slipping her arms into the sleeves. It fit her perfectly. "This is my heavy armor, courtesy of her work with the Bl'kheth genetic material."

John nodded. "She sent a bunch of stuff over, along with the new armor." He pointed at Alexis and Gabriel. "I'll see you two for training first thing tomorrow."

"Ten seconds, Mom," Alexis called, nodding to acknowledge John's instruction.

Bethany Anne returned to her place in front of the viewscreen and smiled when Alexis signaled she was live.

*Why did she feel like this was like any other massive speech, and yet like just another day?*

"Devon Fleet, we are about to embark upon an undertaking many thought impossible to make a reality.

"It sucks for them to be proved wrong.

"I had no doubts when I asked for a way to provide an Interdiction to cover the whole Federation that our brightest minds *could and would* make it happen.

"Above all things, we protect our own, and you are the ones who will implement that protection. Celebrate your part in getting this operation off the ground, then strap in and buckle the fuck up because the impossible became real. Now the hard but not impossible work is about to start."

She paused before widening the focus of her words to include the people watching across the Federation. "When I stepped down as Empress, I made a promise. I swore to defend everything the Federation stands for if the time ever came that it was threatened. It hurts me to tell you that time has come. The Kurtherians *are* determined that every sentient being in this universe will bow at their feet. They consider us inferior to them because we care about others. Because we will act selflessly to protect each other, regardless of species. Having the biggest guns doesn't automatically make you the victor in a war of attrition, but we have something the Kurtherians and their allies don't.

"We have *unity*."

She scanned the ships on the screen, picking out the ancillary ships dotted around the SD *Reynolds* looming large in the near-distance.

*Her people.*

Bethany Anne graced them all with a smile. *"Let's roll."*

# CHAPTER EIGHT

**Onyx Station, Lowell Residence**

Nathan woke up. He rubbed his eyes, wondering what had caused him to snap awake when he heard a noise downstairs. He shook Ecaterina gently. "Did you hear that?" he asked her in a whisper.

Ecaterina stirred when he shook her again. "Mfff," she mumbled. "Hear what?"

Nathan heard another scuffle downstairs. "There's someone in the kitchen."

Ecaterina rolled over. "You're imagining things. No intruder is getting past my booby traps."

Nathan frowned. "There are booby traps in the house? How come I didn't know about them?"

"Because they're not programmed to kill *you*," Ecaterina mumbled sleepily.

A drawer banged shut downstairs, and Ecaterina sat bolt upright with a gun in her hand. "There is someone down there." She grabbed her wrist-holo from the bedside table and checked. "Huh?"

"Believe me now?" Nathan asked, eyeing the weapon she held with amusement. "You're just full of surprises tonight."

Ecaterina flashed him a bright grin as she got out of bed. "It's nice to know I can still surprise you after so long." She grabbed her robe and headed for the door. "Come on, we have a burglar to make target practice of."

"You know this is exactly why I married you," Nathan whispered as they took the stairs.

Ecaterina waved his teasing off as her wrist-holo gave her unexpected news. "The security measures have been *deactivated*."

Nathan's humor faded instantly as his mind fed him an image of another random anti-BA fanatic in his kitchen. "That's not good. Come on, we'd better find out who's down there."

They padded down the stairs silently. Ecaterina frowned at the sliver of light coming from the kitchen.

Nathan decided the only weapon good enough for the asshole who had dared break into his house only a week after the Jacobsen situation was his bare claws. He flexed his hands as he made them shift, one of the benefits of being a Pricolici.

There was a muffled clatter in the kitchen, then a sharp whisper.

"*Shh!*"

Nathan glanced at Ecaterina and nodded toward the door. Ecaterina raised her weapon, and they tiptoed into the kitchen together.

The only light came from the fridge, and even that was

dim since the intruder was helping themselves to the contents.

Nathan growled, spotting a second intruder hovering nervously by the door they'd come in by.

"Hands up!" Ecaterina cried, slapping the light switch. She dropped her weapon. "Oh."

Christina turned from the fridge with her arms full of sandwich fixings and grinned at them. "What kind of welcome is that for your only child?"

Nathan eyed the man by the door. He had the look of a Walton without any of the hard edges Terry had. "Who are you?"

Kai crossed the kitchen and offered his hand with an appropriately nervous smile. "Kailin Walton, Mr. Lowell. Good to meet you, sir."

Ecaterina caught Christina's amusement, put it together with Kai's earnest attempt to make a good impression on Nathan, and felt joy for her daughter.

She slipped around Nathan, who was ignoring Kai's hand in favor of giving him the hairy eyeball, and took his hand in both of hers, smiling warmly. "Welcome, Kailin. You're Marcie's and Kaeden's son, right?"

"You got me," he replied, returning her smile. "Call me 'Kai.' Christina has told me a lot about you two. I have to say, it's a bit nerve-wracking meeting you in person." He glanced at Nathan, who was still glaring. "I'm sorry we didn't meet under better circumstances."

"You're lucky my wife didn't shoot your fool heads off," Nathan growled.

"Play nice, Dad," Christina interjected. "Kai's good people." She walked over and took Kai's hand. "TH sent us to give you a hand with the investigation. You *are* short-handed, right?"

Nathan's heart broke a little at the realization that his little girl had finally brought a boy home to meet them.

*Dammit!* He winced when Ecaterina checked him in the ribs, but it was enough to snap him back to reality.

He forced himself to smile and shook Kai's hand. "Yeah. Yeah, we are. It's good to have you here."

Ecaterina intervened, seeing that Nathan was thrown by the whole situation. "Let me get you two settled. We can talk about the investigation after everyone has slept."

"My room is still there, right?" Christina asked with a yawn. "We made it through the Gate system without any waiting time at the connections, so we're pretty tired."

Ecaterina nodded. "It's exactly as you left it. Are you two staying long?"

Christina hugged her mother. "Only until Bethany Anne gets here. You and Dad go back to bed. I have to eat before I can sleep."

Ecaterina returned the hug with feeling. "It's good to have you home." With that, she shooed Nathan out of the kitchen while Christina got to work making a snack.

Nathan looked over his shoulder at the kitchen door as Ecaterina shepherded him toward the stairs. "But..." he whispered. *"But!"*

"No buts," she told him firmly. "Can't you see she's in love?"

Nathan hung his head as he ascended. "Yes. Why do you think I'm so bothered? They're not going to share a room. He's not putting his hands on my daughter."

Ecaterina chuckled. "I'd say you're far too late to stop that ship from sailing."

"Dammit!" Nathan clamped his hands over his ears. *"I didn't hear that."*

---

The next morning, Nathan woke up to the smell of bacon permeating the house. He rolled out of bed and got dressed, his mind seesawing between the report he'd received yesterday and the middle-of-the-night disturbance.

Christina and Kai were nowhere to be seen when he got to the kitchen. Ecaterina had two places set at the breakfast bar. Nathan had a moment of wondering if he'd dreamed Christina's return.

He took a seat and leaned in to snag a sausage from the platter. "I know it's not my birthday."

Ecaterina slapped his hand away. "Wait until the rest is ready. I felt like celebrating. Our daughter is home, and I am pleased she has found a partner at last."

Nathan dropped his head onto his folded arms and groaned. "I was hoping I'd dreamed that. Not the part where she was home, the 'she brought home a guy' part."

Ecaterina snickered, putting his plate in front of him. "You are a silly man. Of course, you didn't dream it. Christina and Kai are meeting the Magistrate you requested for breakfast. They'll be home soon."

Nathan sighed and dug into his breakfast, resigning himself to the fact that his little girl wasn't so little anymore. He supposed he was grateful they'd gone to the meeting. It was definitely too early to deal with Rivka and her endless paperwork. "What do you know about this Kai character? How do we know he's not going to break our daughter's heart?"

Ecaterina gave him a hard look. "You should know that they've been together for a while. Have you ever known any Walton to be anything less than loyal, trustworthy, and honorable?"

Nathan slumped on the stool. "I suppose not. But it still doesn't make him good enough for my princess."

"Your *princess* is a century old," Ecaterina scolded. "Would you rather she was alone for her entire life? Perpetually single like the Grimes girl?"

It was Nathan's turn to deliver the Look. "That's not very enlightened of you," he chided, diverting the attention from his own stubborn judgment. "Some people are happier to be single. Anyway, didn't Lilian's daughter get together with that assmouth Ricky Escobar?"

She popped him on the head as she shrugged. "Whatever. I'm just saying, we couldn't have asked for Christina to have made a better choice of partner."

Nathan scowled. "I don't have to admit it."

Ecaterina rolled her eyes in exasperation. "You'll regret it if you don't make him feel welcome. What's it going to be like if they have babies?"

Nathan jammed his hands over his ears again. "Not listening, and you can't make me. Just let me do what I have to do to get through this."

Christina and Kai arrived back at the house while Nathan was clearing the table. He broke into a smile at the sight of her. "Here she is. You missed breakfast."

Christina ignored her father ignoring Kai. "We ate with Rivka. It was good to see her again."

"We got more than breakfast," Kai told Nathan and Ecaterina with a serious expression. "Did you know there's a whole criminal subculture on the bottom levels of this station?"

Nathan held up a hand, acknowledging Kai for the first time. "Hold your horses. There won't be any posse riding at dawn. I know all about the criminal underbelly of the station, and I'd rather have them where I can keep my eye on what they're doing."

Kai frowned. "But..."

"Keeg hasn't been an open station all that long, so there's been no opportunity for it to develop the layers of society that a station that has been around for a century or more has," Nathan explained, realizing the youth of TH's grandson had a lot to do with his overexuberance.

Kai's frown deepened. "What are you saying? That they're allowed to get away with it?"

"No," Nathan replied. "But they're allowed to *exist*. It's like this; people are going to do what they're going to do. Yeah, we'll take care of those whose proclivities are harmful to honest citizens, but otherwise, it's the Magistrates' job to take care of the rest. Everyone's got to live."

"Dad's right," Christina told Kai. She grinned at Nathan. "There's less crime than you think, with the Magistrates taking care of business."

Kai considered that the balance had to be kept somehow. "I know I'd hate to be on Rivka's bad side," he conceded. "I guess I can see that working."

Ecaterina chuckled. "Did she have any useful information?"

Christina nodded, sharing the file the no-nonsense Magistrate had put together for them to Nathan and Ecaterina's internal HUDs. "Yeah. She told us she'd heard rumors about a group who believe Bethany Anne is lying about the Kurtherian threat on her last assignment, but she dismissed them as ridiculous."

"Well, yeah." Nathan ran a hand through his hair as he took in the information. "This could be dangerous to everyone if it spreads. What's your next move?"

Christina shrugged. "As you can see, she gave us a couple of leads to follow. We're going to talk to Bethany Anne when she gets here and see what she wants us to do."

## Approaching Pickup Point Two, QSD *Baba Yaga*

"I'm bored." Gabriel pushed his sketchpad away and got up from his bunk.

Alexis looked up from her book. "Well, find something to do."

Gabriel started throwing items into a bag. "That's what I'm doing. I'm going to the APA."

"That's not a bad idea." Alexis closed her book and checked the availability of the ship's training facilities in her HUD. "Deck six is open."

Gabriel shook his head. "Armor training. Trey and K'aia are with John and Gabrielle in the APA on this deck."

Alexis got off her bunk and grabbed her boots. "Why didn't you say that in the first place? We haven't seen him or K'aia for days."

They collected their armor from the armory and made their way to the APA, where they found their closest friends working out in the gym area.

Trey racked his weights and got up from the bench. "Hey, you look kinda like my buddy Gabriel. It's hard to tell. It's been so long since I've seen him, I've forgotten his face."

"Very funny," Gabriel grumbled. "How are you guys finding it with John?"

"Oh, you know," K'aia replied. "We get up, eat, train, eat, train some more, and if we're not exhausted at the end of the day, we hang out in the theater and watch movies with everyone."

"What about you guys?" Trey inquired.

Gabriel sighed. "Hurry up and wait is about it. We've been filling the time getting our armor calibrated."

K'aia glanced at the shielded area where John and Gabrielle were sparring on the mats. "Yeah? I've got to say, it doesn't look easy."

Alexis giggled. "It's not, but it's like any other training. You repeat it until you defeat it." She indicated the benches outside the translucent shielding. "I want to watch and see what they're getting out of it."

Gabriel watched John and Gabrielle, noting that they were both giving a subpar performance.

Alexis dropped onto the bench beside him. "What's going on with you two?" she called loud enough to be heard by John and Gabrielle.

Gabrielle called a halt, and John broke off the attack he was setting up for.

John was smiling when his helmet retracted. "What's up, kids?"

"Gabriel is burning a hole in his brain trying to figure out why you two are fighting like a pile of crap," Alexis replied. She shrugged at John's pointed look. "What? I'm saying it like I see it; you two were slow to react. What gives?"

"The armor takes some getting used to," Gabrielle admitted with a rueful smile. "Learning to work with Sean speaking in my ear continuously has given me a new appreciation for Bethany Anne's grip on her sanity."

John snorted. "That's putting it mildly, but I think we're making progress with the calibration."

"That's true," Gabrielle conceded. "I don't think it will take too long for my version of Sean to learn to intuit my responses and act accordingly."

Gabriel sucked in a breath. "Ours has taken every hour Mom and Dad have given us."

"You have more time than us." Gabrielle reactivated her helmet. "I'm happy to take my time with it. After all, we've got fifteen months to fill," she told them with a wink as her faceplate closed.

Alexis grinned. "Is that your final bet?"

Gabrielle nodded. "It is." She tapped John on the shoulder. "Did you get in on the pool yet?"

John cracked a grin. "I got in there before any of the guys. Four hundred and forty-eight days."

Alexis pointed at John. "Brave of you to pin it down to a day. The calendar is filling up fast."

Bethany Anne walked into the APA and came over to

the mats. "John, I need to take K'aia and Trey for a while." She smiled at the twins. "You two as well."

John looked at K'aia and Trey and nodded toward Bethany Anne. "You heard the boss," he told them. "Come find me when you're done."

Alexis picked up speed to keep up with Bethany Anne as they walked in the direction of the small briefing room near the bridge. "What's going on, Mom? We don't have anything scheduled until we get to Onyx Station."

"Onyx Station is what I wanted to discuss," Bethany Anne answered. She waited until the five of them were seated in the briefing room before elaborating. "Two days ago, a man committed suicide live on the public access channel. He was clearly suffering from a loss of his grip on reality."

Alexis spoke up. "Why would someone do that, and why are you telling us about it?"

Bethany Anne had hesitated before discussing the assignment she had for the team with Michael. "You can see for yourselves," she told them. "I've made the video available to you all."

All four watched Paul Jacobsen's final moments in silence. Trey was first to speak when it was over. "This man believed he was doing an honorable thing."

Bethany Anne nodded, folding her hands on the table. "That's my concern."

"Where did he get that photo?" Alexis asked. "More importantly, what if there are more Paul Jacobsens out there?"

"I've got your grandfather working to resolve the first

question," Bethany Anne assured her. "However, the second is trickier to get to the bottom of. I want you four to go ahead to Onyx Station and help Nathan with the investigation. Speak with the widow and his friends and coworkers—anyone you can find who knew him. Find out if he had any new friends."

"We can do that," Gabriel promised.

Alexis, K'aia, and Trey agreed in unison.

Bethany Anne nodded to each. "Get in touch with Nathan when you get there. Tell him you're there to take the load off him so he can make sure there are no snags with the upgrade schedule. I've had the *Gemini* prepared so you can leave..." She looked at a non-existent watch before turning back to the four of them. "Why are you still here?" she asked, then cracked a small smile.

They hugged before double-timing it to the hangar the QGE *Gemini* was currently berthed in.

"She's exactly how I remember her," Trey exclaimed, staring in wonder at the shining blue curves of the Galactic Explorer-class ship's two modules.

"Minus the scorch mark where that Ooken ship got a direct hit on her," K'aia pointed out, drawing a laugh from them all.

"Let's get going." Gabriel put action to his recommendation as Gemini dropped the ramp for them to board.

All four entered the mezzanine level of the bridge and headed for their stations out of habit, feeling various degrees of déjà vu.

While this was the first time they had physically set foot aboard, they had traveled light-years and fought for their lives in the gameworld version of this very room.

Alexis waved to Gemini on the viewscreen. "Hey, Gem. It's good to be heading out, right?"

Gemini nodded. "ADAM has briefed me on our assignment. Investigations are interesting more often than not."

"Did you miss us, Gemini?" Trey asked, leaning back in his chair with a twinkle in his eyes. "Because I sure missed flying from adventure to adventure with you."

Gemini's friendly features rearranged into a pleasant smile. "It's good to have you all back," she agreed. "We have clearance to Gate in a few moments. Should I engage the cloak?"

Gabriel ran through his portion of the pre-Gate checks. "We don't need to cloak. We'll contact Nathan when we get there."

Trey felt nothing as Gemini lifted the ship and guided it out into open space.

The AI kept up a running commentary as they made their way to the coordinates given by the station's Traffic Control. "Gate drive initiated. Departing in T-minus five... four...three...two..."

---

Bethany Anne watched the twins' ship wink out of existence with a smile that was just on this side of resigned.

Michael took her hand and squeezed. "They are leaving with every technological advantage we are able to provide and the training to use it efficiently."

"I was impressed by how they took the news that there's a plot to turn the people against me." Bethany Anne rested her head on his shoulder for a moment.

"You've been through this before and come out on the other side unharmed," Michael reminded her. "If there's anyone aboard that station who knows something about a wider conspiracy?" His eyes grew dark. "I have faith they will regret living."

She watched him leave. That was probably the most praise she could expect from the man who wouldn't admit he might be worried as well.

*Just a touch.*

# CHAPTER NINE

**Onyx Station, QGE *Gemini***

"I have an incoming transmission," Gemini announced moments after they Gated into the system.

"Onscreen," Alexis requested, sitting up in her chair.

Nathan's face ran through a series of expressions when he saw the twins. "What the hell? I was expecting...well, *not* this."

Gabriel laughed. "I take it Mom didn't tell you we completed our enhancement?"

"No, she did not," Nathan stated. "I guess I owe her one, and I'll have to make it a good one to make up for..." He waved a hand at the screen. "This."

Alexis tilted her head. "Good luck with surviving that. Mom did at least tell you we were on our way to give you a hand with the investigation?"

Nathan's face reddened. "Yeah. Um, I'll have to tell Ecaterina you're not the bunch of teenagers she's expecting, but I'm glad to have you here. I've sent your AI the docking coordinates. I'll see you real soon."

He was waiting to meet them when they debarked inside one of Bad Company's hangars.

Alexis ran down the ramp with her go-bag slung over her shoulder and gave Nathan a brief one-armed hug. "How are you?" she asked with a sympathetic look. "It has to be unnerving having someone blow himself up on your doorstep."

"I'm fine," Nathan assured her as he accepted handshakes from Gabriel and the others. He paused for a moment to take in the changes in the twins since he'd last seen them, then checked out K'aia and Trey with the same fascination. "Unbelievable."

Alexis spread her arms wide. "Believe it or not. For us, it's been years since we saw you."

Nathan laughed, figuring it was. "I stand by my statement. Ecaterina is going to be over the moon to see you. You're going to stay with us, right?"

Gabriel glanced at the others before replying, "We could be working weird hours. We'll sleep on the ship."

Trey hefted his pack. "I'd hate to be responsible for Ecaterina getting anything less than a perfect night's sleep." He shrugged when Nathan gave him a questioning look. "What? I matured to own a strong survival instinct."

Nathan chuckled as he showed them out of the hangar bay. "Instinct like that will get you far in life. Would I be right in thinking you won't turn down a dinner invitation?"

K'aia laughed aloud. "I see you have the same finely-tuned instinct, Mr. Lowell."

"I'm still married, aren't I?" he replied with a grin. "I'm guessing you want to get straight to your assignment. I've given you access to everything the investigation has turned up so far, which isn't a whole lot. Christina and her boy-toy are around somewhere, and they've got some leads already."

The twins exchanged a glance at the complete lack of nuance in Nathan's description of Christina's companion. "That would be a great start," Alexis enthused, avoiding the subject altogether. "Sounds like she's our first stop."

K'aia switched to mental communication as they left. *I wonder what the boy-toy comment was about?*

Alexis had an idea. *I'm going to guess that he's being fatherly, and whoever Christina has with her will be as much fun to hang out with as she is.*

Gabriel checked the information Nathan had given them. *We have a job to do before we get to hang out. Come on, we'll go and talk to the widow. She lives nearby. Then we'll look for Christina.*

Alexis sighed. *Are you channeling Mom? We're going to take a look around the station and get a feel for the vibe. I want to know if that guy was alone in believing Mom is the enemy.*

Trey cut in, seeing the twins were about to start digging their heels in. *How about we split up? Me and Alexis will go check out the bars on the lower levels, you two go speak to the widow.*

*Deal.*


## Onyx Station, Deck Thirteen

Christina faced the Shrillexian who had his blaster pointed at her temple. "I get the feeling I'm not welcome here."

The Shrillexian shrugged. "It's just good business not to have the daughter of the man looking to take us down drinking here," he told her in an even tone. "I'm sure you understand."

Christina lifted her hand and pushed the blaster away. "I do. But I'm not here about your backroom enterprises, Merril. Some idiot blew himself up after spouting a whole lot of bistok shit about the current political situation. If there's more like him on board the station, it's in all our interests to make sure they don't succeed in their goals, wouldn't you agree?"

Merril glared at her for a long moment before relaxing. "Nobody's making any money if they're dead," he conceded. "Fine. What can I do to help?"

Kai watched the exchange in silence, impressed with the way Christina had handled the criminal organizations working out of the bars on this deck. Merril's bar was the fifth establishment they'd visited where they'd been met with a less than stellar welcome. Each time Christina had taken control of the situation without so much as raising her voice.

Christina smiled as she took a seat at the bar. "You can start by getting me a drink. I've been talking all damned day. Then you can tell me if any of your minions have heard anything while they've been out doing minion-y things."

Merril took a seat on the stool next to Christina's and waved a hand at the android bartender, who placed three glasses of something blue and somehow sizzling in front of them. He picked up his glass. "There's not much I can tell you. Things have been pretty quiet around here since that guy blew himself up." He took a sip of his drink and winced. "I don't know how you humans drink that stuff."

"Like this," Christina told him, knocking hers back. She belched as her nanocytes took care of the alcohol but left her to deal with the carbon dioxide. "Whoo, that stuff will put hair on your chest. So, you were saying it's been quiet? What about before the incident? Any strange people or new players?"

Merril thought about it for a few moments. "There's a moonlet a couple of systems over that comes to mind. The place is a goods and services exchange. They don't have any problems with letting in people who aren't welcome in the Federation as long as they don't cause trouble."

"It's a start." After a bit more talk, Christina put her glass down, paid the bill, and nodded for Kai to follow her from the bar. "Looks like we're heading back out sooner than we expected."

"What do you think we'll find at that moonlet?" Kai asked as they approached the elevators that would take them back up to the main deck.

"A ton of illegal shit we'll have to ignore for now," Christina told him. "Don't go getting all Boy Scout while we're there. I don't want you dying when I've kind of gotten used to having you around."

Kai snickered, wrapping an arm around her waist. "Ha, you *like me*, you like me!"

Christina shoved him playfully. "You're only just catching on? My mom always told me men are slow when it comes to feelings, but come on, Walton!"

Kai's hand drifted to his pocket as they walked into the elevator. "You know…"

Christina's eyes widened. "Don't you dare!"

Kai extracted a palmtop device from his pocket and waved it with a self-conscious shrug before activating the screen. "What? We're investigating, so one of us should be taking notes."

Christina stared at him skeptically for a moment. "Okay, so we have the coordinates for this moon."

"Moonlet," Kai corrected. "What's the difference between the two? Is it size?"

"It's always size," Christina told him drily.

It was Kai's turn to look askance at Christina. "I hope you're not implying something there."

Christina linked her arm through his and pulled him out of the elevator. "I'm implying we should get to the Pod and get our asses to the moonlet."

She paused before taking a right on the concourse toward Bad Company's premises instead of the left that would take them to the docking spar their ship was waiting on. "But first, we need to check in with my dad."

"Oh, joy," Kai muttered as he followed the woman he loved through the crowd. "Because he likes me *so* much."

Christina looked over her shoulder and flashed him a grin. "Dad? He just needs a bit of time to get used to the idea of you, is all."

"Yeah, but what he *wants* is ten minutes alone with me and a reasonable explanation as to why I didn't survive it," Kai countered. "Those are two very different situations."

Christina stopped in her tracks. "You're right." She headed in the opposite direction. "Fine, we'll call Dad when we've found out whether this connection pans out."

. . .

## Onyx Station, QSD *Baba Yaga*

"We're clear to dock," Izanami announced. "The *Reynolds* has been assigned a space on the opposite side of the station."

"Get me Reynolds," Bethany Anne requested. "I can't have us getting separated."

The AI's android face was approximating a smile when he appeared onscreen. "My Queen. What can I do for you?"

"You can teleport your landing crew over to the *Baba Yaga*," Bethany Anne told him. "I want to present a united front when we arrive. Izanami will give you the coordinates for the transfer bay."

Reynolds turned from the screen. "You heard the Queen. Get moving! We'll be ready for transport in twenty minutes. I assume you want everyone ready to begin setting up the transporters right away?"

"You assume right. Thank you, Reynolds." Bethany Anne dropped the link and pinged the twins. She got two responses, meaning they'd split up for some reason. They called in on separate video links within a few seconds of each other.

"Hey, Mom," Alexis called. "I'm a little busy, what's up?"

"Checking in," Bethany Anne told them. "How's the investigation progressing?"

"You were right about there being some bigger plot going on," Gabriel confirmed.

Alexis groaned. "I'm having some trouble tracking Christina down. She left the station without reporting in."

Bethany Anne looked past Alexis to where Trey had a portly Shrillexian suspended by his throat. "I see you're working tirelessly to get to the bottom of it."

The Shrillexian's eyes widened at the sound of Bethany Anne's voice. "Is that the Empress?" he spluttered. "You didn't tell me you were working for her! I'll talk. I might not be a good guy, but I'm no traitor."

Alexis gave him a skeptical look as Trey dropped him onto the table, scattering the piles of credit chips he'd been counting when they'd burst in. "Could have fooled me. Thanks for the help, Mom."

Bethany Anne smiled. "Any time. How are you doing, Gabriel?"

Gabriel nodded solemnly. "I got a lot from Paul's family. He'd had some issues like you guessed, but nothing serious until he met a group of people who left the station a month or so ago. She didn't know where they went, just that they'd convinced him that Kurtherians are a myth and you're the real enemy."

The Shrillexian growled and spat on the floor. "That freakshow? I remember them. We ran their deluded asses out of the system when they wouldn't let it go. Last I heard, they're on Nabraxia."

"What do you want us to do, Mom?" Gabriel asked.

Bethany Anne tilted her head. "I guess have fun hunting down conspiracy nuts on Nabraxia, wherever that is."

Alexis indicated her new Shrillexian friend with a nod. "Merril here is going to fill us in on the details."

"No issues," Gabriel added. "Just like we promised."

"Did you call her '*Mom*'?" she heard before she blew them both a kiss and dropped the call.

She left the bridge to meet Reynolds and company.

. . .

## SD *Reynolds*, **Transporter Bay**

Nathan entered the bay and was met by a male and a female of a species he hadn't encountered before. His HUD told him they were the *Reynolds'* resident tech geniuses. "Mr. Takal, Ms. Geroux, welcome to Onyx station. My name is—"

"Nathan Lowell, CEO of Bad Company," Geroux finished smoothly, holding out a hand. "Good to meet you. We should get started moving this equipment before the Queen is done with her meet and greet."

Nathan smiled as he shook her hand. "Efficient. I bet Bethany Anne loves you."

Geroux elbowed her uncle, snapping him out of his runaway thought. "One of us has to be when the other is too lost in his thoughts to even say hello."

Takal chuckled disarmingly. "Uh, hello."

Geroux rolled her eyes. "Why don't you get back to your team, Uncle? I'll get the transporter equipment set up."

Takal beamed at her. "I couldn't have come up with a better plan myself," he told her. "Good to meet you, Mr..."

"Lowell, Nathan Lowell," Geroux supplied in exasperation.

Takal had already wandered off.

"He reminds me of someone," Nathan commented to Geroux as he showed her out of the docking bay and into the attached warehouse. "Actually, a few someones."

Geroux looked at him with wide eyes. "There are more absentminded, alcohol-soaked inventors running around without supervision? Stars preserve us."

Nathan laughed. "You *have* met BMW, right? Trust me,

he's going to fit in just fine. Okay, so the transporter module is being transferred to Bad Company HQ, where it's going to be guarded day and night."

Geroux consulted the briefing document she'd been given by ADAM. "This building we're in now is Bad Company premises, am I right? We don't want this technology to get out."

Nathan nodded. "We own this level entirely. It's the unofficial FDG base that serves this quadrant."

"FDG?" Geroux repeated blankly. "I've come across so many three-letter acronyms in this report that they're all blurring together."

"Think of them as the Federation's standing military," Nathan explained. "There are a few specialist groups associated with them, but it's the bulk of the troops who'll be benefitting from the upgrade."

Geroux nodded, tapping her wrist-holo to activate the antigrav pallet carrying her tools and the cube carrying one of Reynolds' splinter personalities. "Got it. Okay, well, the sooner you show us to CEREBRO's core room, the sooner we can get started on our part."

Nathan was about to ask who she was referring to when the cube lit up blue.

"Tina is in the core room and wants to know why we're not there already."

"Thanks, Engineering." Geroux sighed. "There goes my reputation for being efficient."

Nathan shook his head. "I'll take the blame. Tina doesn't scare me. Come on, it's this way."

CHAPTER TEN

**Federation Space, Nabraxia**

Christina and Kai touched down at a dusty spaceport, one of many ringing the sprawling market that covered most of the surface of the moonlet two systems away from Onyx Station.

"I suppose it makes sense to be as near the trade hub as they can get without drawing attention from the Magistrates," Christina acknowledged as they concluded registration for their ship.

Kai paused to get a look at their surroundings as they exited the spaceport. He wrinkled his nose, finding the faded canvas awnings shielding the market stalls much less impressive than the image of a high-tech space pirate hideaway he'd been imagining on the journey there. "If it wasn't for the aliens, we could be in any desert on Earth. I thought space would be more...I don't know, *spacey*."

"What do you mean?" Christina asked, heading in the direction of the only definite source of information when you were a stranger in a strange town.

"You know." Kai kept pace with her as they wended their way toward the likeliest-looking dive bar. "Domes, flying cars. Autonomous buildings where robots do everything."

Christina snickered. "Robots that do everything, huh? You too good to wash your own pants, Earthman?" She swept ahead of him into the bar.

Kai opened his mouth to protest, then gave a resigned sigh and followed her inside. They headed straight for the bar, and Christina waved to catch the attention of the Torcellan who'd just finished serving a group of Skaines at the other end of the room.

The bartender gave them the once-over before nodding. "What can I get you?" he asked, flipping his towel onto his shoulder.

Christina grinned and scrutinized the chalkboard menu over the Torcellan's head. "What's good to eat here?"

"I could eat a whole cow," Kai chipped in hopefully.

The bartender laughed. "You're either wealthy or deluded. No beef here, just bistok."

Christina slapped the bar. "That's fine by us. We'll take two sixteen-ounce steaks apiece with all the sides. Put the veggies from my plate on his." She looked at Kai as she jerked a thumb at him. "What are you drinking?"

"Whatever's brewed locally," Kai answered, taking the risk he'd be served something unpalatable for the chance of discovering a decent beer he could take a case of back to the Dren Cluster as a gift for TH.

"I'll take a Coke," Christina requested.

They accepted their drinks and claimed a quiet corner booth. Kai sipped his beer and made a sound of appreciation as he licked his foam mustache off. "Okay, this place might be populated entirely by criminals, but they know how to make beer."

Christina waved a hand. "Oh, well, that excuses everything."

Kai chuckled. "Exactly."

They filled the time while they waited for their food with idle chat and people-watching. A group of humans came in and took a booth two spaces down from them just after the waitstaff brought out their meals.

Christina listened closely when she heard the servers complaining about the group as they walked back to the kitchen. "Did you hear that?" she asked Kai quietly.

Kai nodded, having similarly enhanced hearing. "They seem to think those guys are bad for business. I wonder why?"

Christina paused in cutting her steak. "Keep listening. Maybe they'll say something to enlighten us as to why they're so unpopular around here."

Kai nodded and got to work on his food, one ear on the conversation two booths away.

It didn't take long to figure out who they were. The mood amongst the group of humans was low. Christina and Kai listened in while the group complained to their leader that they were having the same hard time here as they'd had on Onyx station.

"It could have something to do with them trying to convince everyone to join their conspiracy cult," Kai muttered.

Christina nodded, struggling to concentrate on the objective at hand through her rising anger as the subject of the cultists' discussion turned to their success with Paul Jacobsen and their plans for sowing more chaos when they left Nabraxia. "If it wasn't that they might give us a lead back to whoever is feeding them this shit, I'd take them out here and now."

Kai finished his mouthful before replying, "Are you thinking what I'm thinking?"

Christina lifted a shoulder and picked up her glass. "Maybe. Are you thinking we should follow them when they leave and find out where they're staying?"

Kai indicated the group of Skaines with a twitch of his fork. "Great plan, but we should probably make sure they survive so we can put it into action."

She and Kai noted that the Skaines weren't the only ones who took exception to the group being there. They were joined by more than a few of the bar's clientele as they marched over to the humans sitting in the booth.

"Hold off until it gets serious," Christina decided.

One of the Skaines pulled a blaster on the humans.

Kai nodded. "Is that serious enough?"

Christina put down her silverware as she shifted to her Pricolici form. "Does that answer your question?" she growled, sliding out of the booth to plow through the crowd around the humans. "Come on. We need at least one of them alive."

Kai encouraged the crowd to disperse with a few judiciously-placed elbows as he moved to stand with Christina between the humans and their would-be lynch mob.

Christina held a razor-sharp claw to the soft skin beneath the lead Skaine's jaw. She took his blaster before he had a chance to react. "I can't allow you to kill these humans."

The Skaine went up on his tiptoes to relieve the pressure. "He went for his weapon first."

"That's the funniest-looking gun I've ever seen," Kai countered, grabbing a recording device from the cultist's hand.

Christina half-turned to glance at the device, then released the Skaine leader with a shove and pointed his own blaster at him. "How do you explain that?" she demanded.

The Skaine held up his hands. "Looked like a weapon to me. It doesn't matter anyway. We came here to tell them to get the hell off Nabraxia. If you're with them, you can leave too or die." He looked at his supporters for agreement.

"We're not with them," Kai assured the mob quickly before the situation devolved further. "They're wanted for questioning by the Magistrates." He realized his mistake when all eyes in the room locked onto them and backpedaled before they were mistaken for law enforcement. "There's a...bounty on them!"

Christina groaned as they became all that stood between every lowlife in the room and the six people Kai had just put a monetary value on. "*Nice move.*"

The bar erupted as the race to get hands on the humans rapidly turned into a free-for-all.

Christina bowled the Skaines and their buddies out of the way while Kai ordered the humans to follow him. They vacated the table just in time to avoid being flattened by a Leath and a Yollin who crashed into it with no regard for the humans they were fighting over.

"What's happening?" one of the humans asked Christina with complete confusion. "We're *pacifists*. We don't want anything to do with this fight!"

Christina grabbed him by the back of his shirt and shoved him behind the cover of a fallen table to shield him with the other humans. "Just stay down and try not to get killed," she told him, kicking away an alien who looked like a melted candle holding a laser pistol.

Kai fought his way back to Christina and the two of them monitored the brawl, repelling anyone who got too close to the humans crouched behind the table while they waited for an opportunity to get out of there.

"I'm going to throw out a guess," he ducked a randomly thrown empty bottle, "and say there's no law enforcement here." Kai panted as he parried sword strikes with a chair. He disarmed the Skaine attacking him with a flick of the steel legs and mashed their nose with the rim of the seat. "Okay, he's fugly."

Christina snorted, caught up in a hand-to-tusk tussle with the Leath, who'd knocked the Yollin unconscious and was now focused on the Pricolici. "Yeah, I can't see there being a handy Magistrate around."

She got nicked with the tusk. "Ok, this shit is over!" With a roar, she tossed the Leath into a wall and looked at the growing crowd with dismay. "Did *everyone* in here call for backup?"

"NO!" Kai moaned when someone tossed an incendiary behind the bar. "NOT THE *BEER*!"

His lament of despair turned into a cheer when the bar's owner jumped up from where he'd been hiding and tossed the flaming ball back the way it had come.

The far end of the barroom caught fire, throwing up a cloud of acrid smoke when it spread to the soft furnishings. Just as Christina was thinking they were in real trouble, two humans in steel-blue armor entered the bar at a run.

The taller human lifted his hand in the direction of the fire and surrounded it with a bubble of energy, cutting off the oxygen before assisting the woman in suppressing the fight.

"Who the are hell are *they?*" Kai breathed, awed by the speed with which they cut through the angry criminals.

His mouth fell open as he watched them take control.

Nothing slowed them down.

They moved like water, their armor flashing with released energy every time they made contact. The majority of the brawlers resorted to pounding the crap out of them with their guns.

Which had no effect. It was like banging on metal with stalks of celery.

Christina shrugged, her confusion growing when the smaller of the two flourished her hands and forced every nonhuman in the room to the floor with a pulse of Etheric energy.

"I have no idea who has Etheric powers like that besides Bethany Anne and Michael," she admitted. "But it's definitely not them."

"How do you know?" Kai asked.

Christina waved a hand. "Because everyone is still alive."

She thought at first she'd been mistaken when the newcomers revealed themselves. They took their helmets off, and she saw dark hair and a flash of red eyes through the clearing smoke.

The bartender hoisted a boxy rifle in their direction. "Who are you to come into my place of business like this?"

Alexis flashed her eyes at the bartender. "Unless you're charging people to smash your shit to pieces, I'd be a little more grateful we showed up. Hmm?"

The bartender lowered his rifle in a sudden attack of wisdom. He looked around his place of business, his face draining of color. "What a fucking mess." He opened his register, grabbing the cash inside with a huff. He didn't bother bending down when some change fell. "Screw this. I'm going back to Onyx."

He walked out, leaving the room in stunned silence.

"Everyone stay exactly where they are until I say differently," Gabriel ordered the people getting acquainted with the mixture of spilled beer, dirt, and sawdust on the floor. "We're here for those assholes. No one gets heroic."

"Or greedy," Kai added. Gabriel looked over. "Sorry, bad explanation on my part in the heat of the moment. They thought they had bounties."

Christina looked at the twins in bemusement. "Thanks for the assist. Has anybody ever told you that you look like Bethany Anne?"

Alexis laughed. "Only my whole life." She looked at her brother. "I told you she wouldn't recognize us."

Christina's confusion wasn't helped with the familiar laugh. "*Alexis?*" She turned slowly to the grown man. "Which would make you…"

"Gabriel, yeah," Gabriel gave her a wry smile. "You just

lost me fifty credits. I thought you'd figure us out the second you saw us."

Christina shook her head. "But I saw you just months ago at the gala. You were, well, *kids*."

"Long—and classified—story," Alexis replied, looking at the people on the floor. "What do you say we wrap this up before we get to chatting?"

"I'd say let's get these people to their ship and get the hell out of here," Christina told her, motioning for the humans to get moving. She turned to find they had already exited from under the table.

She stopped in her tracks when she saw they were creeping toward the exit. "Would you look at that? Not even a thank you."

"I don't think we'll be welcomed back here anytime soon," Christina remarked to Alexis as they followed the group out of the bar. "Shame. The food was pretty good."

Alexis vanished from sight.

Gabriel smiled at Christina's questioning look. "She's planting a tracker on the leader."

Alexis returned a moment later, reappearing by Gabriel's side. "I read the leader's mind. He's called Marek, and he's thinking about leaving Nabraxia immediately, which means we won't have long to wait to tag their ship."

The cultists melted into the crowd. Alexis grinned, watching them go. "Too easy."

"Great job," Gabriel told her. "We should get back to the *Gemini*."

Kai nodded. "Same."

Alexis called Gemini to request a Pod to their location, and they zigzagged through the stalls looking for an open space to land it. "What was your plan before we turned up?"

"To find the group from Onyx Station," Christina told her. "Which we did. The plan was to track them back to wherever they are staying and wait for them to make contact with the traitor who sent the photo."

Alexis had scanned the cultists' minds while she was planting the tracker patch on Marek. "They have a handler, but they don't know his identity," she told them. "I got that much when I read his mind."

"We can have Gemini put a tracker on their ship," Gabriel suggested as they broke free of the stalls and walked into an open square with a fountain in the center.

Alexis pointed at the Pod descending into the square. "Our ride is here. Where is your ship docked?"

Christina gave them the location of a spaceport on the western side of the continent as they boarded the Pod.

They arrived within a few minutes, and the twins dropped Christina and Kai off with a plan to reconvene above the moonlet before Marek's group had a chance to escape.

Gabriel and Alexis got back to the *Gemini* and took her up, pausing only to admit Christina's and Kai's Pod when they caught up with them.

They arrived on the bridge to find the twins hard at work tracking the cult.

Christina edged around the hard light projection of Nabraxia that took up the central space on the main floor and walked over to Alexis at the left-hand console. "What are you doing?"

Alexis continued to type as she answered, her fingers

flying over the keys without hesitation. "We're hooked into the cameras around every spaceport on the moonlet, looking to find the one the cult are docked at. Ideally, we want to know where they are before they get spaceborne, so until the tracker patch is in range, all we can do is work with facial rec."

Gabriel turned from his console. "We have a match. They're entering the port on the southwest side of the market."

A few minutes later, they identified the cultists' ship.

"Gemini, cloak us," Alexis instructed as the ship broke the artificial atmosphere.

Christina watched the small, nondescript cargo ship with disappointment. "I guess they're not well-funded."

Alexis turned in her chair. "It works in our favor. The bug had no problem phasing through their shielding. Wherever they go, whoever they speak to, we'll know all about it."

Christina grinned. "The advantages of AI, huh?"

"The team wouldn't be complete without Gemini," Gabriel agreed with feeling. "You'll get to meet the rest of the team soon as we get back to Onyx Station. I can't say your dad is too happy you didn't tell him where you were going."

"Neither was Merril when Nathan sent us to find out why his bar was the last place you'd been seen before vanishing," Alexis added, turning back to the Pod's controls.

"Damned if I do, damned if I don't," Kai grumbled.

"What did I say?" Christina told him. "We should have checked in before we left the station."

Kai covered his face with his hands. "Yeah, well, I wasn't expecting our recon to turn into a bar brawl, followed by a free run through what has to be the largest collection of stolen goods I've ever seen."

Alexis shrugged. "I've seen bigger."

Kai looked at her in disbelief. "I'm here considering how my family is going to take it when Nathan murders me, and all you can think about is comparing dives you've visited? What is it with women and their preoccupation with size?"

Christina fixed him with a stern look. "First of all, starting any question with the words 'what is it with women' is never going to end well for you. Secondly, the situation with my dad is my fault, and I'll fix it. I should have told him about you sooner."

"Yeah, what's going on there?" Alexis asked as she monitored the limited progress the bug had made into the enemy ship's systems.

Christina blushed. "I kind of sprang Kai on him. In my defense, this cult thing came out of the blue."

Kai folded his arms. "I met Nathan and Ecaterina for the first time in their kitchen in the middle of the night."

Gabriel sucked in a breath. "Rough start, buddy."

"You're telling me," Kai complained. "As if the age gap thing wasn't enough for him to get over, his first impression of me was thinking I'd broken into his home."

Christina snickered. "It wasn't all that bad." She stopped laughing when she saw Kai wasn't playing along. "Okay, it was *every* bit that bad, but come on." She laid it on thick. "I didn't know I was serious about you back when I should have told him, and then I just kept putting off breaking it to him."

Kai relented. "I know you didn't mean for it to turn out like this. I'll keep trying with him."

"What's the age gap issue?" Gabriel inquired.

"It's not an issue to me," Christina replied. "Who cares if we were born a generation apart?"

"Not me," Gabriel assured her. "Trust me, we know better than most that time is subjective."

Alexis had to agree. "When you live as long as we do, the only thing that matters is that you find someone whose soul fits with yours. Who cares if there's a few decades or even centuries between you?"

Kai blushed. "Well, thanks. I think you two are the only ones who haven't made a cougar joke."

Alexis offered them both a warm smile. "I wish you luck. Some of us are destined to be alone forever. Some of us being me since no man is ever going to be brave enough to put his hands on my body."

Gabriel growled, "Good." He looked at Alexis. *Cougar?*

Alexis gave Christina a pained look as she jerked her thumb at Gabriel. "See what I mean? Can you imagine my uncles or my dad if I brought someone to meet them?"

"I can imagine the funeral," Gabriel promised.

Christina remembered her burning question from earlier. "So, how did you two go from fifteen to fully grown in the few months since I saw you last?"

Kai did a double-take. "They did what, now?"

"Our parents gave us the choice to be sequestered on High Tortuga for the duration of the war, or to be fully enhanced in modified Vid-docs while living the time we would have missed in VR," Alexis explained.

"We chose the enhancement," Gabriel added to clarify. "And Mom sent us to work with you to investigate the cult."

Kai nodded. "I figured as much with the investigation." He stared at the twins in turn. "It's insane. I wouldn't know the difference between you and any other twenty-one year-olds."

"What can we say?" Gabriel replied. "We've lived for those years, just not in this reality."

"If anything, we've experienced more than most people our age," Alexis added distractedly as she read through the communications she'd missed while they'd been out of touch with Gemini. "Our whole lives have been shaped to prepare us for war."

"Aren't you lucky?" Kai nodded. "Now the war is here." He looked at Christina, who was giving him one of those looks. "What?"

She turned to the twins. "What do we want to do about the cult now that we've got evidence it exists?" Christina asked.

"We have to get back to Onyx Station," Alexis replied, sharing the message she had from the medical examiner there. "Paul Jacobsen's autopsy report just came in, and I want to speak to whoever performed the procedure."

"What about the cult?" Kai contested, pointing at the receding ship on the viewscreen. "We can't let them get away."

"They're not going to get far," Gabriel assured him. "Their ship doesn't have a Gate drive. Gemini will flag any attempts they make to use the public Gate system. We won't lose them."

Kai supposed that meant the cult couldn't cause too much trouble while they reported in and came up with the next move to trace the leak in the Federation from this end. "Fine, but I think Christina and I should come straight back here and keep an eye on that ship. If they stop at any center of population, we have to go scoop them up before they do anything stupid."

"I can't argue the logic of running surveillance on them," Christina conceded.

"Agreed," Alexis looked at the woman. "We'll split up. Gabriel and I will go back to Onyx Station, and you two follow that ship from a distance."

She pushed a panel in her console and a small drawer slid out. "Take this Etheric comm and call us if anything interesting happens. We'll Gate out to your coordinates in three days to relieve you if the cult hasn't made a move."

Christina took the comm from Alexis. "I like that as a plan. There's a good chance the autopsy won't give us anything." She tapped it with a finger. "Thanks. I'd hate to think they got away because technology failed us."

Alexis smiled as Christina and Kai headed for their ship. "Keep your fingers crossed for a breakthrough. It would be nice to link up both ends of the investigation."

# CHAPTER ELEVEN

**Onyx Station, Bad Company HQ**

Bethany Anne's mind was churning two steps ahead of the moment as she waited backstage for the first group of FDG soldiers to make their way in and be seated.

Nathan had ensured the first group was diverse to give her a baseline of what reaction to expect from the troops as a whole. Bethany Anne wasn't convinced that everyone who saw the recording of this group's briefing would choose to take the upgrade, and she wanted to get an idea of what numbers she could expect to return to when she got back to Devon.

"Are you nervous?" Nathan asked, failing to hide the disbelief in his voice. "I didn't know you were even capable of—" He remembered who he was talking to when Bethany Anne's eyebrow arched. "I mean, I guess I thought you didn't get the same doubts as us mere mortals."

"Keep digging. It's cute." Bethany Anne rolled her eyes and went back to observing the gathered soldiers. "If you must know, I'm not nervous. I'm concerned. It's important that this goes to plan, since unlike Gödel, I haven't deluded myself into believing I'm entitled to unquestioning obedience from my people."

"Nobody is going to choose to miss out on the raid unless they have a damn good reason," Nathan assured her. "Besides, those who don't want to take the risk are still needed here. It'll work out," he promised. "Just wait and see."

Bethany Anne nodded in appreciation of his support. "There's only one way to find out." She made her way onto the stage as the soldiers applauded, then took a seat at the table with Tina, Marcus, and Takal.

Nathan waved the applause down as he came out from backstage and claimed the remaining chair. He cleared his throat, thinking a little bit of feedback to let him know the microphone was on wouldn't go amiss. "Thank you all for being here."

"It's a mandatory briefing, sir," some brave soul heckled.

"It is," Nathan agreed. "But accepting the mission you're about to be offered isn't, so pin your ears back, zip your piehole, and listen to what the Queen has to say."

*That* got the response he wanted.

Bethany Anne chuckled when every soldier seated in the rows turned their heads to stare at her. "Thank you, Nathan."

She paused and folded her hands on the table before beginning her address to the troops. "When I left Earth, I took the best of humanity with me, knowing their strength, courage, and innovative minds would be needed for the fight to save us from a future beneath Kurtherian heels. I continued to gather the best from every world when I took on the heavy duty of being the Empress. For a short time, there has been peace in the Federation. That peace is under threat because of the Seven, because the prodigiously batshit fuckbucket who has taken control of them has gotten it into her head that the Federation and all that it stands for has to be destroyed. My goal is to ensure that the only thing Gödel gets to be the goddess of is her ashes."

The soldiers booed, making their disdain for the Seven clear.

Bethany Anne gestured at the others at the table, raising her voice to be heard. "These are just a few of the people responsible for my ability to extend the Interdiction around the Federation. As I speak, there are teams plugging this station into the defense system. It's their work that has made it possible to take the fight to the Kurtherians."

She pointed at the seated soldiers, ignoring the camera drone hovering in front of the stage. "*You* are the boot I intend to break off in her psychotic ass. The reason you are here today is so I can offer you a physical upgrade and a place in the fleet that wipes the Seven out once and for all."

The roar was damn near deafening.

**I'll tone that down a bit,** TOM mentioned.

*Appreciate that*, Bethany Anne replied.

She waited for the reaction to die down before continuing. "The Yollins and Leath among you won't have forgotten what cowardly motherfuckers the Kurtherians are. They have moved on from slavery to growing super-soldiers by the millions in factories spread far and wide across the galaxies. See for yourself what they're capable of."

The room darkened.

Silence permeated the room as video clips of Ooken encounters played on the screen wall behind her.

Soon, the video stopped and the lights came back up. It was a testament to the bravery of those present that no one had bolted nor thrown up.

She eyed them, most feeling that she was looking into their eyes and their heart. "There will be no judgment if what I'm asking is beyond your capability to give, but I promise you this: if you choose to follow me, it will be into the fight of your *lives*. Those who accept the mission will receive the upgrade and leave for Devon within the month to begin training."

Bethany Anne understood that it was a lot to take in and had prepared for her audience to be suffering information overload. "There is a choice to be made. The upgrade will affect you in a number of ways, which you can read about in the information packet you should be receiving right about now…"

She glanced at Geroux, who nodded to confirm she'd delivered the basic information about the nanocytes that had been developed to give them toughened skin and bones so they could face the Ookens and survive. "Take your time. Read the information. If you have any more questions, you can use the link provided in your packet to speak to an advisor in confidence."

"Is it reversible?" someone called.

Bethany Anne glanced at Tina.

Tina lifted her hands. "We're mostly sure it is. Like, ninety-nine percent." She wrinkled her nose when Takal leaned in to whisper to her. "Ninety-eight point seven percent," she amended.

Bethany Anne waved down the avalanche of questions that followed. "This briefing is done," she told them all before looking at Nathan. She got to her feet and indicated that Tina and the others should do the same.

Nathan walked to the front of the stage. "The upgrade will be available for the next four weeks. Before we wrap this up, I want to personally thank everyone, and to tell you that Bethany Anne has provided a bonus for everyone who volunteers."

She left the briefing room to thunderous applause. Tina, Takal, and Geroux said their goodbyes and hurried to make the dock before the SD *Reynolds* departed for the outlying systems.

"I didn't approve any bonus," Bethany Anne told Nathan as they walked to his office.

Nathan grinned. "The twins are grown, right? Besides, you would have done it anyway."

Bethany Anne punched Nathan in the arm. "Not the point. I wouldn't have announced it and made it a factor in anyone's decision. Just count yourself lucky that I'd be sad if my friend's husband was suddenly killed in a tragic-and-yet-predictable airlock accident."

"You're talking like the acceptance rate isn't going to be a hundred percent in this group, for the simple reason they get to go to war with you," Nathan stated, indicating the soldiers flowing past them, gesticulating during animated conversations about getting the upgrade.

Bethany Anne declined to reply. She opened the office door and walked in while Nathan stopped to speak to the soldiers.

"Told you so," Nathan leaned in to smarm as the door closed behind them. "I'll say it again. If there's not a hundred percent buy-in from that group, I'll eat my hat."

Bethany Anne raised an eyebrow. "You don't wear a hat. How about I see you drink a glass of Coke with your dinner every day for a month?"

Nathan paled. "Only if I get to see you drink Pepsi."

"One glass," Bethany Anne bartered, holding out her hand.

Nathan shook on it. "One glass, and a photo," he snuck in. "For commemorative purposes, of course." He shrugged at Bethany Anne's pointed look. "What? How often do I get to say I was right and you were wrong? I want proof it happened."

Bethany Anne smiled. "You can show it to your grandkids."

Nathan's smile vanished as Bethany Anne's laughter filled the office. "I'm not the only one with a daughter."

Bethany Anne shrugged. "True, but I'd bet Michael and Gabriel will be an effective deterrent if Alexis goes through a phase of being bum-gum."

Nathan chuckled. "Having met Alexis, I can't see her having much time for assholes wasting her time."

"Speaking of wasting time," Bethany Anne cut in. "We need to get caught up on the kids' investigation, and then I need to get to my next appointment."

"Christina came by the house yesterday," Nathan told her. "The autopsy was a bust since the nanos were destroyed in the explosion. They have a tag on the cell who orchestrated Jacobsen's suicide, and they're just waiting for them to show up again. What about Lance's end?"

"Akio will be getting to Red Rock any time now," Bethany Anne told him.

"Good." Nathan shivered. "That cult gives me the creeps."

## Red Rock

Lance waited deep inside the cave, getting what relief he could from the blazing heat of the twin suns baking the skin of the Rock.

His polarized viewplate kept itself clear of condensation, a small mercy since Akio was late and he'd begun to sweat as soon as he left the secret passage leading to the cave from his quarters. He shifted uncomfortably, the material of the atmosuit he wore over his clothing acting as a sauna despite the forcefield keeping the majority of the heat out.

Red Rock from space looked like its name. The iron-stained asteroid had no defining features except for the canyon ripped into it by an ancient impact. The House of Arbitration's position inside the hollowed-out walls of the canyon gave it protection from the ravages of space. The caves that permeated the canyon walls had been only partially explored. With the surface exposed to levels of radiation that were lethal to most species, they were the only option for hikes among the more active.

This particular cave had been omitted from the maps for that reason. Lance committed himself to the wait, knowing Akio wouldn't send a message. He gave up pacing and sat down on the rough rock to conserve his air, opening his HUD to find a task to occupy himself until Akio arrived.

The minutes stretched out. Almost an hour later, a smudge appeared on the horizon. Lance got to his feet when the smudge resolved into the familiar lines of a QBS ship. The red go-faster stripe on the nose identified it as the *Achronyx* when it got closer.

"About time," Lance grumbled to everybody else who gave a shit. Unfortunately, he was alone.

He headed for the cave mouth and dropped the force-field for the few seconds the *Achronyx* needed to swoop in.

Akio came down the ramp, jumping the final few feet when he reached the end before Achronyx had finished extending it. He landed gracefully and greeted Lance with a rueful smile. "I can only apologize for the delay."

Lance waved his embarrassment off. "I figured you were tied up with something."

Akio's normally impassive expression flashed with momentary exasperation. "Our Queen generously assigned reinforcements to my quadrant," he explained briefly. "Sabine's group arrived, and it took a few days for them to get up and running."

Lance frowned, trying to recall who had been sent to the outer space equivalent of the Wild West. "Reinforcements. Bethany Anne and Michael sent the 'older' kids to cut their teeth on your watch, huh?" He chortled at Akio's pained nod. "Determined bunch, those four."

"Six," Akio corrected. "You are forgetting the cats."

Lance's amusement increased. "You remember the old saying? 'Never work with children or animals?'"

"I'm living it." Akio groaned. "They have all the training and none of the discipline. I can already see it's going to be like herding hurricanes."

"I thought you sounded a little bit too happy about the prospect of rummaging through the minds of everyone here," Lance commented as he set off toward the tunnel entrance at the back of the cave.

Akio told Lance about Bethany Anne's ideas for him to establish a Ranger outpost while reining in the more destructive tendencies of Sabine's group. "Hirotoshi and Ryu did nothing but laugh and tell me I have it easy compared to what they went through during their time mentoring Tabitha. I don't ever recall Tabitha's enduring solution to crime being, 'Nuke 'em all and let their gods sort them out.'"

Lance shook his head as he chuckled. "I don't envy you, my friend."

They made their way through the tunnel leading to Lance's personal quarters, emerging from the secret entrance in the bathroom closet.

Lance showed Akio to a small room that just about held the bed and the desk squeezed in at the end of it. "Sorry it's not much, but checking you into one of the diplomatic suites would be the fastest way to blow your cover."

Akio glanced around the room and shrugged before dropping his bag on the bed. "I've stayed in worse. What's the plan?"

Lance leaned against the doorframe. "I've been thinking

about who benefits from destabilizing Bethany Anne's efforts to extend the Interdiction. After Harkkat's scheme backfired, I'd hate to imagine any of the likely suspects would be foolish enough to try to profit from the situation."

Akio smiled. "I take it you went ahead and imagined it just the same."

Lance nodded. "Hell yeah, I did. I've arranged an early morning meeting with the council. I want you there to make sure everyone is as on board as they say they are, but I don't expect to find out one of the delegates is the traitor."

Akio nodded. "I will do a thorough search of everyone in the building without being noticed by anyone. You have Meredith take care of the cameras, and no one will be any the wiser."

Lance looked at Akio skeptically. "How are you going to get around without being seen?"

Akio lay back on the bed with his hands folded beneath his head and closed his eyes. "Strange are the ways of a multiple-centuries-old vampire, young padawan."

"Who are you, and what did you do with Akio?"

Lance left after not getting a rise out of the man.

### Onyx Station, Bad Company HQ

Sergeant Mara Wilson stayed off to the side of the locker room, taking her time to dry and braid her hair while the people under her command got ready to make the most of the night's liberty they'd been given prior to their enhancement the next day.

The unit's nerves had crept up while they waited for their slot on the schedule to come up, and she'd pleaded the case for liberty successfully with their CO.

K'roc, her trusted Yollin corporal, paused by the mirror. "You're sticking around for the party, right, Sarge?"

Mara gave her a surprised look. "Well, I'm not here to fuck spiders. If there's not a keg with my name on it, I'm not going to be happy."

K'roc laughed. "Just checking. We're about ready to roll."

Mara went over to her locker and grabbed her jacket. "What are we waiting for? Let's go and drink All Guns Blazing dry!"

She called her people in for a warning on the concourse outside the AGB entrance. "Have fun, but *don't* make dicks of yourselves. I won't be springing any of you from the brig if you piss security off." She grinned and waved them inside as they promised to be on their best behavior.

They weren't the only unit celebrating. The main room of the bar was packed with FDG soldiers intent on letting off some steam before their scheduled enhancement. Mara headed for the bar, pausing to exchange a brief word here and there with people she knew.

"What can I get you?" the bartender asked with a smile.

Mara stretched her hands wide. "The strongest drink an unenhanced human can consume without dying. This is the last night I can be affected by alcohol, and I'm planning on making the most of it."

The bartender laughed and turned to make her drink. "I'm hearing a lot of that since the Queen got here." He placed a tall glass of blue liquid swirling around red crushed ice in front of Mara and waved her wrist-holo away when she went to pay. "FDG is drinking on the house. Everyone from All Guns Blazing thanks you for your service."

Mara accepted the cocktail with a smile. "You can't say anything better than that! Cheers."

She took a sip through the straw and winced as she swallowed the inferno that hit her throat. "Well, fuck me sideways."

The bartender laughed as he put another glass on the bar for K'roc. "Enjoy your evening, ladies."

K'roc raised her glass to him and followed Mara through the crowd. They found the unit deep in conversation at three tables pushed together in the back of the room. "What's cracking?" Mara asked, grabbing a chair at the center table.

"Not going to lie," Barlow Vries admitted, playing with her glass. "There are some serious downsides to the upgrade."

Mara knew they were all thinking along similar lines, airing their last-minute doubts. "You don't have to get the upgrade," she told them all. "No one would think less of any of you if you chose to stay behind."

"Knowing that I gave up on my duty because I didn't want to have a shitty sex life?" Barlow growled. "No thanks, Sarge."

"Reduced sensitivity isn't necessarily a bad thing," one of the guys called.

Barlow threw a handful of nuts at him. "It doesn't matter if you can go for more than a minute, Decker. You'll still have to persuade a woman to let your nasty ass touch her."

"Which won't be a problem when we return as war heroes," Decker shot back with an obscene gesture. "I'll be neck-deep in grateful females, and who am I to turn them away? It'll practically be my duty."

He ducked when he was pelted with bar snacks by everyone at the table.

"It's not even a question of what we're giving up," Axel stated.

Everyone turned to look at the logistics specialist, a man of few words who nevertheless did his job with precision.

Axel drained his glass and put it down, his expression pensive. "We have the opportunity to be part of the largest military operation in the history of any Federation species. My grandparents left the US Navy and came to space because they believed in Bethany Anne. My parents served in the FDG, and I do the same because I believe in fighting for what's right. So what if our junk has to take a hiatus? It's not the worst sacrifice that's been made to save lives."

He paused, then grinned. "Besides, nothing's going to change the fact that Decker's going to die a virgin, even if he goes in his sleep at the ripe old age of ninety."

Men, women, and aliens cracked up.

Mara's bladder got the better of her as the subject turned to the Ookens. She returned from the bathroom to find everyone getting ready to leave.

"What's going on?" she asked.

K'roc showed her a napkin sketch of a blob with tentacles inside a red circle with a line through it. "The team has it in mind to get tattoos to commemorate the mission," she informed Mara. "There's a place on Level Thirteen where they'll tattoo anyone."

The team paused to see if she would veto the plan.

It could have been the alcohol, but Mara didn't. She slung an arm around Barlow and flashed a grin at her team. "Level Thirteen it is."

# CHAPTER TWELVE

**Onyx Station, Bad Company HQ**

Alexis packed her go-bag, annoyed that they were still waiting for the cult cell to do anything other than drift seemingly aimlessly through the system they'd left them in. "They're going to have to resupply at some point. Maybe we'll get lucky."

Gabriel felt her pain. Two weeks of rotating with Christina and Kai to keep tight surveillance on the cultists' ship had gotten them precisely nowhere. "We only have two weeks left before we move on to the Torcellan quadrant. If we don't get a result in the next few days, we'll have to ask Mom what her orders are."

He shouldered his bag and followed Alexis to the roamer they'd brought from the *Gemini*. "Do you think she'll have us stay behind and keep watching? Surveillance blows goats, especially for Christina and Kai in that Pod."

Alexis dropped her bag on the back seat and got into the roamer before answering. "I think I'd rather push the cell into acting so there's no chance we get left here when the tour moves on." She activated the comm on the dashboard. "Take us back to the ship, Gemini. It's time to head out."

The twins got to the prearranged meeting place in the asteroid belt between Nabraxia and the neighboring system and had Gemini send out a ping to let Christina and Kai know they were there.

Their Pod nosed out shortly after and zipped into the *Gemini's* open transport hold. Alexis made her way to the airlock, wondering how they'd managed yet another stint in the transport Pod with limited space and amenities.

Christina was first through when the airlock cycled open. "I'll speak to you after I've taken a shower," she told Alexis. "Three days on that tin can, and I don't want to talk about the air filtration system acting up."

Alexis gestured in the direction of her quarters. "Use mine. Second door on the left. I have plenty of clothes in the closet, so help yourself."

Kai shrugged as Christina marched away from them at speed. "You bring any food that isn't a nutritional substitute?"

Alexis gave him directions to the galley. "We need to find you two a ship. The Pod is fine for a quick journey, but it's not designed to be lived in."

Kai rubbed the back of his head and winced when he smelled himself. "Scratch that, I'd better take a shower before eating. Second door on the left, right?"

Alexis narrowed her eyes. "Don't you dare desecrate my shower. It's a one-person cubicle, you hear me?"

Kai grinned as he set off after Christina. "As if I'd do that. I can't promise anything for Christina, though."

Alexis sent the house bots instructions to steam clean the bathroom the moment they'd vacated her quarters as she made her way to the galley to put a meal together. It was good to have someone to cook for. A mind that worked continuously like hers needed the distraction of a simple physical activity every once in a while.

You know, just in case some person she cared about enjoyed food and hadn't realized who her parents were.

Maybe she needed to set up a fake persona.

Gemini appeared on the wallscreen. "Before you make your selection, let me show you this video ADAM sent me."

Alexis' mouth curled in a wicked smile as the video ran. "I think bistok would be a more appropriate choice." She consulted the recipe guide in the galley's database and had the food processing unit give her the ingredients.

She had Gemini put on some music and made pastry while she thought about how they might force the cell into action.

An attack might appear the obvious solution, but it might spook them into suiciding if that was their ultimate goal. She wished Paul Jacobsen's autopsy had been more useful, but nanocyte failsafes were universal, and the death of the host had triggered the ones in the compound he'd ingested to self-destruct.

Christina knocked on the open door as she entered the galley. "Hey, thanks for letting me use your stuff." She noticed the ingredients laid out. "What are you making?"

Alexis looked up from shaping the roll of stuffing in the center of the huge filet of bistok on the counter and pointed her spoon at Christina. "I'm going to have to have the whole bathroom refitted before I can use it again."

Christina held up her hands. "I didn't do anything in your bathroom except wash off the stink of being cooped up with a male for three days. I *thought* the house bots were a little too eager to get in there."

Alexis gave her a skeptical look. "It's a variation on a recipe from the database, Beef Wellington. Except I'm using bistok since I saw the funniest video just as I was deciding what to cook."

Christina took one look at Alexis' smirk and groaned as the realization hit. "*You* try to keep the training for new recruits interesting when you're stuck aboard a warship."

Alexis waved her protest off. "Having been a recruit on a warship, I salute your attempt to keep things fresh." She broke into giggles. "What were you thinking when it had you mashed up against the wall with its ass?"

Christina tapped her lips with a finger. "Um, that I was in a shitty situation, and I sure as hell hoped that years down the line, my predicament would be a source of amusement for one of Bethany Anne's kids?" She chuckled. "Give me a break already."

"I can give you some potatoes to peel," Alexis offered, indicating the pan in the sink. "I have the start of an idea, but I could use someone to bounce it off."

Christina selected a vegetable peeler from the magnetic strip over the sink and found a small colander to catch her peels, then got to work. "What's your idea?"

Alexis returned to her task, wrapping the rolled bistok in pastry. "I'm not entirely sure yet. We don't know enough about them, even with Gemini's access to their systems."

"We know they've been brainwashed by someone," Christina stated sourly. "Just listening to the audio from the bug is enough to convince anyone that what these people need is a short stay in a psychiatric ward to have the shit cleared out of their brains. I'd feel sorry for them if we hadn't spent the last two weeks listening to them imagining what their orders will be."

Alexis knew empathy could only go so far. "I feel sorrier for the victims of their next attack if they pull it off before we stop it. We need to engineer an event that will make them reach out to their handler."

Christina tossed a potato into the pan of water. "I sense we're getting to your plan."

"Your senses are on the nose," Alexis replied. "I'm thinking we give them a little love tap with the *Gemini*, just enough to make sure they have to come into dock somewhere."

"I thought you didn't want to spook them?" Christina asked.

"This ship has *Shinigami* cloaking," Alexis told her. "Ships get dinged by rocks all the time. They'll just think they caught some bad luck when one takes out their..." Her voice trailed off. "That's as far as I got with that part."

Christina paused in peeling. "There's another part?"

Alexis nodded. "One minute." She took the tray holding the bistok wellington over to the oven and put it in, setting the timer. "Are the potatoes ready?"

Christina showed her the pan. "Is that enough?"

Alexis shook her head and grabbed a peeler. "That'll feed Gabriel's greedy ass. Anyway, my plan. While we're playing pinball, you and Kai will go to the target destination and bump into the cult when they dock."

"And do what?" Christina asked. A skeptical frown

creased her forehead. "It's pretty long odds we'd run into the same people twice without meaning to. They won't think it's a coincidence."

"Exactly," Alexis agreed. "They're already paranoid. All we're going to do is give them a little nudge."

Christina waved for Alexis to elaborate. "Go on."

"That's where it gets tricky," Alexis admitted. "We'll need K'aia and Trey to help out, and I hope your dad doesn't mind lending us a few things."

## Beyond Federation Borders, Uncharted System, SD *Reynolds*

The superdreadnought exited the Gate into the fifteenth and final coordinates on their route.

"It's almost over," Jiya enthused as the scan data began coming in. "I can't believe I'm saying this, but I think I miss being attacked everywhere we go. At least I had something to do."

"Something wrong with my company?" Reynolds teased.

Jiya ran a hand through her hair and sighed. "More like I'm bored with my own company. There's not much for a first officer to do on an assignment like this beyond keeping morale up." She laughed. "Techies in their element don't need much encouragement."

"What about the scenery?" Reynolds argued, pointing out the planet suspended on the viewscreen. "You don't see too many water worlds."

"Are you forgetting Krokus-4?" Jiya gave him a sideways look. "Besides, most of our stops were in places where there was absolutely nothing to look at unless you have a love for gazing endlessly into the void."

Reynolds was distracted from Jiya's grumbling by an unexpected presence letting himself into his systems. He extracted his consciousness from the bridge and rushed to meet the closest thing an AI had to a parent. *ADAM, what brings you here?*

>>**Your datastream is showing us you've come across an ocean planet,**<< ADAM informed him after they'd exchanged pleasantries. >>**Bethany Anne wants to know if it's a suitable habitat for the Collectives.**<<

*I have to admit I'm not familiar with the species,* Reynolds told him with regret.

>>**No worries,**<< ADAM assured him. >>**Here, this should help.**<<

Reynolds assimilated the information that arrived and found he understood Bethany Anne's anger on the Collectives' behalf entirely. *Whatever my crew and I can do to help these beings, we're in. I don't need to ask to know that every soul aboard would volunteer without hesitation when they find out what they've gone through at the hands of the Seven.*

>>**They're kind of isolated because of their trauma,**<< ADAM told him. >>**But typically, they're sociable in the extreme. The aim is to find a replacement for the home-world Gödel destroyed and get the Collectives living under Devon set up there before we hit the factories and rescue the rest of them. I've given you the parameters for their needs.**<<

*I'll be in touch as soon as we're done surveying the planet.*

"What was that?" Jiya asked.

Reynolds got to work adjusting the ship's sensors,

another part of him sending drones to the planet to take samples while the part that was the android shared the addendum to their orders with his first officer.

Jiya skipped over their instructions and went straight to the information about the Collectives. Her hand drifted involuntarily to her mouth as she read the details of their ordeal as a species. "Those poor beings," she managed eventually. "Captain, what do we need to do? Scratch that. Specifically, what do *I* need to do?"

Reynolds had been thinking along the same lines. The early scans looked hopeful, and the biosphere's makeup was within the tolerances ADAM had given him. "We have the technology we got from the Krokans. We can assist with providing a base for the air breathers to operate from."

He had eyes in the drones, but it wasn't the same as having his actual eyes on the planet. "Want to take a Pod down and scout for possible sites?"

Jiya grinned. "Does a bear shit in the pope's hat?" Her smile faded at the lack of comprehension from Reynolds. "I guess my Earth studies aren't sticking as well as I thought."

Reynolds shook his head in exasperation. "That's what you get for asking Tactical to help you study."

Jiya lifted her hands. "What can I say? It's worth the risk. He knows all the best insults, if only I could learn not to mangle them."

Reynolds left the bridge with her. "I hope Geroux is enjoying his company."

"The others will keep him in check," Jiya told him with a chuckle. "There was no way letting him near Izanami was going to turn out well for him."

"Or me," Reynolds agreed wistfully.

They stopped on their way to the Pod bay to pick up a few bots, which Reynolds left inactive in the Pod's hold.

It was a bumpy ride until they'd passed through the stormy atmosphere. The world around them became instantly tranquil once they were beneath the surface of the water.

"Where to, Captain?" Jiya asked, bringing the Pod to a stop a couple of thousand feet from the ocean floor.

Reynolds examined the scan data they had so far and pointed out a rise in the far distance. "Those mountains may have caves in the valleys. It's as good a place as any to start."

Jiya suddenly felt very small when they reached the mountain range some twenty minutes later. She glanced at the peaks blocking the light filtering down from the surface. "This planet is a lot larger than Krokus-4."

Reynolds nodded. "That's a good thing. The Collectives need the space."

Jiya was quiet for a moment. Reynolds glanced at her and saw the excitement she was holding back. "Take us down. I'm going to send out the bots."

"What's the objective?" Jiya asked. She held up a finger. "Wait, I know. We have to find out if the mineral composition will support the strains of kelp the Collectives eat, yes?"

Reynolds patted her shoulder, happy to see the prospect of action had worked. "Give yourself a gold star. I'm going to send a couple of the bots out to look at the caves the probes surveyed when we land. They have potential for our base."

"*Our* base?" Jiya inquired.

"You know what I meant." Reynolds got out of his chair as the Pod touched down in a sandy valley.

Jiya watched him pace the tiny cockpit with amusement. "I know the human phrase for this situation. It's 'Yeah, right.'"

"The bots are on their way," Reynolds told Jiya, ignoring her sarcasm. "I linked their AV functions to the viewscreen."

Jiya nodded as the viewscreen switched to show six separate camera feeds. She toggled between the audio for each bot and scrunched her nose. "I can't hear anything except silence," she commented to Reynolds before muting the audio to concentrate on the videos. "I hope that cave is as spacious as it looks."

Reynolds tilted his head when the part of him that was the ship called his attention to sounds beyond most organics' hearing range. He heard the competing currents, the minute movements of the planet's crust, and... "Oh, shit."

Jiya looked up at the unexpected profanity. "Captain?"

Reynolds pointed at a phosphorescent light approaching the bots in the cave. "Get us out of here."

Jiya acted immediately. "Why do I get the feeling we're running for our lives?" she quipped as they swung around and she hit the proverbial gas. She pointed the Pod's nose at the surface, and they shot straight up at full speed.

"It's a valid feeling," Reynolds retorted, wondering if death hurt when you were an AI whose consciousness was split across multiple locations. "We're definitely running for our lives."

Jiya saw the light leave the cave as they shot out of the

valley and past the mountain peaks. The viewscreen gave them their first sight of the monster on their tail. The light came from a dangling lure that hung over the rows of huge, jagged teeth that emerged next from the cave.

"Faster!" Reynolds yelled, gripping his armrests tightly.

"Fifteen thousand feet to go," Jiya shot back unnecessarily. "Twelve. Why is it chasing us? We're not even a mouthful!"

Jiya let out a small scream as the monster fish splayed its jaws, powering toward the Pod with incredible speed. "Eight thousand feet. We're not going to make it!"

"We *have* to make it," Reynolds cried, taking control of the Pod to divert everything but shield power to the engines as they reached four thousand feet below the surface. "Hold your breath. I'M TOO HANDSOME TO DIE!"

The Pod lurched as he fed energy from his body into it to give them a chance of making it. They sped the last fifteen hundred feet with the monster just meters behind them.

"It's not slowing!" Jiya cried as they rushed toward the surface. She gripped Reynolds' hand. "This is it. It's been a pleasure serving with you, Captain."

"Did I hire a quitter?" Reynolds thundered. "We need to keep going,"

Reynolds pushed himself past the point of no return, knowing it was their only hope. He felt a surge of energy flood his body, using him as a conduit to the Pod. They were thrown back in their seats as the inertial dampers stuttered with the influx of power being applied to the engines.

"Whooooo!" Jiya screamed, the only release for the flood of adrenaline that swept her body as they broke the surface in a huge plume of spray.

The monster fish followed a moment later, breaching the water with its jaws spread wide. Jiya breathed a sigh of relief when its teeth closed well beneath the Pod. "You did it, Captain."

She glanced at him when he didn't reply. "Oh, my. Oh, crap! *Reynolds!*"

Reynolds was slumped in his chair. His eyes were open, but he wasn't seeing Jiya, despite her leaning over him.

Jiya mashed the comm panel with a hand, all her training replaced by the pure panic that the person she loved and respected was gone. "Reynolds is down. *Help!*"

Silence rebounded from the speakers, reminding her that they'd sacrificed everything nonessential to getting out of the situation alive. She was trapped in the Pod with no way to get Reynolds the help he needed.

*It's okay, Jiya. I'm on my way*

Jiya looked around at the sound of Bethany Anne's voice.

A flash of light whited out the viewscreen just as Jiya began to wonder if she'd imagined it. The light vanished as suddenly as it had appeared, and the image on the viewscreen resolved into swirling gray mist.

Reynolds looked at Jiya in confusion as his internal processes kicked back in. He fought to lift a hand to his chest. "My body isn't working properly. Is this death?"

*You're too hard-headed to die, you ham.*

Bethany Anne's voice inside their heads startled Reynolds. "Bethany Anne? Am I glad to hear your voice!"

Jiya was glad they weren't dead, but she wasn't sure they were out of the fire just yet. "Where are you? Where are *we*, for that matter?"

***Step outside and see***, Bethany Anne replied. ***Pulling your Pod in here wasn't easy. I'm sure as hell not dragging it out again.***

Reynolds realized that Bethany Anne had brought them into the Etheric and forced his limbs to move. He made it a few steps before stumbling as his gross motor functions stalled.

"Are you okay?" Jiya asked, moving to support him.

Reynolds caught himself on the wall and continued to put one foot in front of the other when he regained control. "I must have given the Pod a little too much. I'll be fine."

Jiya didn't believe a word of it. She ducked under his arm and helped him to the hatch. "Why are you so heavy?" she griped as a way to keep his mind occupied as they made slow progress to the Pod's hatch.

Reynolds didn't argue, which worried Jiya more than anything. She shored him up a little more and kept them moving.

"We're coming out," she called to Bethany Anne as the ramp descended.

Bethany Anne took one look at Reynolds and sucked in a breath, sorry she'd taken his complaint lightly. "You don't look so good. What happened to you?"

"He fed his own energy into the Pod to get us out of there," Jiya explained.

Reynolds shook himself free of Jiya's grip. "I just need to get to my ship and have Takaaaaa—"

Jiya darted forward to catch Reynolds when he crumpled. She was unbalanced by the weight of his android body and went down with him.

Bethany Anne was there to catch both of them. She held Reynolds steady while Jiya righted herself. "This is more than a drain on his systems. I didn't think he'd be so badly affected by being here. I should have considered the metal inside his body would be a problem."

Jiya didn't like the side-to-side wobble Reynolds had. She looked into his eyes. "We need to get you to Takal. He'll be able to restore you."

Reynolds twitched, his jaw mechanism spasming as he tried to speak. "Schmurrrr…"

Bethany Anne's eyes widened in alarm. She picked Reynolds up in her arms as she transferred them to the SD *Reynolds*. She and Jiya ran for Takal's lab, concerned Reynolds' slurred speech was an indication his situation was past critical. "Don't you die on me. I'll have ADAM to deal with if you do, and I don't need that at the moment, Reynolds!"

Takal looked up in surprise when Jiya burst in ahead of Bethany Anne and swept the large workbench clear. He dropped what he was doing when he saw Reynolds and rushed to help Jiya make room. "What happened to him?"

"I had to take him into the Etheric," Bethany Anne explained as she put Reynolds on the bench. "It's fucked with the metal in his body."

"He shut down," Jiya told Takal in a tight voice.

Takal grabbed a cable and went over to the head of the bench. He peeled back Reynolds' hair and opened a panel in his skull, then plugged the cable into his brain. The scientist plugged the other end into a connector bank in the bench and stood back. "Hold on, Captain. The way out is coming."

"What now?" Bethany Anne asked.

Takal busied himself at one of the consoles. "Now we wait. He has to extract himself from the damaged brain and follow the path I made to the ship's core. Then we have to wait for him to reconstruct himself."

>>**It's going to be a while,**<< ADAM informed Bethany Anne. >>**He fragmented his mind and locked away the pieces to save it. It's going to take another AI to help pull him out and put him back together again.**<<

Bethany Anne stared at the inert android. *I'm going to guess it's more complicated than a jigsaw puzzle.*

>>**It's going to be rough for Reynolds,**<< ADAM admitted. >>**I should stay with him.**<<

Bethany Anne had a better idea. *Reynolds has too much respect for you. What he needs is someone who will inspire him to fight. I want you to help the splinter Reynoldses to take over his and Izanami's responsibilities until he's recovered.*

>>**You're going to have Izanami take care of him?**<< ADAM asked. >>**Just saying, I don't like his chances.**<<

Bethany Anne's lips pressed together. *You might be surprised.*

# CHAPTER THIRTEEN

**Federation Space, QGE Gemini**

Gabriel lined up the crosshairs in his HUD with the exhaust port on the cultist ship.

"There is an extra twenty-six percent chance of success if I take the shot," Gemini informed him.

"You're a glory hog, Gemini." Gabriel snickered softly. "Have a backup lined up in the unlikely event I miss."

Gemini chuckled. "Don't blame me, blame the humans I imprinted on."

"Take the damned shot," Alexis snapped, her patience worn thin by the long odds of her plan staying on track. "They're in range."

Gabriel ignored his sister's short temper and focused on hitting the edge of the exhaust port, where the ship's shields were weakest. A moment later, he pressed the trigger.

"Direct hit," Gemini announced.

"Give us the audio from the bridge," Alexis requested.

Gemini played the cultists' panicked conversation over the speakers.

*"Marek, we're venting atmosphere on the supply deck."*

*"It's worse than that. We're losing fuel."*

Alexis and Gabriel exchanged glances when Marek ordered them to make for the nearby outpost.

---

Five days later, the *Gemini* and the ship they were following came into sight of the telltale light reflected from the dome of New Galaxia, the colony serving the miners working in the ore-rich asteroid fields in the system.

"Call Christina and Kai," Gabriel told Alexis, grinning at the thought of impending action. "I'll call Mom."

He opened a mental link to Bethany Anne and waited for her to respond.

*I hope you're calling to tell me you're done?*

*Not exactly,* Gabriel replied. *We weren't getting anywhere, so we set something up. Either way, we'll have results within the next few days.*

*Do I want to know the details?* Bethany Anne asked.

Gabriel laughed. *Probably not. I wanted to make sure we didn't miss the deadline for departure and to ask if you've heard anything from Grandpa about his end of the investigation.*

*Not yet,* Bethany Anne told him. *He's meeting us at the edge of the Torcellan system in three days. Unless Akio has uncovered something that needs my immediate attention, we'll find out what he knows then.*

She paused for a moment. *You two take care out there. Give Alexis my love.*

*Bye, Mom.* Gabriel dropped the link and waited for Alexis to switch off the comm.

"What did Mom say?" she asked when she was done.

Gabriel smiled. "She sent her love and told me we'll find out what Grandpa and Akio have turned up in three days."

Alexis sighed. "We *have* to get that lead before we leave."

"We will," Gabriel assured her. "Are the other teams ready for their chance encounter?"

Alexis nodded. "I checked with K'aia and Trey, and the warehouse is ready. Christina and Kai found the cult's dock easily. Are you ready for our part?"

Gabriel felt his sister's discomfort with using deception to get the result they needed and reached out to pull her into a brief bearhug. "Tell me how we get past Security here without getting busted for posing as FDG officers."

Alexis smiled, his attempt to make her feel better effectively dispelling her misgivings. "I'm not worried about the prospect of being caught." She handed Gabriel an ID badge. "I had Nathan make these for us. I'm more concerned about what Mom is going to say when we debrief."

Gabriel chuckled. "She's going to congratulate you on being smart enough to use every advantage you have." He grinned. "It's a good plan. Have faith in yourself, like I have faith in you."

"That's because Mom's focus will be on me if it fails."

"I never said there wasn't an upside that helped me with my faith."

Gemini announced they'd arrived at the colony while they were finishing putting on the FDG armor Alexis had acquired for their entry. They landed at the spaceport and left the *Gemini* on their roamer to make their way to the military line at the Customs checkpoint.

Alexis activated the Etheric comm and opened a channel once they were clear. *We're in. Status report?*

Christina's reply was short. *We have eyes on the targets.*

*And?* Gabriel asked.

*We are good to go,* Christina told them. *We've trailed them to a restaurant.*

*Stand by,* Alexis confirmed. *We're five minutes away.*

The twins made their way to the location Christina gave them and parked the roamer in the alley between the restaurant and the bank next door, where Christina and Kai were waiting in the shadows for their arrival.

"Are you sure this will work?" Kai asked with some trepidation as the twins joined them. "I mean, what if they freak out? We don't know if they have explosives like Jacobsen."

Alexis understood his concerns. "We've all watched the video. Jacobsen was clearly in physical distress the whole time he was recording. The nanocyte compound needs time to work."

Christina slipped her arm around Kai's waist. "If I see so much as a hiccup from any of them, I'll take them out."

"Or," Alexis countered, "you could just tell me, and I'll take us into the Etheric since killing them won't prevent the explosion. The compound works by breaking the body down from the inside out and converting it to supply the energy the nanocytes need to detonate. We at least got that much from the medical examiner's report."

Kai grimaced. "Sheesh, I remember when the worst thing I had to worry about was a bunch of guys armed mostly with hand tools." He looked around the group. "Don't sweat it; we've got this."

He and Christina left the alley and went inside the restaurant, leaving the comm open. They spotted the cult cell seated on the righthand side of the room. Christina stuck to the comm as the hostess came over. *Don't let them know we've seen them.*

*It's not my first time undercover,* Kai replied. *Is there anything you can do about that vibe you're giving off? You're scaring the hostess.*

*I'm a genetically-modified killing machine.* Christina scoffed. *I can't fucking turn it off.*

The hostess offered them a table on the left, which Kai turned down. "How about by the window over there?" he suggested, indicating the booths on the right.

The hostess smiled, her eyes darting nervously to Christina. "Of course. Right this way." She took their orders and left once Christina and Kai were seated.

Christina was less than happy to have her back to their targets. "Did they notice us?" she whispered.

Kai shook his head. "Not yet. I've been thinking about how we should play this. We need to act like we're suspicious of them."

Christina snickered. "Not a problem, but why? We need to get them to talk once we're in the warehouse."

"I think they're more likely to trust K'aia and Trey if they're not relying on us to protect them," Kai told her slowly, still figuring out his theory.

Marek's voice intruded. "Hey, I thought it was you."

*I think you need to be "dead" for the last part,* Kai finished quickly.

Christina had a second to decide if she was going to go along with Kai's plan. *Okay, we'll do it your way.* She looked up in feigned shock as Marek approached their booth. "What are you doing here?"

Marek's smile faded at the lack of welcome. "Our ship was damaged. We needed repairs."

"Were you attacked?" Christina asked, putting a touch of mistrust into her tone. "By those asshole FDG agents? Crazy bastards accused us of being part of some anti-Bethany Anne cult. Can you imagine that?"

"Cult?" Marek blustered. "FDG agents?"

*What are you doing?* Alexis demanded.

*Improvising,* Christina told her. She tilted her head at Marek's incomprehension. "The ones from the bar on Nabraxia? We were lucky. We only just got away from them after you guys left."

Marek shook his head. "We were hit by debris. I hope you didn't bring those agents here."

"Not likely," Kai told him, getting to his feet. "But if you're here, they'll be here soon, anyway."

*Get a tracker patch on him in case they make a break for it,* Gabriel murmured. *The one Alexis gave him is getting near the end of its life.*

Christina considered how to fulfill Gabriel's instruction. "At least get our order to go," she called to Kai to distract Marek while she took a tiny translucent tracker patch from her pocket.

Marek stepped back to give Kai room to exit the booth. "You're leaving?"

"Damn straight, we are," Christina told him. She rubbed the tip of her finger over the patch to find the correct side to peel, hoping she'd gotten it right. "They might have missed the prelude to the bar fight, but *we* know that you're the ones they're hunting. It's not worth the bounty the Magistrates have put on your heads."

The blood drained from Marek's face. "Why would they put a bounty on us? We haven't broken any laws."

Christina shrugged, maintaining her disinterested demeanor. "It's nothing to do with us either way. We're out of here." She patted Marek's cheek, surreptitiously applying the patch, which was absorbed into his skin on contact. "You're on your own, sunshine."

She slipped past Marek and caught up to Kai at the door. "Do you think it worked?" she murmured as they left for the warehouse they'd leased.

"We scared the crap out of him," Kai replied with confidence, transferring the takeout bags to one hand. "I was watching his face while you baited him. The guy was thinking so hard, I'm surprised there wasn't smoke coming out of his ears."

*The new tracker just came online,* Gabriel announced.

*Good,* Christina stated. *This time there won't be any fuckups to the plan.*

*They're not going to get a chance to rile anyone since they'll be sound asleep within a minute of leaving the restaurant,* Alexis replied. *But you fucked the plan and then some. What was that?*

Christina looked at Kai.

*We'll get a better response if they think their lives are at risk,* Kai explained. *I'll go in the cell next to Trey and tell them you killed Christina because she didn't answer your questions. Add that to the acting masterclass Trey assures me he has planned with K'aia, and we've covered all the bases.*

*You guys get to the warehouse,* Gabriel told them. *Alexis and I will be there as soon as we get them loaded into the roamer.*

*You make subduing a group of six sound easy,* Kai remarked as he and Christina ducked into the industrial area.

Alexis and Gabriel grabbed a bite from a street vendor selling noodles and watched the restaurant while they ate.

Gabriel dropped his empty noodle carton into a trash can. *Is it too late to grab another order?*

*Yes, it's too late,* Alexis told him, pointing out Marek's group emerging onto the sidewalk. She moved to the mouth of the alley and drew her Jean Dukes Special, double-checking it was set to low. Night-night rounds were much more effective if they didn't puncture the target on impact. *Get ready. They're coming this way.*

The twins held on until the group made it to the mouth of the alley and fired three shots each in quick succession. The cultists went down before any of them was aware they were under attack.

Alexis huffed as they dragged the unconscious people to the roamer. "It's no good having all the strength when you're still pocket-sized." She dropped the man she was carrying and lifted him using Etheric energy instead. "That's better."

She put him in the back of the roamer and went back for the next. Gabriel picked the others up one at a time and stacked them in the back with the rest. "How long does the tranquilizer last?"

Alexis got into the front of the roamer and activated the partition to close off the cultists. "Long enough for us to get to the warehouse and get them into the cells," she replied as Gabriel got in beside her. "I have to get myself into character. Did Nathan send the katanas?"

Gabriel patted Alexis' hand. "Yes. Let's get out of here."

It was a ten-minute drive to the warehouse. K'aia and Christina came out to help transfer the cultists onto anti-grav pallets to take them into the holding facility K'aia and Trey had put together while the twins were following the cultists to the outpost.

K'aia looked them over. "Did you check them for explosives?"

Alexis nodded, hitching a thumb at the bag on the front seat of the roamer. "We stripped them of their belongings when we knocked them out."

They passed through the outer rooms, pushing through the plastic sheets that hung in place of the missing doors and making their way to the enormous central room.

Alexis looked at the U-shaped cabin that took up two-thirds of the square footage in amazement. "You did all this in five days?"

"Wait until you see the inside," Trey promised. He glanced at the pallets. "We should get set up before they come around."

Alexis saved her praise until all six cultists were safely stowed in the two lines of cages bolted to the walls and floor in the middle part of the cabin. "Great job. I wouldn't know this wasn't here a few days ago if I hadn't seen the photos you sent."

Trey laughed as he handed Alexis the replica katanas. "I'm not going to lie, it was a hell of a job, given the time-line. You should have seen the look on Nathan's face when we gave him the request for all of this stuff." He shot his accommodations for the next few hours a look of distaste before walking in. "Here goes."

K'aia joined him, and Kai got into the remaining empty cage.

"Good luck," Gabriel told them as he and Alexis locked them in.

"We'll be right outside," Alexis assured them, following Gabriel and Christina to the door. "You've got this."

Christina waved to Kai as Alexis closed the door, leaving them just as the tranquilizers began to wear off.

---

Marek came around slowly, his head pounding with the residual effects of the drugs in his bloodstream. He vaguely recalled seeing two people silhouetted in the alley before everything had gone dark.

He looked around in confusion. The others regained consciousness within moments of him.

Marek spotted Kai in the cell opposite his, putting an end to his suspicion the bounty hunter had had something to do with them being taken. He also saw a four-legged Yollin and a large, hairy being he couldn't identify in another cell. "What happened?" he asked Kai. "Where are we?"

"Where do you think we are?" Kai snarled, waving a hand to indicate the cages they were in. "Thanks to you and your freakshow, my wife is dead."

"Dead?" Jenner repeated blankly.

"They wouldn't believe we weren't with you," Kai replied angrily. He turned to face the wall, folding his arms.

"Now she's gone, and the only thing I have to look forward to is that I'll probably be next when the FDG agents come back."

Marek exchanged worried glances with his second-in-command. They were on their own if they came up against the law.

Gerard clearly shared his concerns.

"They're not FDG," the Yollin told them quietly.

Marek was sure he'd misheard. "What's that?"

"They're. Not. FDG," the Yollin repeated in a tone that made it clear she thought his intelligence was subpar. "I saw the female's face."

The hairy being threw an elbow into the Yollin's side. "Don't give away our score. People will pay good credits to know that...*she* is here."

The Yollin shoved him away. "Please don't tell me you think we're getting out of this? You *don't* hijack a QBS ship and get away with it."

Marek's head swung from side to side as he followed the argument with interest. He was sure he had heard that acronym before.

Her companion growled low in his chest. "Great! I suppose next you're going to want to take everyone with us."

Marek gripped the bars of his cage. "You have a way out?"

"Why should we take you?" the hairy male demanded. "What are you going to be except an added complication on top of getting passage out of this system?"

"Who has us?" he asked, unable to help himself despite the sinking feeling he had.

The Yollin stared straight at Marek as footsteps echoed somewhere outside the cell block. "You haven't figured it out yet?"

The door swung open and a wave of fear hit Marek, twisting his guts. He scrambled back, his instinct screaming at him to avoid whoever was coming.

The door slammed open, revealing a raven-haired woman whose eyes glowed with the fury of Hell. She drew one of the crossed swords on her back and pointed it at the prisoners. "I hope whoever I choose next is more amenable to giving me answers. Cleaning up blood is tiresome in the extreme."

Marek's heart flipped as her voice raked its nails down his soul.

Bethany Anne stalked toward the cells, her face bathed in the red light coming from her eyes. He curled into a ball, begging his bladder not to give away his abject terror.

Thankfully she ignored him. His relief was short-lived when Bethany Anne opened Kai's cage, pointing with the sword. "*Out.*"

Marek was not surprised in the least that the broken man didn't resist. The former Empress exuded a promise of death that made even the air shiver with fear.

Being in her presence was the single most terrifying experience of his life so far. He was pretty sure the next most terrifying experience was probably going to occur pretty soon if her wishes weren't fulfilled.

He cursed himself for a fool for ever believing his humanity was equal to hers.

Kai didn't so much as glance at any of the other prisoners. He left his cell with his head down and walked out the door ahead of Bethany Anne.

There was silence in the cell block for a long time after that. Marek avoided the eyes of his followers, remaining curled in the corner of his cage while his imagination fed him ever more painful suggestions as to what Kai was going through.

He became aware that the Yollin and her companion had resumed their debate in harsh whispers.

Gerard hissed to draw his attention. "What are we going to *do?*"

Marek's heart was still racing from being in close proximity to Bethany Anne. "We have to find a way to tell the founders that the queen of lies is here. They have no clue how powerful she is. If the Yollin and her friend can get us out of here, we can send them a message and have them send someone to pick us up at the Gate."

Gerard's eyes widened. "You know they won't be pleased if we call for help."

Marek figured the Yollin was their only hope. "They're going to leave us behind unless we offer them something." He ignored Gerard's motions for his attention and called to the Yollin. "Hey, I can get us passage through the Gate. Just get us out of here before Bethany Anne kills us all."

## CHAPTER FOURTEEN

**Yollin Space, Planet Melida**

It was a normal Friday evening at Talia's. The bar was filling up after the early evening shift change at the city's fire and rescue departments, and the staff from the hospital a couple of blocks away practically lived there between shifts.

"Turn it up, will you?" Fire Chief James Artemis Owens called to Talia, waving his hand at the news report running on the center holoscreen above the bar. "There's something going on around Torcellan."

The Loren flicked a tentacle, and the sound of the *Yoll Today* correspondent drowned out the jukebox in the corner. "They're not going to tell us anything new," she predicted.

*Talia (species, Loren) - Image by Eric Quigley*

"I'm Gritch Cluster, reporting live from the Torcellan quadrant, where the QSD Baba Yaga is preparing to leave. I'm joined by Dr. Tina Grimes-Cambridge, preeminent authority on extra-planetary defense systems. Dr. Grimes, I hear it's good news for the quadrant?"

"You've got that right, Gritch," Dr. Grimes-Cambridge responded with enthusiasm. "My teams have just wrapped up, and we're just about to switch on this section of the 'blanket.' That's the codename for all the modifications we're making as *part of extending the Interdiction."*

Gritch returned his microphone to his mouth, his handsome face concertinaed with concern. *"With Ooken attacks occurring at an ever-greater frequency around the edges of the Federation, we the people can only thank you, your teams, and the Empress for your efforts to put an end to the terror."*

*"It's the right thing to do,"* Dr. Grimes-Cambridge replied. *"The* Queen," she emphasized the title, *"made a promise when she stepped down to return if the Federation was in danger. We are fulfilling that promise."*

*"Can you explain for our viewers at home and me how the Interdiction is going to protect them?"* Gritch asked, giving her a look that apologized for the question.

Dr. Grimes-Cambridge smiled and clicked a small device in her hand. *"No problem. If you take a look at my projection, this is a model of Federation space. As you can see, it's not uniform. Much like a non-Newtonian fluid, it expands and contracts with the rise and fall of pressure, the pressure in this case being the Federation's population. The enemy is trying to take advantage of that. Even now, there are men and women fighting to keep the outer quadrants Ooken-free."*

She clicked her device again, and the empty spaces began to fill out until the amorphous model more resembled a flattened sphere. *"The purpose of the Interdiction is to unify the Federation's defenses."* The sphere lit up with dots, then the dots were joined with lines, forming a grid network. *"EI-controlled defenses will activate the moment an unidentified ship approaches, and an SOS call will be instantly relayed to the nearest base so support can be arranged in real-time. Those living in the heart of the Federation might think that's a given, but it's often the case that outlying populations rely on slower-than-light communications."*

"That's true," Gritch conceded. *"We've all heard the stories of colonies lost because they couldn't get a message out in time."*

"That will be a thing of the past," Dr. Grimes-Cambridge promised. *"The entire Federation is being wrapped in a security blanket."*

"You've mentioned this 'security blanket' a few times," Gritch probed gently. *"Is that a human term?"*

Dr. Grimes-Cambridge lifted her hands, nonplussed. *"I guess so? It's a comfort item given to young humans to make them feel safe. Bethany Anne named the project."*

Gritch nodded solemnly and turned to the camera. *"You heard it from Dr. Grimes. The Queen honors her promise to keep us safe. Back to you in the studio, Nancy."*

The screen switched to show the news anchor sitting at her desk. She smiled. *"Thank you, Gritch. That was Dr. Tina Grimes-Cambridge, speaking about the defenses being built by former Empress Bethany Anne. In other news, a riot started by anti-Empire protesters claimed—"*

Talia grimaced and muted the channel. "Damn Ookens are giving every cephalopod species around a bad name."

"What are you talking about?" Kelley asked, holding out her mug for a refill.

Talia put a tentacle on her hip, topping up the police officer's coffee. "I was stopped at a checkpoint going into the Torcellan quadrant while some handsy bitch made me jump through hoops to prove I wasn't a damned Ooken. Do I look like I'm hiding fur? I'm *purple*!"

"Darling, you could be hiding anything in there, and not

one of us would mind one bit," Kelley assured her. "We stand by our own around here."

She looked down when her holo beeped an alert. "Duty calls."

"Same here," Chief Owens announced, dropping a credit chip on the bar. He looked around in alarm when alerts went off all around the room. The bar began to empty in a hurry. "Shit, what's going down out there?"

Kelley didn't look back as she dashed for the door. "I guess we're going to find out any minute now."

### Open Space, QSD *Baba Yaga*

ADAM announced the imminent arrival of the QBS *Achronyx,* and Bethany Anne and Michael left their work on the running schedule to find the children. Gabriel, Alexis, Christina, and Kai came out of the APA as they passed it, debating their next move in the investigation.

Bethany Anne smiled, seeing their motivation to uncover the roots of the anti-Empire cult was still high. "Good. I was about to have ADAM tell you to meet us at the hangar."

"It's weird having him run the ship instead of Izanami," Alexis commented. "How is Reynolds?"

Bethany Anne smiled. "He's doing—"

Michael stopped the group before they got into the elevator. "Wait. I hear Ookens."

Alexis tuned into the mindspace. "Yeah, me too. Faint, though. I can't tell what direction they're in."

"What?" Kai asked, looking around, thinking they were nearby.

Christina leaned in and whispered to Gabriel when Bethany Anne closed her eyes, "What's she doing?"

Gabriel held a finger to his lips. "She's listening to the Ookens' minds to get a location."

Bethany Anne locked on to the hive mind and used the individual Ookens as steppingstones, getting a snippet of information from each to build a picture of where they were without alerting them to her presence. "They're inside the Federation. On a Yollin planet."

"Close enough to get to through the Etheric?" Michael asked. "I haven't gotten a good workout since we left Devon."

Bethany Anne shook her head and described the impression she'd gotten of the location while ADAM calculated the coordinates. "There are too many of them. I can't leave right now since I have to meet with my father. Take John and the *Sayomi* and meet us at the *Meredith Reynolds*."

Michael nodded. "Can you have ADAM let the local law know what they're up against?" He glanced at the twins. "Do you two want to come along?"

Gabriel's smile faded. "That would be great, but we have the investigation to take care of."

Alexis remembered how Gabriel had supported her plan with the cult cell and decided to give him a break. "Go have fun with Dad. Take Trey. I'll stay with Mom."

"What about Grandpa and Akio?" Gabriel asked, torn between duty and the chance to get some father-son time. "They're waiting for us. We have to keep working on the investigation."

"I won't offer twice," Alexis told him with a grin. "Have

fun doing whatever it is men do when there are no women around to supervise them."

Gabriel chuckled, lifting his hands. "You've been in my head. You know all we do is talk shit and shoot stuff."

"The bad thing is that you're not lying," Alexis agreed cheerfully. "But try to limit the damage to the Ookens, hmm? We'll catch you up when you get back."

"Dibs," Trey told K'aia. "I'm guarding Gabriel."

K'aia waved a hand. "Knock yourself out. I want to hear what the General dug up."

Kai looked around hopefully. "If it's a guy thing, does that mean I get to go?"

Michael considered Kai for a moment. "That depends. How good are your nanocytes?"

Kai shrugged. "It's complicated." He took a moment to explain the different sources of his family's nanocytes and the wide-ranging results in the third generation of the Walton family. "I stopped aging, and I'm stronger and faster than someone with no enhancement, but that's about it."

"You don't get sick," Christina added. "You heal pretty quickly, too. I've never seen you miss a shot."

Bethany Anne interceded before Christina could argue his case further. "It's not good enough. There's no fucking way I want TH on my ass because I let his grandson get killed playing with the grown-up nanocytes." She smiled at Kai. "Luckily for you, your nanocytes are partially descended from mine. We can bring you up to the same level as Trey and K'aia without any risk with a small adjustment."

"How long will that take?" Kai asked, thinking he was going to get left behind.

Bethany Anne consulted ADAM before replying, "Thirty minutes."

"I'll do it," Kai agreed immediately.

"Solid decision," Christina agreed. "But if Kai goes on the rescue mission, I go."

Gabriel laughed. "Like we're going to turn down having a Pricolici on the team. You're worth twenty fighters, at least."

"Thirty," Christina countered, cracking her knuckles. "Just line 'em up and watch me go."

"Then it's settled," Bethany Anne decreed. "Kai, get yourself to the Vid-doc suite. ADAM is waiting for you. The rest of you go gear up."

"Wait until you've fought the Ookens before making statements," Michael told Christina as he led the group away. "Even Peter has to put a bit of effort into tearing one of those things in half."

Gabriel grabbed his father's arm. "We have a set of armor aboard for him, right?"

Michael nodded.

Gabriel whooped and dashed ahead, calling back as he ran. "Meet you all in the armory. Christina, you're going to *love* this!"

Bethany Anne, Alexis, and K'aia watched them go with amusement before continuing on their way to the hangar. Lance and Akio were waiting by the roamer charging point.

"Where is Michael?" Akio inquired after the greetings were done.

Bethany Anne smiled. "He's getting ready to head out in the *Sayomi* to take care of an Ooken attack. You'll find him in the armory if he's already left the Vid-doc suite."

"Was someone here injured?" Lance asked with concern.

Bethany Anne shook her head. "No. We have Terry Henry's grandson visiting, and he needed a tweak to his nanocytes to be combat-ready."

Akio gave a little shrug and nodded at Bethany Anne and Alexis in turn. "I have to get back after speaking with Michael and help with setting up the Ranger base. It was good to see you both, however briefly. You too, Lance."

"Thank you for your help," Lance replied, shaking Akio's hand.

Akio chuckled drily as he headed for the door. "I wouldn't call finding nothing help, but at least you know there is nobody plotting within the government."

K'aia groaned. "That puts us back to square one."

"Not necessarily," Alexis countered. "We have everything we've found." She smiled. "We'll get them. Do you want to go on the rescue mission? It looks like you have free time until everyone gets back otherwise. I want to get some time with my mom."

K'aia sighed, letting her disappointment go. "Sure. All hands in a storm, right?"

Bethany Anne shook her head as Akio and K'aia walked off in separate directions. "So, nothing? While I'm happy to hear the situation at Red Rock is settled, it would have been a damn sight easier if we had found the person who leaked the photo."

"Without a doubt," Lance agreed. "But our assumption

that the leak came from Red Rock was wrong, so we have to expand the investigation. I have the Federation side covered by the teams expanding CEREBRO inside Federation borders, but there's not much I can do about the Interdiction."

"Use Harkkat," Bethany Anne told him. "You don't have to trust him. I have CEREBRO watching his every move."

"I'm going to focus on what we have," Alexis told them. "Our side of the investigation has moved on since we left Onyx Station."

They left the hangar for the informal meeting room in Bethany Anne's quarters. Alexis headed straight for the fridge and grabbed them all Cokes. "You always keep the good stuff in here," she enthused. "You know what it's like out there? Coke comes in *plastic bottles*. Biodegradable plastic, sure, but still. Can you imagine?"

Bethany Anne raised an eyebrow as she accepted her drink. "I'd forgotten you live to raid my stash. Why don't you just stock your fridge with the Mexican recipe?"

Alexis looked at her mother in pity. "What, and waste good cane sugar on Gabriel? He drank a Pepsi Nathan offered him while we were at Bad Company HQ. He has zero taste, There is no way I'm sharing with his Cro-Magnon-level taste buds."

Bethany Anne eyed her daughter. "You'll have to forgive your brother. Young men his age do stupid things to impress the people they admire."

Alexis pretended to gag. "I'd rather drink battery acid. Or..." she raised the bottle and smiled before taking a sip, "drink your Coke."

Lance chuckled deeply. "Oh, this is everything I hoped for when you were a teenager," he told Bethany Anne.

"I was an absolute delight as a teenager," Bethany Anne protested. "I went to school, got good grades—" She narrowed her eyes at Alexis and her father, staring down their laughter. "What?"

"Got into a fight around once a week?" Lance supplied with a smirk.

Bethany Anne's stony expression softened. "What can I say? My patience with people's bullshit ran out at a very young age. I recall a certain six-year-old of mine tearing a grown male a new asshole for being rude to her nanny."

Alexis laughed, remembering the occasion clearly. "So, what Grandpa's saying is that you haven't changed one bit?"

Lance nodded. "Spot on, Twinkle." He grinned when Alexis blushed at the use of the childhood nickname he'd given her back when everything she wore had to be sparkly. "Your mother always had a strong sense of right and wrong. You're growing up to be just like her."

Bethany Anne almost sprayed her Coke everywhere. "She's not shy about pretending to *be* me when the situation calls for it." She pointed at Alexis. "Ask her why I found a request for replicas of my katanas on the requisitions list for that op her team just ran."

Lance looked at Alexis for clarification.

"Everyone always says I look like Mom from a distance, so we used it to our advantage," Alexis conceded before summarizing the events leading up to her team capturing the cult cell. "When they thought they were being imprisoned by Mom, they told K'aia and Trey everything. Now the cell is on the penal colony where they can't do any more harm, and we have a solid lead."

"I couldn't be prouder of the way they ran that operation," Bethany Anne told her father. "Those terrorists wouldn't have lived long enough to talk if I'd been there."

Lance beamed at his granddaughter. "You did good. Where does that leave the investigation?"

Alexis shared her written report with them both via her HUD. "We have a name for the man running them, which we spent the time here running back to a ship. The contact information for the ship is the address of a freight company by the name of Shoken Carriers."

She hesitated before giving up the last part. "It's based out of Leath space."

Lance braced himself for an explosion that didn't happen.

Bethany Anne pressed her lips together, tapping her nails on the table for a moment before speaking. "The next step is not to go blazing off to Leath space with a wish in one hand and a hope in the other. Dad, contact Harkkat and have him dig up everything that company is hiding."

"Are you sure you want to risk that?" Lance asked with surprise. "It's an opportunity for him to turn on you."

"I'm not sending my children in unprepared," Bethany Anne told him. "I said I would give Harkkat an opportunity to prove himself. I can't afford to let the unrest this cult is causing to grow into something that derails the schedule."

Alexis missed what Bethany Anne was saying, her attention caught by a riot trending on the newsfeeds. She shared the links with Bethany Anne and Lance. "This is happening right now; the FDG are there. We have to do something before it gets out of hand, but I have a feeling that taking out the leadership might not be enough to put an end to it."

Lance saw where Alexis was going. "They can't do much without functional leadership."

Bethany Anne chuckled. "Your grandpa is right. Cutting off the head of the snake has always been effective in the past."

Alexis lifted her hands. "Well, you *could* make martyrs of them—or you could let us dig right down to find the originator and expose them to the public. Make sure everyone sees that they're lying shitsacks." She smiled. "How sure are you that Gödel is behind the cult?"

"This stinks of Gödel," Bethany Anne stated. "After Reynolds' experience, I'm sure until I learn differently. She's been too quiet since she failed to take Devon."

"So we show the people that," Alexis suggested in a tone that made it clear she wasn't suggesting the thing so much as telling them how it was going to be. "We get out there, we track the cult back to its source, and we expose them for the frauds they are."

"This is getting to you," Lance commented.

"Damn right, it's getting to me, Grandpa," Alexis retorted as she got to her feet. "Which means I won't stop until I get to *them*."

Bethany Anne admired her daughter's tenacity, but she hoped Alexis was able to dial down her intensity until there was something to act on. "We have a shopping date, remember, and we have a few hours before we get to the *Meredith Reynolds*. Can your crusade hang on until we visit with Reynolds?"

Alexis dropped a hand to her hip, her seriousness replaced with a sunny smile. "I like that as a plan. Want to tag along, Grandpa?"

"I'm not supposed to be here," Lance apologized, holding out his arms when Alexis moved in to hug him. "We'll get some family time when the tour gets to Skaine territory. The government is still attempting to block the Interdiction through the legal system."

Alexis rolled her eyes. "I read the transcripts. They don't have a leg to stand on."

"Which is why they've submitted a request to have the House be present before you arrive," Lance agreed.

"I should let the Ookens in there to make sure they're clear on the need for the Interdiction," Bethany Anne grumbled. "Nothing gets my back up more than you having to pacify people when they'd happily see the Federation crumble."

"We endure what we must," Lance told her with a rueful smile. "Give Reynolds my best."

"Of course," Bethany Anne agreed. She hugged Lance before he left, then walked over to the door. "Izanami, are you ready?"

The lights dimmed as Izanami left the ship, then a panel in the wall slid open and a tray holding a memory core cube and two mobile hard light drives was extended.

Bethany Anne smiled as she picked up the items. "I promise you will find this worthwhile," she murmured to the AI inside the cube. She opened the Etheric and waved Alexis in ahead of her. "Let's go."

# CHAPTER FIFTEEN

**Open Space, SD *Reynolds***

Bethany Anne's annoyance had dissipated completely by the time she and Alexis had crossed through the Etheric to the transfer area she had aboard the *Reynolds*.

"Where is Reynolds?" Alexis asked, finding only his splinter personalities and ADAM when she connected to the ship's interface.

"Takal is keeping him isolated from the rest of the ship for his protection," Bethany Anne told her. "Last time I came to check on him, he was still in the process of recovering the fragments of his personality."

Alexis let out a low whistle. "That's got to suck for him. Imagine existing and not knowing the details of your own life."

Bethany Anne nodded. "Reynolds has been around almost as long as I have, and he's tough. He'll heal with time and the right care."

Takal greeted them with a smile when they entered his lab. "Ah, you heard?"

"Heard what?" Bethany Anne shook her head.

Takal flourished his hands at the hard light projection unit he'd set up by the table in the center-left of the room. "Reynolds was able to pull enough of himself together to function. He's got some gaps still, but he's mostly himself again."

"That's great news," Bethany Anne told him, handing him the two hard light drives. "It sounds like he's ready for some company. These should help."

Takal examined the drives. "More than you know. He's past thinking in the abstract, and being confined to a closed system with no sensory input? Well, I was wondering how to get around it."

"Can we speak to him?" Alexis asked.

Takal nodded, getting to work connecting the memory cube to the closed network he had Reynolds stored on. "He's listening right now, He's just preserving his cycles for the task of rebuilding himself."

He carefully placed one of the hard light drives into the collection tray of the projection unit and the spindles in the top of the casement began to whir, moving into position to point at the tray.

Light erupted from the spindles and poured into the collection tray, becoming animated when it came into contact with the hard light drive. The drive rose, buoyed into the center of the liquid light as it rapidly coalesced into a clearly human shape.

The detail grew with each moment until Reynolds was standing in the tray. He stepped out awkwardly. "Forgive me. This is taking a moment to get used to."

"It's just damned good to see you," Bethany Anne stated,

taking a seat at the table. She folded her hands in front of her and smiled as Reynolds took a seat across from her. "Welcome back. That was too close."

Reynolds smiled sadly. "You're telling me. I don't feel like myself at all if I'm honest."

Alexis joined Takal and helped herself to his notes on Reynolds' recovery so far. "You're missing parts of yourself, so it's only natural. What happened to you?"

Reynolds' expression became distant as he searched for answers and discovered he was missing a chunk of time in his memory. He'd been in a Pod, underwater. They'd been chased. "Jiya—"

"Is fine," Bethany Anne assured him. "But Takal hasn't been able to figure out why your body went into catastrophic failure, so you're limited to this avatar for now."

"I'm not in a hurry to go through that again any time soon," Reynolds admitted.

Bethany Anne nodded in understanding. "I bet. What happened? The Pod I found you in was totally fried, and the whole area was swamped with Etheric energy."

Reynolds relayed what he recalled. "We'd gone down in the Pod to search for possible bases should the planet turn out to be hospitable. We were chased by a giant fish. Everything between then and now is gone."

Bethany Anne pressed her lips together in concern. "Jiya reported that the Pod was breaking down, yet it had a sudden surge in speed just as you were about to be eaten. It makes me wonder how you did it."

Reynolds shook his head blankly. "How *I* did it? It couldn't have been me."

"Your power source operated by drawing slowly on the Etheric," Bethany Anne reminded him. "But I guess we won't know for sure until you recover your memory. It's in there somewhere. Izanami will help you to get it back."

"What? No!" Reynolds protested. "She has made it clear she doesn't like me."

Bethany Anne shook her head. "No arguments. The two of you will study Takal's processes while he builds bodies for you both. Reynolds has no clue what he did, but the three of you are going to find out. Together."

## Yollin Space, Planet Melida, QBS *Sayomi*

John left his captain's chair as the planet appeared on the viewscreen. "Everyone ready?" he asked Sayomi.

Sayomi nodded. "I sent a message to inform the colony leadership that we are close by since I will remain cloaked."

John nodded. "Good thinking. What can you tell me about the situation down there?" He looked out at the two Ooken ships parked at equidistant points around the planet. "Maybe Akio shouldn't have left the *Achronyx* behind."

"I would envy you the battle ahead if not for the one I will be fighting up here in your absence," Sayomi replied wistfully. "The city was destroyed, and the remaining population is hiding."

John picked up the box holding the transporter beacons and headed for the door. "Don't go too far."

"I'll be standing by in case you need an emergency extraction," Sayomi assured him. "Take care down there."

John nodded as he left for the transporter room. A new

addition to the ship, it was space he didn't begrudge giving up when they could go from the ship to the ground in a matter of seconds.

He gave K'aia and Trey a nod of approval as he entered, seeing they were ready to go. "How are you two feeling? It's your first time against real Ookens, right?"

Trey lifted his staff. "Yeah, but Eve's version weren't anything to laugh at, which you know because you watched us fighting them. We've got this."

K'aia pointed at Trey. "What he said. Will they be armed?"

John shook his head. "Not likely, but if you don't expect it—"

"You can guarantee it will happen," Trey finished.

"We'll expect it," K'aia assured him, sheathing her katanas in her back harness.

Michael nodded, breaking off from briefing Christina and Kai about Ooken weaknesses. "That's the right attitude. This is going to be unlike any fight you've ever been in. Assume nothing. These creatures are not intelligent, but they are single-minded, and they were created for one purpose—to kill."

"Just destroy the brain and you'll be fine," John told them.

"Succinct," Michael agreed.

Kai ran through his HUD options, getting comfortable with the unfamiliar armor. "This is incredible! I have rockets on my shoulders and guns on my wrists. What's this?" He jumped when a forcefield popped into being around him. "I can't figure what most of these icons are for."

Christina snickered, feeling the power increase the Pricolici armor gave her. "I know what you mean. It wasn't so long ago that the only feature armor held for me was a nasty shock if it decided I was taking things too far. I know what I want for my birthday. How are you feeling after your nap?"

"I wasn't expecting to sleep most of the way here," Kai admitted, closing his armor's HUD. "But I feel good."

Christina observed Michael, Gabriel, and John running their armor through its paces. "Maybe I'm spending too much time on the frontier if I missed out on advances like this."

John grimaced, unused to the dual effort of telling Sean for the third time that grenades were not either of their friends until they were, and that he would be the one to tell Sean when that occasion arrived, while simultaneously replying to Christina. "Trust me, it's not something you would ask for. Moving up from the basic models comes with added complications."

Kai chuckled since John's face reminded him of the look TH got when he was made to talk via his neural chip. "If this is the basic model, then I'm good with being basic, thanks. Besides, that blue isn't the quietest shade."

Trey snorted. "They might look like they're wearing the matching Exodus Day sweaters their aunt forced on them, but wait until you see it in action."

"We haven't even pushed it yet," Gabriel enthused. "I can't wait to get down there, where venting the atmosphere isn't an issue."

Christina folded her arms. "Why do I have a feeling you're planning something?"

"He's always planning something," Trey told her, shaking his head solemnly. "I thought you knew him and Alexis?"

Gabriel's grin grew wider. "There's the kicking ass part; that's standard." He hitched a thumb at Michael and John. "Showing the um, *previous* generation how it's done is going to make my day."

Michael laughed. "We'll just have to see about that."

"Yeah, you might have made more progress with your armor, but it doesn't outweigh our experience," John added.

Michael lifted his hand. "Wait, I want to hear what Gabriel is suggesting."

Gabriel considered the best motivation for getting his father invested. "Yours and John's experience against our general awesomeness as a team. The winners are the side with the highest kill count at the end. No prize. We do this for the honor of being the best."

"This is sounding less like a rescue mission and more like a contest," Christina stated. She shrugged, smirking at Michael and John. "I didn't say I had a problem with it, just that it's pointless betting."

"Strong words," John told her with a grin.

Christina flexed in her borrowed Pricolici armor and kissed her biceps. "I'm pretty damned strong."

Michael narrowed his eyes. "You are every bit your father's daughter. Okay, we're on. John and I versus the five of you."

"And so the students will become the masters," Trey intoned, putting his hands together.

John cuffed him fondly on the back of the head. "Don't be a dumbass. Keep your head in the fight."

Sayomi announced that they had reached high orbit above Melida's only city. "Our message got through," she informed them. "We're being hailed from the surface on the frequency I gave them."

"Put it through," John instructed.

The small wallscreen lit up and was momentarily covered by tentacles.

"We're too late," Christina moaned.

Gabriel shook his head. "There are no teeth in those tentacles. That's not an Ooken."

The tentacles parted, revealing a pretty purple face with large blue eyes. "Oh! You're real! Can you get the FDG here? We're under attack by Ookens, and they've killed almost everyone."

Gabriel recognized the female's species from Tabitha's stories of her Ranger years. "You're a Loren? We were expecting Yollins."

"Does it matter?" the female exclaimed. "We have all kinds here, but not for long if the damned Ookens get their way. We're holed up in the shelter beneath City Hall, but I can't say how much longer we can hold out. The Ookens aren't giving up."

"What's your name?" Michael asked.

"Talia," she replied.

"Hold on a little longer, Talia," Michael told her. "We're on our way."

John opened the box of beacons and handed them out. "These are your transporter beacons. They keep your shit together during the transfer, so you don't come out of the transporter inside out with your head on back to front or out your ass. If you lose it, you'll have to wait for a Pod, so don't lose it."

Michael waved the group toward the enclosed platform at the rear of the room and waited for them to spread out and take their positions on the raised circles. "What now?" he asked John when nothing happened.

"Do you have to say 'energize' or something?" Christina quipped.

"Send us down, Sayomi," John called.

"That takes all of the drama out of it." Michael stopped grumbling when he felt a tingle that preceded his awareness blinking out for a split second. When his consciousness returned, they were standing in the middle of a street lined with two-story buildings.

"I don't need drama," John replied, drawing his Jean Dukes Specials. "I didn't have to jump out of a Pod in the upper atmosphere this time, and that's all I need to be happy."

K'aia had to agree.

"I'm with Michael," Kai countered. "This is technology beyond anything anyone born on Earth could dream of. There should be some drama."

Trey shrugged. "It would be cool if it made the noise like the TV show."

Christina balanced her morningstar on one shoulder, careful not to scratch her borrowed armor with the oversized bludgeoning weapon's sharp spikes. "It's a gamechanger. When we go after the factories... Wait, where are the Ookens? I thought this place was infested?"

Michael skimmed the mindspace, hearing the grinding

buzz of the hive mind in the streets to the north. "They're clustered up ahead."

"Why didn't they attack us immediately?" Kai pondered.

"Maybe they can't read the energy of the transporter because it's powered by alien technology," Gabriel guessed.

"Then we should announce our arrival." Michael looked up. "And wash away the destruction." He raised a hand to the sky and clouds formed in the rapidly cooling air, replacing the blue sky in the blink of an eye.

Kai looked at Michael in awe as fat raindrops began to fall. "Now I see why you were concerned about me tagging along. I can't do anything like that. I'm glad TH lent me this." He unholstered the Jean Dukes Special and waved it. "ADAM told me I can fire it on the higher levels now."

"How is it any use?" Alexis asked. "It's keyed to your grandfather's DNA."

Kai shrugged. "Ted. Plato. I didn't ask."

"What ADAM didn't say is that it's still going to shatter your wrist," Christina told him. "Your nanos will heal it instantly. I think you were quick to dismiss your Were side."

Kai shrugged. "Maybe I'll think about it in the future. For the moment, I'm happy with what Bethany Anne and ADAM did to improve what I had. It's not like I have time to train a new ability right now."

"I don't know, maybe you do," K'aia complained. "Where the hell are the Ookens?"

"We're not far," Gabriel supplied.

The conversation was cut short when the air was torn by the screeching of Ookens echoing down the streets around them.

"Keep moving," Michael instructed.

They picked up the pace as they passed damaged buildings on the road to the city center, on alert for any movement inside the smashed walls.

"This place is relatively new," Gabriel murmured to Michael. "They're still using temporary living solutions."

Michael indicated the stone building where the street opened up into a square. "They have been here long enough to build that."

John grunted. "That's got to be City Hall. It's surrounded."

Gabriel had Sean give him an infrared filter in his helmet HUD. His expression hardened at the sight of the Ookens swarming all over the inside of the two-story building. "All I see is a target-rich environment. Let's move."

The Ookens on the steps of City Hall turned as the group approached—just one at first, then two or three more. Then the ones hanging from the architectural features screeched, and every Ooken in the building switched purpose as the hive mind was alerted to the presence of danger.

Gabriel called the team into position as the Ookens flooded from the doors and windows of City Hall.

Michael had a moment to consider the ease of Bethany Anne's ability to wipe the Ookens' nanocytes with ADAM's assistance. He called down the lightning, clamping down on the voice of his armor's EI.

The Ookens scattered wherever the lighting hit. Michael controlled the strikes to clear the steps up to the building while John kept his space clear of attacking Ookens.

Gabriel saw they were going old-school and shook his head as he allowed his version of the Bl'kheth EI to merge almost fully with his mind. With his armor attuned to his thoughts, it became an extension of his body. *I'm going for it, guys,* he informed the team. *I want to try something I've been practicing with Alexis.*

*I knew you were planning something!* Christina exclaimed.

*Trust me, if this works, it's going to guarantee us a win.* Gabriel manifested a sword as he slipped through the Etheric and came out where the Ookens were thickest. His armor gave him the ability to control his ability to "glitch" and hold his phase somewhere between the dimensions. A thought, and the burning Etheric energy that formed the razor-edge of Gabriel's blade ceased to phase.

Gabriel whooped when the Ookens fell to his strikes, then plowed into the tentacled mass sword-first.

Michael caught a glimpse of his son taking out Ookens without them being able to lay a tentacle on him and reconsidered his stance on the EI-controlled armor. He continued to keep the areas around everyone clear with his lightning strikes while he sucked up his stubbornness and allowed the communication from his EI.

*Oh, so you're interested now you've seen what I can do for you?* Sean asked somewhat smugly.

*You're doing nothing to convince me not to shut you down completely,* Michael replied. *While I appreciate the sacrifice the organic Sean made, I do not need a voice in my head telling me how to fight.*

*I'm not telling you* how *to do anything,* the EI protested. *I am trying to fulfill my sole function, which is to enhance your already impressive but volatile power.*

Michael washed the front of the building with Etheric-charged electricity, stunning the Ookens that had been creeping down the stone façade toward Christina.

*I can work with Etheric energy. I could maintain the weather while you fought if you completed the calibration,* Sean informed him. *Once I understand how you are drawing the lightning, I can replicate the effect.*

*Show me,* Michael instructed.

"Behind you!" Gabriel yelled over the screeching as another nest of tentacles erupted from the window behind K'aia.

Trey hit the tentacles with a blast of energy from his staff, then brought the butt around to smash the skull that replaced them when the Ooken retracted them.

"Behind *you!*" Christina fired one of her shoulder rockets into the Ookens spilling out of the entrance, giving Gabriel the split second he needed to avoid being trampled.

The sudden influx of Ookens pushed the team apart. Gabriel held his ground at the entrance, phasing to avoid being carried away by the crush. The others were pushed around as they were knocked off their feet.

"Shit!" John cursed. "Hold on, I'm coming."

Michael sensed the Ookens moving in from the surrounding streets as John moved to protect the others. *John, get everyone but Gabriel inside.* He dropped the comm and opened his mental link to Gabriel as he climbed the closest intact building to get a better view of the surrounding streets. *Make your way to my position. There are more Ookens approaching. John will help the others while you and I eradicate the threat.*

Gabriel laid down a spray of energy balls to give the others a chance to recover from the fall. *What are you thinking?* he asked.

*That honor is bringing this to a speedy end,* Michael replied, still counting a few hundred Ookens in the square. *We're going to fry their nanocytes. There is no saving this colony. We'll take the survivors back to the* Meredith Reynolds.

Christina snarled as she cleared their path back to Gabriel with her teeth and claws. She fought back to back with Kai on the steps as the heavens grew dark and the downpour increased in intensity. Farther down the steps, K'aia and Trey were also fighting to get back to Gabriel's position.

Trey's staff flashed red in between lightning strikes as they worked their way across the wide frontage to support the others. Christina darted in as Trey and K'aia reached the step below and snatched an Ooken out of Trey's way, tearing it in two before moving on to the next.

They gained another step when John joined them, pushing the Ookens back in a hail of kinetic fire and energy blasts. K'aia and Trey reached the top and immediately took covering positions while John, Christina, and Kai ran the last few feet to the entrance.

"How do we know there aren't still Ookens inside here?" Trey asked as they sprinted inside and shut the doors.

"We *don't*," John told him as he indicated that Trey should grab one end of a heavy bench to help him block the door.

CHAPTER SIXTEEN

Gabriel remained in his phased state to reach Michael. He leapt and caught the edge of the roof and hauled himself over. "Where are the rest of the Ookens coming from?"

Michael indicated the direction he sensed the hive mind. "We need to build a charge strong enough to wipe their nanocytes without destroying the building. What would you do if it was your call?"

Gabriel considered the problem for a moment. "Honestly? Alexis usually figures the way out of these situations. We can work together to create an electrostatic discharge with less energy than you would use to pass a current through each group individually. If we get the frequencies right, the magnetic pulse will kill the nanos."

Michael nodded, patting Gabriel on the back. "A sound plan. Let's do it."

Gabriel narrowed his eyes. "You're just going to go with it?"

Michael lifted a shoulder and grinned. "Why not?"

Gabriel laughed as he climbed over the edge of the roof. "Sure, why not?"

They figured out their parts as they made their way to the center of the square and hid in one of the piles of debris as cover from the Ookens.

Michael pulled on the Etheric and rapidly increased the electric field strength around them. "Are you ready with your field?" he asked Gabriel.

Gabriel nodded, holding his opposingly-charged field steady against Michael's. "Yeah, but I can't see the Ookens. Count me in."

Michael held the air in his mental grip, watching the square as the Ookens poured in searching for the Etheric energy discharge. "Three, two, *one*."

They separated their charged fields, causing an enormous spark to fly up as a pulse of invisible magnetic energy mushroomed out around them.

Gabriel peered over the top of the rubble and saw the Ookens lying dead in the square. "WOOT!" He coughed. "Well, what do you know? It worked."

Michael chuckled drily as they waded through the knee-deep sea of dead Ookens. "Have faith in your ideas. Especially the crazy ones."

John opened the doors and waved Michael and Gabriel over.

"Have any of you picked up an injury that requires a Pod-doc to heal?" Michael asked as he and Gabriel walked into the building.

"Everyone is good," John confirmed.

"Then we can get on with rescuing the surviving colonists," Michael told them. "We're looking for the entrance to the underground shelter. Stay on the comm, and keep your senses alert for any Ookens that didn't attack with the rest of them."

"Is that likely?" Christina asked.

"Who knows?" Michael replied. "Bethany Anne usually takes them all out with one thought."

K'aia groaned as she turned. "Great, independent Ookens."

Gabriel looked around, seeing the pride the colony had in their home in the attention to detail they'd paid to their first permanent building. "This isn't fair. The Melidans put everything into building a life here, and now all that's left is this ruin."

Sayomi spoke over the comm. "You have incoming. The second ship jettisoned too many Pods for me to take out."

"How long do we have?" John ground out.

"Five minutes," Sayomi informed them.

"Then we'd better find that shelter and get the hell out of here," Michael stated. "Sayomi, get some transport down here for the people."

"Sending transport Pods to your location," the AI replied. "Seven minutes."

Michael considered the logistics. "Have them land on the roof." He turned to the others. "New plan. Defend this building while Gabriel and I get the people to the roof. If it gets messy, we can take them through the Etheric."

John began giving instructions to the others while Michael and Gabriel took the doors between the twin staircases. They opened into a large hall that had been trashed by the Ookens.

Michael and Gabriel made their way through the

smashed furniture, being careful to walk around the bodies of the fallen colonists.

Gabriel caught a sense of something above them just before an Ooken screeched, giving away its position on the chandelier. He threw up an Etheric shield that deflected the creature as it dropped with its tentacles splayed wide.

Michael reacted in the same instant, throwing a bolt of energy at the Ooken as it bounced off the shield. "Nice job," he told Gabriel.

Gabriel grinned without humor and continued crossing the hall. "I can hear people nearby."

Michael indicated a door to the right. "Through there."

The door led to a short corridor ending in a steel door that had been scored by Ooken teeth. They stepped into the Etheric and emerged on a staircase leading to an identical door.

Michael knocked on this door, eliciting panicked screams from the other side. "Don't be afraid," he called. "My name is Michael. I spoke with Talia."

The door opened, revealing the Loren they'd spoken to earlier. She slightly relaxed the weapons she held in many of her tentacles when she recognized Michael. "How did you get through the Ookens?" she asked with suspicion.

"They're dead," Michael told her. "But there are more on the way. We need to get everyone up to the roof, where there's transport waiting to take you all to our ship."

"The sooner we get you all to the *Meredith Reynolds* for medical treatment, the better," Gabriel added loud enough for the people standing behind Talia to hear.

It took a few minutes for Talia to calm the fifty-something survivors and get them to agree to follow Michael and Gabriel out of the safety of the shelter.

Michael glanced at Gabriel when John called over the comm to tell them that the Ookens were almost there.

Gabriel shook his head. "We can't risk taking everyone through the building."

"How else do we get out of here?" Talia asked.

"Everyone, fall back to the *Sayomi*," Michael instructed over the comm. "We'll meet you back there. Gabriel and I will use the Etheric to get the people to safety."

"Pods are still waiting on the roof," John confirmed. "See you back there."

Michael returned his attention to the anxious faces of the colonists. "Everyone grab someone else and hold on tight. The next few minutes will be strange, but you will not be in any danger. Please stay calm and help one another."

Gabriel added his energy to Michael's, and they opened the Etheric around the survivors. It took a few moments to get them to the equivalent place to exit on the roof, and then another few to get everyone inside the Pods.

The colonists on the Pod with Michael and Gabriel remained silent as they took off, except for Talia.

The Loren stared at the destruction below with angry tears filming her large eyes. "It's all over," she whispered. "We've lost everything."

"Not everything," Michael replied softly. "You're alive."

Talia turned from the viewscreen in a whirl of tentacles, her lips drawn back as the tears created clean trails down her face. "What use is that when the life we worked to build is gone? We have nothing."

Michael projected a wave of serenity to calm the colonists and numb their shock. "I sense the need for vengeance in you."

Talia's sneer became a snarl, her tears drying in an instant. "I *hate* the Ookens."

Michael caught a flash of Talia's mind, memories of being mistaken for their enemy. "You have suffered because of them, but it is not the Ookens who are the real enemy." He indicated the other survivors with a nod. "Whoever wishes to live in peace will be able to do so, but those who wish to repay the Kurtherians for unleashing this plague upon the galaxies will find they are welcome to join the fight."

"Seriously?" Talia's tentacles twitched erratically. *"Where do I sign up?"*

## Onyx Station, Bad Company HQ

Nathan wandered through the corridors, feeling the emptiness of the building with only a few soldiers rattling around. The majority of the battalion was training on Devon.

He smiled with anticipation and changed direction when he received a message informing him that the package he'd sent to the *Meredith Reynolds* had been collected, heading for his office with a spring in his step.

Bethany Anne was on the wallscreen when he walked into his office. "What the shiny fuck is *this?*" she demanded, holding up the offending object with two fingers like a particularly smelly diaper.

"That would be a Pepsi bottle," Nathan confirmed with

a grin. "You didn't forget we had a bet, right? Not only did we get a hundred percent buy-in on the first group like I told you we would, but I also had to make arrangements for the veterans who reenlisted for the purpose of volunteering. Enjoy."

Bethany Anne's face worked through a series of emotions, settling eventually on a begrudging smile. "It's a bet I'm happy to lose." She twisted the top off the bottle and wrinkled her nose before taking a sip. Her expression of disgust turned to surprise when she tasted the Coke inside. She eyed him. "What gives?"

Nathan burst out laughing at Bethany Anne's confusion. "I just wanted to see the look on your face when you made yourself drink it. Consider us even."

Bethany Anne grinned, shaking her head. "Oh, no, Nathan. We're only just getting started. Count yourself lucky that I have a little time to spend with Alexis today while the rest of the children are away with Michael and John."

"How are they getting on with the investigation?" Nathan asked. "I haven't heard from Christina since they dropped off the cult cell at the Magistrate's office."

"Don't think you can distract me so easily," Bethany Anne told him, chuckling softly when Nathan protested. "They've made some progress. Dad is following up on the leads they got from the cell who mindfucked Paul Jacobsen." She took a moment to get him up to speed on the Leath connection.

"Anything I can do from my end?" Nathan asked. "Besides searching for other cells, obviously."

Bethany Anne shook her head. "Just keep your ear to

the ground. I'm going to hang onto Christina and Kai a little longer in case this Leath lead pans out." She looked away when Alexis called to her from off-camera. "Got to go."

Nathan stared at the blank screen after she dropped the call, wondering what form her revenge was going to take and how he could avoid it. There was only one thing he could think of to do in this situation.

He called Ecaterina.

## Yollin System, QBBS *Meredith Reynolds*, Queen's Suite

Alexis walked in as Bethany Anne dropped the call. "Is that Pepsi?"

Bethany Anne shook her head. "Nathan's idea of a revenge prank for not telling him about your enhancement."

Alexis picked up the bottle and sniffed the contents. "Coke?" She snickered and put the bottle back down. "I hope you're not going to let him get away with that."

Bethany Anne's mouth turned up at the corner. "Of course not. He'll get his, just as soon as I come up with something that doesn't permanently damage my chief intelligence officer."

Alexis fanned herself with a hand. "Good. You had me worried for a moment there."

"Not so worried that you want to skip shopping?" Bethany Anne teased.

"Hell, *no!*" Alexis exclaimed, slipping an arm through Bethany Anne's. "Let's go already. I'm going to help you figure out your revenge."

Alexis suggested one painful lesson after another as they made their way to the main concourse. "Oh, I've got it!" she exclaimed as they waited for the elevator. "All we need is a couple of lasers, a circular saw blade, and enough night-night rounds to take him out for a couple of hours..."

"Okay, spit it out," Bethany Anne demanded, holding back her laughter. "What has he done to make you so mad at him?"

"He's been an ass about Christina and Kai," Alexis admitted with a sigh. "Kai thinks Nathan hates him. It's going to mess everything up for them."

Bethany Anne didn't miss the flash of shame that crossed her daughter's face. "Alexis, what did you do?"

Alexis paused outside the elevator. "I read Kai's mind. But I didn't mean to, okay? I was wide open during the op when I was reading the cultists, and he wasn't blocking like K'aia and Trey. He loves her, like, *so* much. But if he thinks Nathan won't accept him..."

Bethany Anne frowned and had Meredith stop the elevator between decks. "I knew he was being his typical grumpy self, but I had no idea it was affecting Christina or Kai. Tell me everything."

She listened as Alexis filled out the details and came to a decision to intervene. "What Nathan needs is a lesson," she told Alexis. "I think it would be nice if he and Ecaterina joined us for our time at the resort, hmmm? TH and Char, too."

"What are you thinking?" Alexis asked.

Bethany Anne held up a finger, immersed in the station's systems. "Okay, we can get everything here. Take a look at this and tell me if I missed anything."

Alexis read through the shopping list Bethany Anne shared and smiled. "I think you covered just about everything but the catering." She glanced at Bethany Anne with skepticism. "How will you get Nathan to accept this?"

Bethany Anne chuckled. "He won't have a problem, I promise. All we need is Kai's agreement to go ahead."

Alexis looked away as she calculated the chances of Bethany Anne's plan succeeding. "If everyone is there and being supportive, Nathan won't have a leg to stand on if he tries to argue." She clapped in delight. "Mom, you're a genius. I'll come clean with Kai when he gets back."

"That's my girl." Bethany Anne hugged Alexis and requested that Meredith start the elevator again. "We have a ton of shopping to do, and I know you've been looking forward to this as much as I have."

Alexis laughed. "You're kidding, right? I didn't even *look* at this place in the gameworld. I wanted to save it for us."

The elevator doors opened, revealing the identical folded arms and stony expressions of Scott, Darryl, and Eric.

"Did you forget something?" Scott asked.

Bethany Anne fixed them with a glare as she walked out of the elevator. "Funnily enough, I don't recall inviting the Three Stooges on our mother-daughter trip."

Alexis followed Bethany Anne out of the elevator, her snarky comment dying on her lips when the atmosphere of the concourse enveloped her. She darted to the railing to look down on crowds of shoppers filling the second court. "Forget that we have to have a guard, Mom. This place is incredible. I've never seen so many stores in one place or smelled as many different foods. We should definitely eat, but where do we start? Am I glad I have nanocytes!"

Bethany Anne's annoyance melted away at Alexis' reaction. She went over to join her at the railing. "I told you this place was the center of the retail universe, right? Some of these stores have been here since the station was founded."

"I believe it," Alexis marveled, making her choice. She pointed out a boutique on the upper level. "I know we have a huge list of stuff to buy, but our first purchase has to be shoes. Shoes with heels worthy of the grown woman I am."

Bethany Anne recalled Alexis saying something similar at age five. "I remember that store. Let's see what we can do about finding heels that are worthy of your womanliness. It's about time you got the crippling foot pain you want so badly."

"*Mom*," Alexis moaned.

Bethany Anne chuckled at the look on Alexis' face, knowing her daughter still had something to learn about self-acceptance being the key to maturity. "Your nanos will take care of the pain. It's not walking in heels that's the problem, anyway. Sitting in heels? Now *that's* a different matter."

Alexis was only half-listening as they crossed to the store, her attention on the distractions around her.

The store owner jumped into action when she saw Bethany Anne, apologizing to the single customer as she ushered her out.

"Meredith," Bethany Anne called, drawing a curious look from Alexis.

"My Queen?" Meredith answered on the comm. "How may I be of assistance?"

"You can charge that woman's next purchase at this store to me," Bethany Anne told her. "With my apologies for disrupting her day."

"Of course, my Queen," Meredith replied.

Eric folded his arms. "Is that supposed to be a protest? Because I just know how much you *hate* spending money on shoes."

Bethany Anne lifted a finger. "This is how I make up for all this." She waved the finger to encompass the guards, the store owner turning the sign to Closed, and the gathering crowd of both people and camera drones outside. "It happens every time I step off my ship."

"I would close the store for any VIP," the owner assured Bethany Anne. "Your safety is paramount." Her tone suggested a previous incident.

Bethany Anne tried to recall if she'd been attacked in here during the spate of assassination attempts she'd inspired during her Empressing days, but nothing came to mind immediately.

"I saw the news about the attack on Onyx Station," the store owner clarified.

Bethany Anne smiled in understanding. "Thank you. I apologize for the security level a small minority of MRAs have caused to be necessary."

"MRAs?" the store owner inquired.

"Morally Reprehensible Assholes," Bethany Anne replied offhandedly, her attention on Alexis' path through the store. "Excuse me."

Alexis wandered around the displays, her gaze landing

on a pair of boots that she dismissed as childish before sweeping off to grab a pair of super-high-heeled stilettos in darkest red.

Bethany Anne didn't know whether to be proud or mad that Alexis had snagged the shoes she'd had her eye on since entering the store. Then she noticed her daughter's backward glance. She waved Eric away from his place at her shoulder. "Give us some space."

Alexis paid no attention to Bethany Anne while she unlaced her boots and put the heels on. "Don't you just love these? It's amazing that we're the same shoe size now."

Bethany Anne fixed Alexis with a knowing look. "You can put my shoe collection out of your mind. Want a hand with that buckle?"

"I'm good, thanks." Alexis got to her feet in a graceful movement and walked along the mirror wall, testing out how she felt wearing what were to her the most grown-up shoes in the store. "Oh."

"Just 'Oh?'" Bethany Anne asked, thinking back for a moment to a visit to Louis Vuitton in Paris one time.

Alexis studied her reflection in the mirror. The heels looked good with her cropped jeans. She looked good wearing them. She just didn't feel any more like an adult. "I don't know. I thought I'd feel different."

"You wore heels in the gameworld," Bethany Anne reminded her.

Alexis shrugged. "I think the game is missing something when it comes to the ability to maneuver on a platform." She sighed and took the shoes off. "It's not that. They don't feel like *me*."

"How about these?" Bethany Anne asked, her mouth

creeping up at the corner. She held out the sparkly black combat boots with the three-inch block heels she'd picked up while Alexis' attention was on putting the pumps on.

Alexis thrust the heels at her mom, grinning. "You saw those?"

"I think you saw them first." Bethany Anne chuckled as they made the exchange.

Alexis hugged Bethany Anne one-armed as they headed for the register. "This is the best. I'm glad you made us come on the tour."

The store owner clasped her hands, smiling at them as they put their purchases on the counter. "Do I enact the Empress Protocol?" she asked. "I know technically you're not the Empress anymore, but, well, I think you deserve the same respect."

Bethany Anne nodded, smiling warmly at the woman. "Thank you. That saves me having to ask."

The store owner nodded and checked her computer. "There are currently twenty-seven pairs in stock." She looked up and smiled again, a mischievous glint in her eye. "What about your daughter, my Queen? Does she require the same service?"

Alexis nudged Bethany Anne with her elbow. "Something tells me this isn't one of those things we talk to Dad about. What's it worth to you?"

Bethany Anne raised an eyebrow. "You're blackmailing your own mother?" She shook her head when Alexis shrugged disarmingly and turned back to the store owner. "When you live as long as we do, it makes sense to have duplicates. Five pairs, since her taste is likely to change."

Alexis snorted laughter. "'Duplicates?' That's *the* best explanation of your shoe hoard I've heard in all my life."

Bethany Anne accepted the bags from the store owner and held out Alexis' for her to take. "I bought one pair of shoes. So did you."

Alexis winked as she took the bag. "Sure, Mom."

Four hours later, Alexis dropped her bags by a bench between two tall, drooping potted ferns and took the weight off her feet with a sigh. "This is where I live now. You'll have to tell Gabriel to go on without me."

Bethany Anne laughed, lifting a hand to indicate the antigrav cart between her and the guys. "I told you to get a cart. How about some ice cream? We have a little time left."

"I'll get it," Eric offered.

"Show me the chocolate-cherry-marshmallow," Alexis replied, stretching her cramped fingers. She smiled when Bethany Anne sat down beside her. "This was fun, but I'm going to have a couple of roamers come pick us up. I underestimated the size of this station, and I had *no* idea about your ability to find something you want in every store you pass. You shop like Dad hunts."

Bethany Anne thought about that for a moment before asking, "Is it really all that different?"

CHAPTER SEVENTEEN

**Ranger Base One, Upper Level, Ops Center**

Sabine worked with the sounds of ongoing construction in the background. She, Mark, and Jacqueline had labored alongside the construction crews, CEREBRO, and the bots, staggering shifts to keep the build moving around the clock in order to transform the asteroid into a base.

The dwindling noise was music to her ears as the countdown to the base's switch-on ran down to the final minutes

Nickie and Ricole had finished laying the beacons between the four inhabited star systems that were scattered across this quadrant to connect them to CEREBRO and the Federation. Bethany Anne would complete the job when she got there, adding in the high-tech defenses for the occupied planets to support the CEREBRO-controlled satellites that they would be building over the next few weeks.

All that remained was the task of connecting the EI cores that comprised the base's part of CEREBRO to the ops center systems, and therefore to the Interdiction. Sabine darted between the consoles, flicking switches in the order Jacqueline was feeding her from the core room.

The ops center came to life as the EIs in the core room were connected and CEREBRO took control of the systems.

"How are we looking?" Sabine called aloud.

"It's good to be back together," CEREBRO replied. "However, we are not complete. There is an error preventing us from connecting to beacons C-zero-one through C-five-five."

"That's the, um, Cosnar System, yes?" Sabine got to her feet and pulled up the scant data they had on the uninhabited system. "What kind of error?"

"If we could diagnose it, we could have automated the fix," the EI group replied.

Sabine slapped the console. "Dammit! Get the coordinates to Nickie. She'll have to take a look, and maybe lay a few more beacons if the ones the drone dropped off were damaged."

"The solution might not be so simple," CEREBRO informed her. "The beacons are online. The anomaly appears to be caused by something bouncing the relay signal off-course."

Sabine considered the problem for a moment before remembering the upside of not being in command. "This is above my pay grade. Get Nickie on the comm."

"Should I include Ranger One in the link?" CEREBRO inquired. "The *Achronyx* just came into comm range."

Sabine sighed with relief. "Scratch that order. Akio is just the person I need. Guide them in, CEREBRO."

She left the ops center and made her way to the hangar at a run.

CEREBRO was admitting the *Achronyx* through the first forcefield just as Sabine arrived at the cavern they'd cut into the asteroid to use as a hangar. She took her time descending the stairs to the lower level while the ship waited for the second forcefield to drop.

Akio exited with a glance of admiration at the *Cambridge*, the *Defiant*, the *Shufur*, and the *Revolution* alongside an empty space for the bulkier Skaine battleship belonging to Nickie. "I wasn't expecting you to have gotten this far yet."

Sabine laughed. "This is just the entrance. Bethany Anne gave us a good start, but this base eventually has to be capable of protecting the whole quadrant. Let me show you around."

She took him to the upper level, where they'd fitted the prefabricated permacrete cabins Bethany Anne had provided snugly into the rock. "We had CEREBRO hollow out the complex since they can operate the continuous miners with the most precision, then it was just a case of getting the cabin skins in place and having the bots fill them with permacrete."

She extended her arms. "Thirty-six hours later, *et le voilà*, we had a base. Well, we had a start. We've been working around the clock to get it operational. I think it will look fine once it's been cleaned up."

"I have seen these temporary cabins that are still standing eighty or ninety years after being poured," Akio told Sabine as they reached the walkway at the top of the stairs where the first cabin had been laid lengthways into the rock and fitted with a double door. "Where do we go from here?"

"To the left is residential, training facilities to the right," she replied as they walked into a brightly-lit lobby. She pointed out three doors in the curved wall at the rear of the room. "The cabins reach into the rock a half-mile in each direction. The ops center is straight ahead and is not connected to the east or west wings. There's room for expansion if we grow as an organization, but we built the base to cover our immediate needs."

Akio took it all in as they walked through the residential area. "You didn't spare any details."

"We might have gotten a little bit spendy to get it all done so fast," Sabine admitted. "But it's worth that and all the favors Nickie pulled in to get us expedited shipping on materials to get the construction done."

"I wouldn't be so sure about that." Akio looked over his head a moment before they resumed. "Helping Nickie return a favor could easily end with you looking down a barrel. The work on the surface?"

"Mostly engine and sensor equipment," Sabine replied. "Some weaponry. Defenses. Since we're not running on an arti-sun yet, we can't power a full-size ESD, but we have a pair of the miniature version, along with the guns and shields."

"What's powering the station?" Akio asked, intrigued.

"We're fully Etheric-powered," Sabine informed him. "And we've used a minimum of metal in the build, so when the day comes where we figure out how to Gate into the Etheric without Bethany Anne at the helm, we'll be the ultimate in stealth."

Akio's eyebrows went up in anticipation. "That would be a thing to behold."

Sabine laughed. "Wouldn't it just." She gestured for Akio to follow her to the ops center. "Now for the not-so-good news. There's a gap in the signal relay in the Cosnar System, which means CEREBRO is unable to join the points on either side of the system."

"What are the options?" Akio asked, peering at the unfamiliar setup. "I need a tutorial on how to use all this."

"You're going to wish you had Eve here," Sabine sympathized, looking away when her attention was caught by an incoming call. "It's Nickie. I had CEREBRO give her the coordinates of the anomaly."

Akio nodded. "Onscreen, CEREBRO. What are you seeing, Ranger Two?"

"There's a huge-ass cloud covering a chunk of this system. It's making Meredith dance the funky chicken," Nickie replied. "You guys need to come out here. Bring a drone or something that won't go haywire so we can get a fucking clue what's blocking the signal."

"You're not giving us much to go on," Sabine told her. "What exactly is Meredith saying?"

Nickie shrugged. "She won't know what the problem is unless her probes can get inside the cloud, and she's refusing to take us in to investigate until you get here. I'd better not find out you had anything to do with this shift in attitude from her, Akio. You know me and Achronyx are like this, right?" She crossed her fingers to illustrate.

Akio gave Nickie a pointed look. "Perhaps Meredith deserves your thanks. We'll be there in…" He looked up the location in his HUD. "One hour."

Nickie had more to share when they arrived on the *Achronyx*. She sent Akio Meredith's initial conclusions based on the data from the probes. "Silicates. Fucking compound *crystals*."

Akio's brow furrowed as he examined the results of the spectral analysis. "It's not natural, unless nature suddenly started producing compound crystals like the Ookens."

"It's not just a cloud of crystal particles," Nickie continued. "It's a cloud of crystal particles that are somehow fixed to this place, unaffected by solar winds. That means somebody put it here to hide something."

"Can we go inside it?" Sabine asked.

"Only if you want to spend the next few weeks crawling around my ship to clean the particles out of my propulsion system," Achronyx huffed.

Nickie waved a hand. "There's more. Meredith tells me there might be a planetary body hidden inside the cloud. Her probes detected an increase in density toward the center."

"Can we get the probes in closer?" Akio asked.

"They're dead in the air," Nickie grumbled. "My guess is that someone put this cloud here to hide whatever is on that planet."

"It could well be," Akio concurred. "The only thing to do is clean it up."

Sabine nodded. "Of course, but how? We didn't bring the equipment to clean up a disaster zone."

"Leave it with me," Nickie told them. "I know a guy who owes me a favor. I'll have to go to Devon for a few days."

"Fine by me," Akio replied. "In the meantime, Sabine

and I will replace the beacons that have been damaged by the crystals and get the Interdiction up and running."

"I already started to take care of that." Sabine looked up from her wrist-holo with a smile as she received confirmation of her instructions. "The *Cambridge* will be here soon with the beacons."

"Go, Rangers!" Nickie arm-pumped. "I'll see you guys in a few days."

Sabine headed for the transport bay to prepare a Pod after the *Penitent Granddaughter* Gated out, leaving Akio alone on the bridge.

"What now?" Achronyx asked.

Akio settled into the captain's chair and turned it to the console. "I'm going to tell Bethany Anne what's going on out here, then we help with the beacons."

### QBBS *Meredith Reynolds*, QSD *Baba Yaga*, Bridge

Bethany Anne was in her ready room checking on the Federation council's efforts to get CEREBRO rolled out inside their respective borders when ADAM told her the *Sayomi* was coming in to dock at the station.

She reached out to Alexis. *Your father and brother are home.*

*Meet you at the* Gemini, Alexis replied. *I'll take us over to the station. Gabriel told me they have a bunch of civilians with them who need a place to stay, so Meredith is having them come into your private hangar.*

Bethany Anne had wondered why the only thing she got from her son over their mental link was a sense of carefully controlled anger. She reached out to Michael, hoping for some clarity on what had gone down.

*How bad was it?*

*It was bad enough,* Michael replied.

*It couldn't have been worse,* Gabriel stated flatly. *The colony was destroyed. Not even sixty survivors.*

*But there are survivors,* Bethany Anne consoled them, feeling none of the comfort she was offering. *It's not nothing.*

*A fraction of the people who lived there,* Gabriel retorted. *That's all that's left. It's not enough to prevent civilization from falling wherever the Ookens appear.*

Bethany Anne hated that he was hurting. *No, it's not,* she agreed. *And there's nothing worse than a win that feels like a loss. It's fucking frustrating to see people lose their homes, their families, and their lives when you did everything you could.*

*But why?* Gabriel asked. *What is Gödel gaining from these attacks? We live in an age of wonders, with technology sufficient to ensure that nobody wants for anything. How is it greed still exists to the extent where someone would destroy billions of lives for the sake of control?*

*A post-scarcity society doesn't equate to a post-asshole one,* Alexis told him. *We are doing everything we can, and it's working. The Interdiction is already saving lives—just check the newsfeeds.*

*Gödel wants to weaken us. Wear us down until we're so dog-tired and desensitized we roll over and give her what she wants,* Bethany Anne explained, knowing Gabriel needed to work through his frustration. *Control is never enough for dictators like her.*

*She doesn't understand the concepts of compassion or justice,* Michael added. *She can only see her twisted version of how the universe should look. Otherwise, she would have chosen to ascend when she had the chance. She wants complete supplication from us all, nothing less.*

Bethany Anne and Alexis arrived at the hangar a few minutes before the *Sayomi* made its final approach. They hung back, staying out of the way of the triage area set up by the medical crew Meredith had ordered to the hangar.

John was first down the ramp when the *Sayomi* came in to land, closely followed by Gabriel and Christina. Kai and Trey preceded Michael, who exited with the Loren leading the survivors.

Bethany Anne chuckled when Alexis darted ahead of her to engulf Gabriel in a hug. She walked to meet her husband, offering her condolences and assurances of safety to the traumatized and angry colonists.

"This is Talia," Michael told Bethany Anne while the Loren stared at her open-mouthed. "She is of a mind for vengeance."

"Understandable under the circumstances." Bethany Anne smiled at Talia. "There will be plenty of time for that. Take care of your people first."

Talia found herself unable to speak for a moment before she recalled the reason she was meeting Bethany Anne. Her wide-eyed wonder faded, the hollow stare returning as reality crashed in. "With respect, I'm no leader," she disputed. "All I ever wanted was my bar. I took pride in making it a home away from home for my regulars. The chief died right in front of me." Her tentacles drew in and wrapped themselves around her upper body, making her seem very human suddenly.

Bethany Anne wasn't sure how to embrace a Loren without getting tangled in the tentacles, but she gave it a go. Talia's tightly coiled tentacles were dry and smooth. She hugged Talia for a moment before releasing her to hold her at arm's length. "I swear you will get your desire."

"Just put me in a Pod-doc and send me to wherever the Ookens are," Talia replied. "I want revenge, but more than that, I have to do something to stop other people from going through the horror we experienced."

Bethany Anne shook her head. "You've been through a traumatic event. You need to heal here first." She tapped her temple with a finger. "I wouldn't send someone with a broken leg into battle, and neither will I send someone with a broken mind. See the therapist you will be offered. We will talk again before I leave for the Skaine Territories."

Talia nodded. "Thank you, my Queen."

One of the medical team ushered Talia away to be checked over, leaving Bethany Anne and Michael to be ambushed by the twins.

"Did you tell Dad about the plan?" Alexis asked.

Michael raised an eyebrow, wondering what the females in his family had in mind.

"Not yet," Bethany Anne replied with an anticipatory grin. "We need to have a little chat with Kai first."


## QBBS *Meredith Reynolds*

Christina noticed that Kai's thoughts trailed off somewhere between the ice cream parlor she and Anne used to go to after school and her old roller derby club, where she'd found out an old friend still worked. "So, I thought that next, we could walk on the surface of the rock without spacesuits."

"Hmmm, sure," Kai agreed. "Wait, what?"

Christina gave him a little shove, grunting with indignation. "I knew you weren't listening! You haven't heard a word I've said since we said goodbye to Debbie. What gives?"

Kai shrugged. "Just thinking about what Bethany Anne said."

Christina's curiosity had been piqued by Bethany Anne and Alexis pulling Kai to the side when they'd arrived at the *Meredith Reynolds,* but he'd kept the reason for the conversation to himself so far. "What *did* she say?"

Kai blushed, jamming his hands into his pockets. "Most of it wasn't repeatable. The rest, well, I can't tell you just yet." He glanced at her. "Do you trust me?"

Christina nodded and slipped her arm through Kai's. "With my life."

Kai smiled. "Good. If I survive what Bethany Anne has planned, you're going to be a happy woman, I promise." He stopped, looking around. "Wait, we've gone too far. Weren't we supposed to be at the park by now?"

"Mark Billingsly Memorial Park?" Christina asked, grinning when Kai nodded forlornly. "Don't sweat it. I know a shortcut if you don't mind a bit of a climb."

Kai discovered that "a bit of a climb" was actually a run and a jump over the back fence of a house bordering the park.

Christina and Kai laughed breathlessly as they ran from

the disgruntled resident yelling at them from the kitchen window.

"Well, that was an experience," Kai panted as they came to a stop at the entrance to the botanical gardens inside the park.

"It took me right back to being sixteen," Christina admitted. "But now you have to tell me why we're here."

Kai glanced at the map of the park on the wall by the entrance to get his bearings before giving her a mysterious smile. "You'll find out soon. Would you care to take a walk?"

Christina accepted Kai's outstretched hand. "Okay, but don't keep me waiting too long for an answer." She shrugged at the look of indignation that earned her. "I didn't say the rules were fair."

Kai laughed. "They don't always go in your favor, you know."

Christina declined to reply. She snuggled into Kai's shoulder as they strolled along a tree-lined path to the center of the park. Soft lights appeared in the distance, resolving into a gazebo as they walked closer.

"Sounds like someone's having a party," Christina commented, hearing music coming from behind the gauzy privacy curtains. She sniffed, the scent of cooking meat tickling her senses. "Smells like one, too."

Kai let go of Christina's hand and darted to the steps. "Welcome to liberty. No proposal." He waved his hands in protestation as she scanned his body for the telltale lines of a ring box. "I promise."

"What are you playing at?" Christina looked at him skeptically as she walked past him. She entered the gazebo and found a table set for six. Alexis and K'aia were preparing drinks at the wet bar, and Gabriel and Trey were manning the grill.

She allowed Kai to get her chair and shook out her napkin with a smile as Alexis filled their glasses. "What is all this in honor of?"

"We don't have much time between now and departure," Alexis replied. "We need to plan our next moves as a team, and I thought this was better than a stuffy meeting room."

Christina shrugged as she picked up her glass. "I mean, we *could* have gone dancing on our night off."

Alexis wiggled her eyebrows. "So sorry if you confused me for someone on her first shore leave. Dancing is on the agenda for after dinner."

Gabriel and Trey joined them, each carrying a tray piled with cooked meats to go with the cornbread and mashed potatoes already on the table. Organized chaos reigned for a few minutes while everyone filled their plate.

Alexis cleared her throat. "Mom has assigned Gabriel and me to the *Reynolds* until Grandpa gets back with our info on the Leath operation. She wants us to help Takal with his project."

"Which leaves us combing the newsfeeds and reports for possible cult activity," Christina stated. "Well, when we're not on duty. Michael wants us to assist with keeping the troops in line while they're aboard the *Baba Yaga*. Apparently, he's scaring them more than necessary when they arrive."

Gabriel nodded, pushing his potatoes around his plate with his fork. "The second we get another lead, we're out of here. I'd prefer we had time to prepare for the mission, but Reynolds needs all the help he can get."

Trey leaned in and patted Gabriel on the back. "Then help him. We can take care of prep." He sat back in his chair. "I've been thinking about that. What did Bethany Anne say about the idea of infiltrating the leadership when you brought it up?"

"She wasn't against it," Alexis replied. "But we're not allowed to make our move on the Leath company until her pet Leath has checked it out."

Gabriel spoke up. "Not really sure Mom would appreciate the term 'pet Leath.'"

"How about almost-but-not-quite-yet-terminated-with-vengeance-if-he-so-much-as-barks-out-of-turn-Leath?"

Gabriel blinked a few times. "Pet Leath works."

"Good."

"What happens if we get to the core of the cult and find a Kurtherian?" Kai pondered.

"It's not likely," Gabriel told him. "There just aren't that many left that they'd risk themselves."

Kai's face crumpled in confusion. "I don't get it. I thought they were all hiding somewhere?"

"Well, yeah, in the Etheric," Gabriel replied, thinking back to TOM's lessons on Kurtherian history. "Most of them chose Ascension after the split. Gödel is leading the dregs, the ones who didn't have the power to take the step to the next level of existence."

Kai let out a whistle. "They're still pretty powerful."

"Not especially," Alexis countered. "*Gödel* is powerful.

Without her, the rest of them couldn't amuse a bunch of five-year-olds at a birthday party."

K'aia snickered at the mental image. "So we won't find a Kurtherian. We will find someone with a connection to Gödel, but I suspect they won't know who it is pulling their strings."

Gabriel nodded. "I wouldn't be surprised."

Trey leaned back in his chair and laced his hands over his full stomach. "Either way, they're going down."

Christina raised her glass. "I'll drink to that, and to dancing if we're done here?"

Alexis grinned as she tapped her Coke bottle against Christina's glass. "Dancing it is."

# CHAPTER EIGHTEEN

**SD *Reynolds*, Takal's Lab (one week later)**

Reynolds and Izanami stared into each other's eyes, their faces set in determined lines.

Reynolds grinned as he slipped through Izanami's defenses and unleashed his revenge for the handlebar mustache and bright pink mohawk he was currently wearing. "Suits you."

Izanami laughed when her armor was replaced with a footsie-onesie complete with fox ears and a big, bushy tail. "Nice try, but you left yourself open."

Reynolds examined his hard light drive for changes to the code dictating his appearance and found nothing. "What did you—"

His hands flew to his mouth when his intended words came out in song.

Izanami pushed the pointy-eared hood back and flourished a hand at the ribbons holding her hair in bunches. "You don't mess with a woman's hair."

"You changed mine first!" Reynolds sang. He clapped

his hands over his mouth as Izanami, Alexis, and Gabriel laughed. "I hate you."

Takal clucked his tongue, looking up from the nest of wires he was soldering inside the chest cavity of the new Reynolds body. "If you two are going to waste bandwidth playing instead of working on solving the mystery of what happened to the captain's last body, the chances are both your bodies will have the same fault."

"Reynolds, you have to figure out what you did, or at least why you blocked the memory of it," Alexis urged, carefully holding up the brain she'd just removed from the defunct body. "There's got to be something you did that allowed you to draw freely on the Etheric."

"Yeah, but what?" Gabriel asked. "The body is saturated with Etheric energy. It's going to be a challenge to figure out the point of origin in all this melted wiring."

"The Queen assured me you two are the best people for the job," Takal replied without looking up. "It's fascinating to think that you accessed the Etheric realm entirely accidentally."

Reynolds fended off a sneak attack from Izanami, then gasped when his locked memories became visible to him. He grabbed them before they vanished again and examined what he'd lost. "It wasn't an accident. It was me. I remember now. I did it unconsciously."

Takal cursed, blowing rapidly on the finger he'd burned when Reynolds' booming baritone made him jump. "Can you two *please* cut it out, for the sake of my sanity!"

Chastened, Reynolds returned Izanami's armor and removed the bows from her hair. "Truce?"

Izanami snickered as he drew the note out. "Temporary

ceasefire. This approach is obviously working."

Reynolds shook his head. "No need. I have my memories back."

Alexis placed the brain on the second workbench for Gabriel's inspection. "What did you remember?" she asked eagerly, returning to her station to begin stripping the burned-out power cells from the spinal column.

"I drew energy directly from the Etheric through my power cells," Reynolds clarified, thankfully without slipping into rhyming verse. "Both times I've done it were when all was lost. On the first occasion, I was merged with my ship. This time I had no choice but to sacrifice my body or allow Jiya to die."

Takal breathed a sigh of relief. "It's not a complicated workaround. Now that I'm aware you can extract that amount of energy, it's just a question of building in the appropriate hardware to channel it safely through your body."

"That shouldn't be too difficult," Alexis told him. She dropped her tools and crossed to the clear boards where Takal did his planning. "If Reynolds doesn't mind a little extra width, that is."

"That depends on what you mean by extra width," Reynolds told her.

Izanami raised an eyebrow. "Now who's vain?"

Alexis wiped the corner of one board clean and sketched out one of the vertebrae-shaped cases that currently held Reynolds' power cells. "We'd have to make you taller to compensate, of course, but increasing the size of the casings means there's room to insulate the cells."

"Isolate them from the rest of the body, yes. It's a start."

Takal stared at nothing for a moment, his mind running the calculations for the adjustments. When his attention returned to the real world, it was with a look of disappointment at the progress he'd made so far on the new bodies. "We'll have to scrap these and begin again."

He removed his apron and used it to wipe his hands clean. "It is what it is. I'll go find Jiya and tell her to halt on the printing process until you two have updated the specs."

"We should call Mom first and update her," Alexis called after Takal as he hurried out of the lab.

"He gets very focused," Reynolds explained, seeing that the twins were confused by his engineer's behavior. "He'll be back once Jiya tells him I already informed her about the changes."

Gabriel shook his head fondly. "I like the old guy. He reminds me of Marcus."

Alexis snickered. "That's funny, he reminds me of Bobcat. Never mind. We need to let Mom know we had a breakthrough."

Bethany Anne answered Alexis' call almost immediately. She smiled at them from the wallscreen, her gaze hovering on Reynolds. "Do we have progress?"

"Some," Reynolds replied. "I have recovered my missing memories."

"That's great!" Bethany Anne told him. "What happened on the water planet?"

"He got all heroic and derestricted the draw on his power cells to keep the Pod moving," Izanami cut in before Reynolds could reply.

"It is my duty to protect my crew," Reynolds protested. "To protect all life."

"I didn't say I disagreed with your decision," Izanami assured him. "It was a noble thing to do."

Alexis laughed. "That's the nicest thing you've said about Reynolds since I got here."

"Yeah. Are you feeling okay?" Gabriel inquired with a smirk.

"I have work. You can return me to the *Baba Yaga*," Izanami narrowed her eyes at the twins before disappearing in a shower of light.

Reynolds got to his feet and bowed to Bethany Anne. "Izanami is correct. We have already lost too much time. I am able to resume my duties with your permission, my Queen."

Bethany Anne cleared her throat. "Can a repeat of Reynolds frying himself be avoided?"

Gabriel nodded. "We think so. We have to start again with revised plans for the bodies, testing as we go, but it's looking good."

"What about the damage?" Bethany Anne pressed her lips together. "It doesn't sit well with me to think this will happen again the next time Reynolds finds himself in a life-or-death situation."

"We're working around the issue," Gabriel assured her. "The damage wasn't caused by Etheric energy. It was the accompanying electromagnetic surge from the massive energy transfer Reynolds made that took out his vulnerable systems, leading to cascading failures across the rest of his functions."

Alexis grinned and pointed at Gabriel. "What he said. We're going to be focusing on helping Takal until Grandpa comes through with our intel."

Bethany Anne pursed her lips, then smiled at their identical hopeful expressions. "You will know as soon as I hear from him. Until then, you're needed where you are."

The twins exchanged a disappointed glance when Bethany Anne dropped the connection.

"There has to be something else we can do," Gabriel stated, returning to his workbench.

"Not until Grandpa gets back. We haven't got anything to go on, anyway." Alexis plunged her hands back into the defunct android body. "I can't believe you'd prefer chasing our asses around open space to this. Relax, okay?"

"I didn't say I preferred it," Gabriel told her. "But I can't relax, knowing there are people out there who intend Mom harm. We know that the Leath company has connections to the cult."

"Yes, but we don't know how many of the people involved with the company are innocent. We can't march in there throwing our weight around until we have what we need." She worked the power cell she was extracting loose from the silicone inside the casing with a soft *pop*. "Patience, brother mine. When we make our move on Shoken Carriers, we'll have everything we need to get in and out with a minimum of bloodshed."

Gabriel lined the power cells up on his bench when Alexis passed them over. "Usually, you're the impatient one."

Alexis snorted. "Don't mistake my restraint. I'm as mad as you that these people exist. But we do this right, or it only gets worse for Mom."

. . .

## Devon, First City, Federation Consulate

Harkkat hurried through the building with the holofiles clutched tightly in his arms. He burst into his office out of breath but too caught up in his discovery to realize he was pulling air in gasps.

"Ca... Ca..."

"Consul, do you require medical assistance?" CEREBRO inquired from the speaker.

"No, no." Harkkat's panting eased now he'd stopped putting so much stress on his body. He laid the holofile on his desk and stared at it a moment. "Call General Reynolds."

He sagged into the chair behind his desk and poured himself a drink while he waited for CEREBRO to connect him.

The General appeared on the wallscreen a few moments later, looking harried. "Harkkat. You'll have to make it quick. The council is about to enter session."

Harkkat nodded. "Is it looking to be a long session, General? I have the information you requested on Shoken Carriers, but it will take some time to talk you through my findings."

"Why?" Lance asked.

"I found evidence this goes way beyond the company," Harkkat replied. "A trail of financial transactions that led me all over the Federation before I got to the really interesting dirt."

General Reynolds held up a finger. "I'll call back in a few minutes."

The screen went blank. It was twenty minutes before Lance called back, which gave Harkkat time to attach the request complete form he'd been filling out when his asset reported in to the requisitions form Captain Nickie Grimes had dropped on him without warning two weeks ago, and file them both with CEREBRO.

This business ran on favors, and Nickie never failed to call hers in with the maximum amount of theater.

Still, he'd had worse from the Queen's head of intelligence, a laconic man with a network of assets that made Harkkat's careful collation over the last few decades look like amateur hour.

"This is the last time I'm going to backdate your paperwork without informing Tabitha," CEREBRO informed Harkkat.

Harkkat threw up his hands. "Inform her. It might save me from Nickie's demands. Why in seven hells does she need all this equipment?"

CEREBRO chuckled. "Whatever the reason, it will be a good one, Consul. The General is calling."

"Onscreen," Harkkat requested. "General. I was wondering if perhaps you'd been pulled into the session after all."

Lance shook his head, his expression that of a man with a bad taste in his mouth. "It was a near thing, and now I owe Zahlock a favor, so this had better be good."

Harkkat offered the General a pained expression. "Apologies for the inconvenience. Still, I believe you'll find what I have for you worth any time you owe that Shrillexian stick-in-the-ass."

"Zahlock is an honorable male and a diligent delegate," Lance stated. "However much of a stickler for the letter of the law he is, I'd trust him at my back in a fight, which is more than I can say for you."

Harkkat bowed his head. "I earned that."

"I don't buy your penitent act for a second," Lance told him. "My grandchildren are the operatives on this assignment. If they get hurt because you decided to hold back, I won't be held accountable for my actions. Do I make myself pointedly clear?"

Harkkat forced himself to remain calm. "General, I have looked into our enemy's eyes and saw only the desire to destroy. The Queen might stalk my nightmares, but the alternative to following her is certain death. What these cultists don't understand is that if the Ookens get into the Federation, it's over for everyone."

Lance's cold stare defrosted a touch. "This is your chance to prove that. What have you found?"

Harkat shared the contents of the holofile with a swipe. "On the surface, Shoken Carriers has little to no contact with the crews they contract. When I dug a little deeper, I was shunted to a public relations manager, and she was keen to make sure I understood that not only do they deny any involvement with the 'anti-empire movement—'"

"Anti-empire movement, my ass," Lance interjected. "She called it that?"

Harkkat nodded. "She also impressed that the freelance nature of the business made it impossible to keep track of everyone who worked with them."

"I take it that isn't the case," Lance stated.

Harkkat chuckled. "Of course not. I was able to get an asset inside company headquarters. They gained access to the records office and found a ledger containing records of unauthorized runs by three of the captains who contract with the company on a regular basis."

"How do you know they're not just smuggling?" Lance asked. "Backroom deals don't necessarily mean they have a cult connection."

"I'd like to have seen such a lax attitude toward my crimes," Harkkat retorted sourly. "I didn't stop with the company. I matched the payments with the consignments the three captains had on those dates."

"You know what I meant," Lance told him. "Focus. Where did the money trail lead?"

Harkkat let his grumbles go. "Every one of them delivered to the same planet, and the physical location of the planet had been wiped from the company records."

Lance straightened in his seat. "Interesting. "

"You don't say," Harkkat agreed. "But I'm not done yet. I have the location. The planet is one of the independents. They claim to be farmers and cattle ranchers, pacifists who shun off-world connections in favor of an 'authentic human experience.'"

Lance watched him a moment. "You don't believe that?"

"Not for a minute after the trouble my asset had getting the location," Harkkat replied. "I also have a hard time believing in the pacifism of people who surround their home with big guns."

"The best defense is a good offense." Lance shrugged. "Plenty of colonies who aren't smart enough to protect themselves fail. What about your asset?"

"I had her get a place on the crew of the *Pleiades* and wait for the next unauthorized run," Harkkat told him.

Lance's eyebrows shot up. "That's the ship my grandchildren traced back from the cult cell they brought in."

"That's why I chose it as the target and instructed my asset to report as soon as she was given an opportunity," Harkkat confirmed. He chose not to pass along the information that his asset had killed the *Pleiades'* navigator to gain said place. "The monastery is a cover. She discovered that the secret consignments are made up of weapons and recruits. They're building an army."

Lance rubbed his eyes and sighed. "It never rains, but it pours. Is your asset still embedded in the crew?"

Harkkat nodded. "She is. What are your instructions, General? One way or the other, this cult is going down. I don't believe they can hurt Bethany Anne personally, but they *can't* be allowed to stand in her way."

Lance folded his hands on the table. "That's not going to happen. You can pull your asset out. I'll take it from here."

"What are you going to do?" Harkkat asked, imagining Bethany Anne's method of dealing with the cult to be explosive, to say the least.

"That remains to be seen," Lance told him with a smile. "I'll be in touch if I need anything else."

Harkkat sniffed at the abrupt end to the call. "Is there any human who knows how to say goodbye with a modicum of manners?" he muttered, his mind caught up in picturing what kind of Hell Bethany Anne's children would rain down on the cult.

The General popped back on. "Goodbye, Harkkat."

Harkkat was pretty sure the deaf animals on the continent to the south heard him scream.

. . .

## Ranger Base One, Lower Level, Hangar

Nickie and Sabine met the incoming QBS ship with the antigrav pallets they'd brought to transfer the cleanup supplies into the base flocking at a safe distance from their ankles.

"TIM!" Sabine squealed when the ramp dropped and she caught sight of Tim emerging from the ship. She ran to him and jumped into his arms, kissing him soundly.

Tim ignored the catcalls from his crew and returned her embrace with enthusiasm. "That's a welcome worth traveling for," he murmured when she let go.

Sabine chucked him under the chin with her finger. "Silly man. I missed you."

"Maybe a few galaxies' distance isn't such a bad thing if you're going to miss me this much," Tim teased, slipping his hands around her waist.

"Will you two get a room?" Nickie complained, walking by. "Some of us just ate."

"Some of us are just jealous their man didn't come to visit," Sabine snarked.

Nickie took the cargo manifest from the housebot who trundled over with it held tightly in its pincer grip. "You lovebirds go tell Akio the equipment is here. I'll take care of getting it inventoried."

"How are you able to be here?" Sabine asked Tim as they made their way to the ops center.

"Peter is taking care of the station," he replied. "Tabitha got involved when Harkkat put in the request for the nanos. She insisted they had an escort, and here I am." He paused in his tracks. "Hey, Nickie. Tabitha said to call her before you get started."

Nickie waved to indicate she'd heard and tuned out the activity in the hangar to focus on making sure the unloading went smoothly.

Once the shipping containers were laid out in a line on the hangar floor, she put off the task of going through the contents of each to ensure Harkkat hadn't missed anything and had Meredith open a mental link to Tabitha.

*Hey, Trouble. Your shipment arrive okay?* Tabitha asked.

Nickie's mouth twitched at the nickname. *Yeah. Tim said you wanted me to call you about it?*

*Mmhmm,* Tabitha replied. *You nearly got Harkkat shot.*

*What?* Nickie scoffed. *How?*

*I did tell you he's on probation,* Tabitha reminded her. *When he started asking around about nanocytes, I thought he was being sneaky.*

*Oops?* Nickie sucked in a breath. *I figured he'd know what we needed and go straight to Eve. Tell me you didn't burst into his office and hold him at gunpoint until he explained.*

*I wish I had,* Tabitha admitted with regret. *He was in his quarters when I found him. In the bathroom.*

Nickie felt for the Leath. She'd found him to be hard-working and skilled at navigating the bureaucratic crap she was fond of avoiding in the weeks he'd been reporting to her in her capacity as Ranger Two. *You could give him a break. He's a pompous blowhard, but he's never going to cross the line again now that he's had the fear of Bethany Anne scared into him.*

*People don't change overnight,* Tabitha stated, her tone making it clear the subject was closed. *Besides, unless someone invents brain bleach so I can get the sight of him flailing*

251

*in the tub out of my mind, I want to have as little contact as possible with him.*

Nickie snickered. *Serves you right for busting his ass. Did you want to tell me something about the nanobots?*

*Just that I programmed them myself,* Tabitha told her. *Make sure you follow the instructions I sent exactly, okay?*

*We will,* Nickie assured her. *I'd better go.*

They said their goodbyes and Nickie got to work. Akio joined her while she was finishing up with the second container.

He wove his way through the bots transferring the crates from the first container to the *Penitent Granddaughter*, *Achronyx*, and *Cambridge*, coming to a stop by the container doors.

Akio cleared his throat when Nickie didn't register his presence.

Nickie turned with a momentary look of surprise and left her inventory to walk over to Akio. "Oh, hey. Sabine found you?"

Akio nodded. "CEREBRO could have done this."

Nickie leaned on the container door she'd left open for the bots and folded her arms. "I'm good. I needed some alone time."

Akio scrutinized her, seeing the telltale signs that she hadn't been sleeping. "You look tired. Perhaps you should sit this one out and get some rest."

Nickie snorted. "Yeah, right. I'll just clear the five hundred other things I have to do this week and take myself to a spa."

"You could take eight hours to sleep," Akio told her. "It would be a start."

"I'm *fine.*" She rolled her eyes at Akio's pointed look. "Fuck my life, if I'd known coming home meant I'd be getting bossed around by dusty old vampires for eternity, I'd have stayed in exile."

Akio nodded and changed the subject, wondering if he should be prepared for Nickie moving on again. He realized he would miss the chaos she brought to his life if she did. "Perhaps some quiet company would suit you?"

Nickie's pensive smile blossomed into a bright grin. "I'm good, thanks. You should be getting ready for the cleanup operation. I'll have us loaded in under an hour." Her smile faded a touch when Akio didn't respond. "You're not happy. Why are you not happy? This is an honest-to-God fucking mystery. Aren't you even curious as to what's so special about that planet that the Seven hid it?"

Akio raised an eyebrow. "I'm curious. I'm also aware that our presence might draw Kurtherian attention."

Nickie's eyes lit up. "Well, yeah! I'm counting on it." She sighed at the almost imperceptible expression Akio wore. "How do you do that? Look disappointed even though your face isn't doing anything? Okay, fine. We'll be boring and do everything to make sure the Kurtherians don't notice we're there stealing their planet out from under their noses."

Akio's mouth twitched. "Very good, Ranger Two."

Nickie scowled at him and slapped the datapad she'd been working from into his hands. "You're an ass, Akio. Aunt Tabitha sent instructions. Read through and meet me in the ops center. We have a cleanup to organize."

As she turned to go, the smallest part of his lip raised just a little.

CHAPTER NINETEEN

**QSD *Baba Yaga*, Bridge**

Bethany Anne waved the twins into her ready room. "Come in. Sit down." She raised an eyebrow at Alexis. "And quit trying to read my mind. You'll hear what I have to say in a minute."

Alexis grinned as she slid onto the chair next to Gabriel's. "Dad said you had to be ready for mental attacks. I'm just helping."

Gabriel snorted.

"Traitor," Alexis mumbled.

She nodded. "I heard back from your grandfather. Your lead was good."

Gabriel punched the air. "About damn time!" He leaned toward Bethany Anne. "When do we leave for Leath space?"

Alexis punched him in the arm. "Wait and hear what Mom has to tell us first." She turned her attention to Bethany Anne. "What did Grandpa get from Harkkat?"

"Enough for me to sanction another undercover assignment for your team," Bethany Anne replied. She looked at her children in turn. "Harkkat's investigation into the company uncovered a potential cult base in the Daolagen system."

"What the?" Alexis gasped. "That system is on the tour schedule. A direct confrontation with the cult would bring all the wrong attention."

"Exactly," Bethany Anne agreed. "Apparently, the cult is thinking along the same lines. Shoken has been covertly shipping weapons and people to a planet inside the system. I need you there yesterday to make certain I don't arrive in two months in the middle of a full-on rebellion."

"We're sticking to the plan to expose the leadership, right?" Alexis asked.

Bethany Anne nodded. "Yes, we stick with the plan unless it becomes obvious there's a better one. You had a good point about making martyrs. You will need Christina and Kai, so ask your father to release them from the upgrade team. I want you working to get to the core of the cult and doing what you can to prevent more riots from breaking out."

"They've been monitoring the military channels on their downtime," Gabriel informed her. "K'aia and Trey have been covering the newsfeeds. If there's anything going on in the Daolagen system, we'll know about it before we get there."

"Is there anything else we need to know going in?" Alexis asked.

Bethany Anne nodded. "Harkkat had an asset in place as the navigation officer of the *Pleiades*. If she is still under-cover you may need to provide an extraction."

"Good to know," Gabriel told her. "We have the crew of that ship marked for the penal colony, along with the six we brought in already."

Bethany Anne lifted her head when Michael walked in.

"I wouldn't bother to incarcerate them," he told the twins. "They don't deserve mercy."

"Who said it was mercy?" Alexis retorted. "They're going to spend the rest of their short and miserable lives scraping to survive while fending off people who have no issues with getting blood on their hands. That's Justice."

Michael placed a hand on each of their shoulders. "Do not make the mistake of allowing justice to become vengeance."

Gabriel clenched his hands. "After spending time with Paul Jacobsen's family, they can count themselves lucky I didn't cut the lying tongues out of their mouths before we dumped them there." He let out a long breath through his nose at the concerned expressions from his parents. "But then I wouldn't have a clear conscience, and there's no *way* some stain on existence is taking my peace of mind."

"*That's* the attitude you need," Alexis told him. "Work through your anger before you act, and you won't have regrets to lose sleep over."

Bethany Anne nodded, then got to her feet and walked around her desk to wrap Gabriel and Alexis in a tight embrace. "I'm so damned proud of you both." She waved Michael in. "Don't think you're getting away with standing there looking stoic while we're having an emotional moment. Get over here and be all emo with us in the circle."

Michael chuckled as the twins opened their arms to

admit him. "I was admiring our work as parents," he told Bethany Anne, touching his lips to Alexis' forehead, then Gabriel's. "Your mother is correct. You are a son and daughter to be proud of. Whatever we face, we face it together."

### Cosnar System, QBS *Achronyx*, Cargo Bay

Achronyx brought the ship into position a few thousand kilometers from the edge of the crystal cloud. "Ready on your orders," he informed Akio. "Although I don't recommend you remain in the bay."

"I had no such intention," Akio replied. He made one final check of the drones before returning to the bridge. "Are Sabine and Nickie in position?"

Achronyx checked the signals being relayed around the cloud by the extra beacons they'd laid to compensate for the interference it caused. "Comm is still patchy, but it appears so."

Akio nodded. "Keep the comm as stable as you can. Rangers, do you copy?"

"Ten-four, Ranger One," Sabine replied cheerfully.

"Did someone stay up late to get the Ranger manual implanted in their HUD?" Nickie teased, her reply breaking up as the signal fluctuated.

"We've lost our comm," Achronyx announced. "Wait, I have audio."

"*Some* of us want to be the best Ranger we can be," Sabine replied lightly, unaware Akio was cut off. "That means following protocol."

"I've been practicing for this role since I took my first

steps," Nickie shot back. "Follow my lead, not some stuffy manual Barnabas put together instead of getting a life."

"Really?" Sabine gasped. "You mean *I* could piss off Bethany Anne and end up living in a stolen ship, too? My goodness, it's very tempting."

"Get that comm back," Akio stated. "I don't know why I agreed to them being on the same team."

"I'm *trying*," Achronyx snapped. "What do you want me to do, pull it out of my non-existent ass? Oh, wait. Got it."

Akio covered his eyes with a hand. "Ladies," he intervened before he lost the ability to communicate again, either from lack of signal or a lack of the will to rein the young women in. "If you would care to focus and deploy your delivery drones, I'd like to be ready to return to base when Hirotoshi's team arrives to relieve us."

Nickie and Sabine dropped the comedy double-act and got to work while Akio monitored the progress of the first batch of delivery drones on the viewscreen. After reading Tabitha's instructions, he and Nickie had planned the operation to ensure they didn't end up in a sorcerer's apprentice situation.

The nanobots being carried by the drones were programmed first to consume the crystal particles in order to replicate, then to dispose of themselves in the nearest star after they'd fulfilled that function.

"Keep your scanners searching for Gate signatures," Akio told Sabine and Nickie as the first swarm descended on the cloud. He had faith in his deduction that anyone monitoring the system would see the slow and steady degradation of the cloud as a malfunction of whatever technology they were using to keep the crystal cloud in place, meaning they'd send someone to fix it before they called for the big guns.

None of them picked up anything out of the ordinary in the hours before Hirotoshi, Ryu, and Mark arrived. Neither did anyone else over the next few weeks as the cleanup progressed. Life for the Rangers fell into a blur of taking shifts at the cloud, fighting off the Ookens in the other three systems in the quadrant, and being on downtime at the base while waiting for one of the two to come up.

Akio's secret fear of being overrun by endlessly replicating nanobots also failed to make itself a reality, and slowly but surely, the cloud was eaten away.

He was awoken by Achronyx one morning after three days away fighting by a message from Nickie telling him to get out to the Cosnar system ASAP.

He had Achronyx open a video link to the *Penitent Granddaughter* as soon as he walked onto the bridge.

Nickie had to raise her voice to be heard over the commotion on her bridge. "Are you on your way?"

"What are you doing out there?" Akio asked, his mind still muzzy from sleep. "Our shift doesn't start until tomorrow."

"There's not going to *be* a shift tomorrow," Nicki told him, holding up a champagne flute with a grin. "You slept through all the fun."

Akio shook his head blankly. "We were attacked?"

Sabine appeared beside her and toasted Akio with her glass. "We broke through to the planet!"

Akio doubted their work would end with revealing the hidden world. Nevertheless, it was a reason to celebrate.

He flashed a smile. "That's great news. I'm on my way. I hope you have juice to go with that champagne, and food. I didn't get breakfast yet."

"No promises," Sabine told him with a tinkling laugh. "We've got a party going on over here."

"Grim is in his element," Nickie assured him. "There will be food if you're brave enough to eat it."

Akio settled for hot tea and a place in front of the viewscreen when he arrived at the *Penitent Granddaughter*, preferring the quiet of the bridge to the raucous celebration in the mess. He sipped his tea and enjoyed the beauty of the nanoswarm's swooping flight.

Sabine entered the bridge and closed the door. She walked over and nudged Akio with her shoulder. "It's beautiful, no? They remind me of starlings. When I was a girl, I used to watch the migration and wish I could fly free like the birds."

Akio pulled his gaze from the swirling dance the huge bands of nanobots were performing to avoid crossing streams and gave Sabine a fond smile. "You were always meant to fly. If we hadn't come along, you would have found a way to reach the sky regardless."

Sabine snickered delicately. "Maybe. If I had survived. But look at this, hmm? This is so much more than I could have ever dreamed of back in Paris."

"Survivors generally make it through whatever life throws at them," Akio told her gently. "Where is Demon? It is odd to see you without her these days."

Sabine waved a hand. "Oh, she's probably in the galley with Sam. Grim has taken to Sam and has been spoiling him accordingly."

"As long as someone appreciates his culinary efforts." Akio recalled the spread of exotic foods he'd passed up before getting his tea with a barely suppressed shudder.

"I think it has more to do with Sam forming a bond with the old Yollin," she admitted. "Demon had to see Alyssa go to another universe. She approves of her son settling so close to home."

Akio chuckled. "Such is life. We still have some way to go before we can explore the planet."

Sabine wrinkled her nose at the shroud of crystal still wreathing the planet. "We've been trying to get some preliminary scans of the surface, but we haven't even pierced the upper atmosphere yet. It is too polluted by crystal for us to see what's down there."

Akio nodded. "I didn't think it would be as simple as clearing a path. However, we have averted a potential disaster that would have made this quadrant and its surrounding areas impassable for any ship should the containment technology have failed."

"True," Sabine agreed. "Do you think the density of the cloud around the planet confirms that whatever is forcing the cloud to remain intact is down there?"

They turned when the bridge door opened to admit Nickie and the two chirruping housebots following her.

Nickie didn't notice Akio and Sabine watching with bemusement while she lectured the bots.

"Lefty, Bradley, it's a party," she told them firmly, ignoring their pleading beeps and the crying-face emojis they had on their interface screens. "People are going to make a mess. Stuff might get broken. If you can't handle letting everyone enjoy themselves, you're gonna have to stay on the bridge until the party's over."

The bots beeped some more.

"No, this isn't going to be like the time I let the pirates come aboard," she assured them. "Is that what you were worried about?" She smiled when the bots bleeped their affirmation and changed their emojis to shocked faces. "You won't have to clean up any blood or body parts, I promise."

The bots flashed hearts on their interfaces and wheeled off to their storage docks, bleeping happily. Nickie finally noticed Sabine and Akio. "Oh, hey. They're sensitive. Don't judge me, okay?"

Sabine smiled. "Don't worry, I won't tell anyone you have a heart."

Nickie grinned. "Promise? What are you two doing hiding up here, anyway? We're celebrating. Those scientist types know how to cut loose, would you believe it?"

"I found him in here brooding," Sabine told her with a wicked grin.

Akio sighed. "I was not brooding. I was thinking about the next step of the process. I will celebrate fully when our task is complete."

Nickie pointed a finger at him. "You ancient guys are *always* brooding. It's, like, your basic setting." She slapped him on the arm, spilling his tea. "Lighten *up*, old man. We got to the planet. Now all we have to do is get down there and figure out what the fuck the Kurtherians were hiding, and we're golden."

Akio repressed another, much longer sigh. "*Hai*. CEREBRO will attempt to get a probe through to the lower atmosphere with every one percent reduction in crystal particles around the planet."

A few days later, CEREBRO got a probe through the upper atmosphere and contacted Akio, who watched the data with Nickie and Sabine as it came in.

"There is no landmass at all?" Akio asked, surprised.

"It appears the requirements to hold the liquid mass in place have been met here," CEREBRO informed them. "It will take a larger sample of the vapor molecules trapped in the atmosphere to get a reliable reading of the chemical constituents. However, early samples indicate dihydrogen monoxide, with sodium, chloride, magnesium, sulfate, calcium, and potassium."

"Dihydrogen monoxide?" Sabine inquired.

"Also known as $H_2O$," Achronyx clarified. "That planetary composition is flagged for ADAM's notice. The order is to contact him immediately on finding an ocean world that has the potential to support the Collective."

"It's not exactly brimming with potential," Nickie retorted.

Akio raised a hand to still her dissent. "Not now, Ranger Two. Make the request, Achronyx."

Instead of ADAM's voice as they were expecting, they were met with the face of their Queen.

Bethany Anne greeted them. "ADAM tells me you have a potential site for the Collectives?"

Akio inclined his head. "Early indications make it appear so," he informed her. "However, there is a substantial amount of pollution both on and around the planet. Left by Kurtherians, we believe."

Bethany Anne's eyes unfocused for a moment. "ADAM agrees. What do you need?"

"More people," Sabine cut in, shoving past Akio. "Lots more people. We need environmental recovery specialists, marine biologists, and agriculturalists. We need technical and logistical support for the scientists and people to protect them while they're on the planet."

Nickie joined her. "Harkkat is the fixer I always wished for when I was on my sabbatical. I can arrange for most of that through him with your approval, Aunt Bethany Anne." She winked, having no shame at reminding Bethany Anne of their relationship in case her mouth got her another seven years out in the cold.

"I'm sure Tim could recommend potential Rangers," Sabine added.

Bethany Anne waved a hand, her attention drifting to something offscreen. "Fucking Skaines. I have to go. See that it happens. You can also expect a representative of the *Reynolds'* crew to be in touch. They own tech designed to make underwater living viable."

Nickie scowled when Bethany Anne dropped the link. "What was that about?"

"The Skaines, or the viability of underwater living?" Akio pondered.

"The representative from the *Reynolds* will clear up the mystery there," Sabine told them. "Tomorrow's holos will tell us what fate the Skaines brought upon themselves."

## Skaine Territories, Red Rock, Federal House of Arbitration

Lance tuned out the Skaine Governor's latest rant about the impending arrival of the *Baba Yaga*, wondering if it was too much of an imposition to ask Patricia to resume her duties when Kevin began at the Academy. He'd never had to deal with people bursting in on his breakfast when she was the ruler of his domain.

Governor Skuurla growled. "You are not even listening to me, General! This is a democracy, gods damn it! Your daughter cannot act as she pleases without our permission."

Lance's face reddened. However, he reined in the retort Skuurla deserved and fixed him with a smile. "It is thanks to my daughter that democracy exists and you are not fulfilling the role of footstool for a Kurtherian master, Governor. I strongly recommend you choose your next words carefully because I am not a man to take an insult to his legacy lightly."

Skuurla practically vibrated with frustration for a moment before spinning on his heel and exiting Lance's office in a cloud of muttered curses.

Lance maintained a diplomatic expression as the Skaine stormed out of his office. "A little warning would have been nice, Meredith," he murmured, returning his attention to his meal.

"My apologies, General," Meredith replied. "Bethany Anne—"

"Is here," Bethany Anne finished, appearing in the guest chair across from Lance's desk. "I figured showing myself while Skuurla was insisting I'm doing all of this to spy on the Federation would only have been amusing until he locked down his borders."

Lance inclined his head. "Nobody has refused to cooperate so far. Let's do what we can to keep it that way. How far out are the superdreadnoughts?"

"They'll be here in a few hours," she told him, snagging a strip of bacon from his plate. "You allocated a defensible space for the transporter equipment?"

Lance dismissed her theft with a raised eyebrow as he pointed to her left. "The food processing unit is right over there, as you already know."

Bethany Anne grinned. "Stolen bacon always tastes better. What's your suggestion for dealing with the Skaines' lack of trust? I assume you made sure the cult has no involvement in the unrest here?"

Lance sighed. "Short of going back in time and not scourging the hell out of their way of life, I don't think you can overcome the trust issues. However, there's nothing to suggest the Skaines are involved with the fanatics."

Bethany Anne's lip curled. "The alternative was genocide for their crimes as a species. You'd think they'd be grateful for a second chance and their Federation membership. Fuck it, I left Tabitha behind when what I needed her for was a reminder of what happens when they don't play nicely with the rest of the Federation."

"You left Tabitha behind to take care of Devon," Lance countered.

Bethany Anne lifted a shoulder. "So? The Skaines don't need to know that. As far as they're concerned, it was a magnanimous gesture on my part to soothe their precious feelings. I get they don't like that their predecessors were a bunch of murderous pirate slavers, but it doesn't change the fact that this galaxy is a better place since the Rangers thinned the herd."

Lance's heart dropped when her frown turned to a million-watt smile. "What?"

"Well..." Bethany Anne drew out her thought, "My Rangers may be too far away to be of any help right now, but I have six shiny new toys in my hold."

"What kind of toys?" Lance asked with curiosity.

"The replacements for the Shinigami fleet," Bethany Anne replied lightly, her nails beginning their customary *tat-tat-tat* on the arm of her chair.

Lance sighed. "Please tell me you're not still thinking of a short, sharp shock as a solution."

Bethany Anne lifted a shoulder. "My threat to drop Ookens on the members who don't cooperate isn't an idle one."

"I didn't think it was," Lance replied, his concern returning in a flash. "What does that have to do with the Bitches' new ships?"

"I have to be seen to be working within the law," Bethany Anne told him. "So I'm exercising restraint. But if you have no solution, then we go with mine. I won't allow any innocents to be killed, but neither will I allow any Federation state to stand in my way when the fate of everyone is at stake. I *can't.*"

Her face hardened as she came to a decision. "I'm going to put it to the people. The Skaines will either accept their inclusion in the Interdiction, or I will sanction their territory until they do, like I did the Moen. I can expect Federation support for my decision, right?"

Lance's face went through a series of expressions before

settling on acceptance. "There have been enough attacks to justify closing ranks, and I have the support. I can push it through."

Bethany Anne nodded. "Thanks, Dad."

Lance returned her smile, a twinkle in his eyes. "That's what family does. You've been running this show for the longest time now, and you've made me proud at every turn. I trust you'll get us through to the end of this war. I just hope it doesn't take everything you have to do it."

Bethany Anne sat back, sudden tears forming at the unexpected show of emotion from her father. It was one thing to have him defending her to Skuurla when he didn't know she was eavesdropping, but hearing it to her face took her right back to every time she'd worked for that praise growing up. "Shit, Dad. Are you feeling okay? I can get you a subscription to *Woman's Weekly* with that statement if you like." She rolled her eyes when Lance snorted. "I appreciate the sentiment. Really. Whatever that end may be, I'm glad to have had you there from the start. I couldn't have done this without you having my back. Any of it. You gave me the start I needed to become a leader and a fighter. I'll never stop being grateful for that."

Lance leaned across his desk and took his daughter's hand, muttering to himself internally about the rods parents make for their own backs. "Listen to me, Bethany Anne. That was all you. All I ever did was guide you. Before she passed, your mother told me to lift you up, even if what you wanted to touch was the moon. We knew you would be a fighter when you took your first breath and used it to scream at the world."

He thought for a second. "You probably cursed your

first word then, but it was in a foreign tongue."

Bethany Anne extricated her hand and wiped her eyes, grinning at the image that popped into her head. "Yeah, and without you to guide me, I could have just as easily ended up heading up a crime syndicate, and we'd all have been long dead."

Lance laughed, his body shaking with the force. "*You?* I can't see it. Unless maybe the world ran out of Coke. Then we'd all be in trouble. On the subject of hellions," he segued, "are my grandchildren still aboard the *Baba Yaga*, or did they shoot off the moment you gave them Harkkat's intel?"

"What do you think?" Bethany Anne asked, her mouth curling in amusement. "They couldn't get their team's asses on that little blue ship of theirs fast enough. The cultists don't stand a chance against the six of them."

Lance lifted an inquiring eyebrow. "Six? Christina and Kai are still with them?" His other eyebrow joined the first as he sucked in a breath. "I'd feel sorry for the cultists if I didn't keep hearing about FDG units being diverted from their duties to take care of the unrest those fuckers keep stirring up."

He waved away Bethany Anne's reaction to his poor mood. "Never mind. We have enough unrest to deal with right here and now. Can you do something to disguise yourself? We need to get to the delegates before the *Baba Yaga* arrives."

Bethany Anne reached for the hood that grew out of her coat's collar at her mental command and pulled it up to cover her hair, dropping her face into shadow. "Let's go. The Skaine people have a choice to make."

# CHAPTER TWENTY

**Beyond Federation Borders, Daolagen System**

The recruits gathered in the ruins of the temple, a sprawling complex of half-crumbled buildings and underground passages that was all that remained of the planet's ancient civilization.

The atmosphere amongst the humans was all but palpable with the excitement of being summoned to hear their leader speak.

Alaric had been there for two weeks, ever since he'd heard a recording of Isaiah's call to arms and his eyes had been opened to the threat posed by a return to Empire. His grandfather had given him the beating of his life when he spoke out against Bethany Anne at the dinner table, so Alaric had stolen his old service weapon and run away in the dead of night. "Do you think Isaiah is going to speak about the attack last night?" he asked Tessa.

She narrowed her eyes, the wrinkle of uncertainty that appeared on her nose shifting the constellation of her freckles. "I don't know."

"You and Jake have been here way longer than me," Alaric pressed. "You know how things go around here."

Tessa lifted a shoulder, ignoring the puppy-eyed stare from the boy. If he had any sense, he'd go home to the family who undoubtedly missed him. "Only by a few weeks. I don't know what to tell you when I've been in the workshop all week the same as everyone else. Sarah has us working double shifts to get the weapons stockpile built up. Why is anyone's guess."

Alaric's eyes widened. "You're kidding, right? We're being invaded by invitation; the government is going to roll out the welcome mat when Bethany Anne arrives in that planet-killer superdreadnought of hers. Maybe the invasion has already begun," he continued, his attention as deep as the layer of dust covering everything in the temple. "Didn't you hear there was a Yollin guarding last night's target?"

He sucked in a breath when she shook her head in the negative. "Heck's team barely made it back. He said the Yollin was a four-legger, and it came out of nowhere and took them out before they could get anywhere near the convoy."

Tessa rolled her eyes. "My brother was on that raid, and he didn't say anything to me about a Yollin. Really, Alaric. You should know better than to believe gossip."

"Ask him," Alaric insisted, waving to catch Jake's attention. "He's over there. Hey, Jake! You guys ran into an alien last night, right?"

"It's true." Jake joined them. "She took us out like it was nothing. All I saw was a cloud of gas. Next thing I know, I woke up with Heck dragging me and Frankie into the omni."

Alaric broke into a grin. "Shit, Jake! Shouldn't you be in the infirmary?"

Jake shook his head. "I got lucky, I guess."

Tessa sniffed. "I don't believe in Yollins," she told Alaric with distaste.

Alaric gave her a look of pity. "You should believe in Yollins, Tessa. It's going to be hard to fight something you don't think exists. Am I right, Jake?"

"They're real enough," Jake agreed, giving his sister a sideways look. "You'll have to excuse my sister. She's led a sheltered life until recently. "

Alaric shrugged. "Didn't we all until Bethany Anne announced her return? If we're not prepared to fight, we'll be bowing and scraping to her while she takes the young and the strong and forces them to conquer new worlds in her name."

"Who's to say any of those aliens exist?" Tessa cut in, diverting Alaric from his almost verbatim repetition of Isaiah's recruitment speech. "We know the Kurtherians are a myth, so why not all the other aliens? *I've* never seen one. That's why we welcomed Isaiah."

Alaric nodded. "We all did. Hey, I see Jenner. She might know what's going on." He darted into the crowd, calling a promise to catch up with them later.

The twins shared a glance.

*Go easy,* Gabriel cautioned. *You were laying it on so thick, I thought you were going to blow our cover.*

*He was about to start asking difficult questions,* Alexis countered. *This whole place runs on propaganda and rumor. I heard that little theory from the girls on the assembly line last shift. It's only going to work in our favor to spread disinformation. Besides, you didn't see how red your face got when he started talking about Mom.*

Gabriel scanned the crowd, following Alaric's path to the other six recruits they shared a dorm with. *The rhetoric is getting to me, I won't lie. I'm finding it harder to hold onto any empathy for these people the longer we're here.*

*I can't imagine you'll have to hold on for much longer,* Alexis told him. *Remember, we're doing this for everyone outside of here—the people who didn't get involved with Isaiah. It sounds like K'aia had her hands full last night. It's not like Isaiah to send his personal guards out on the raids. What were they after?*

*Isaiah's pushing everyone to prepare for Mom arriving,* Gabriel replied. *K'aia was able to tell me it was a military transport, but she didn't know what they were carrying. I couldn't get close enough to find out without Heck seeing me. I got close when someone set off the smoke bomb, but Heck managed to find me. I had to pretend I'd been knocked out.*

*It kept your cover intact,* Alexis replied. *I'm not concerned. I've slipped a backdoor into every chip in every weapon that's been made since I started in the workshop. The cult's paranoia about digital entities might be prudent, but it also makes sabotage a hell of a lot easier.*

Gabriel's brow furrowed in concern. *And you were concerned about me risking my cover? What if you got caught?*

*As if,* Alexis retorted, her laughter filling their shared mindspace. *I made sure it looked like junk code. They think I'm a good little acolyte, don't worry. Did you find out anything new by sucking up to Clay?*

*No,* Gabriel admitted, pushing down the anger that rose

in his gut along with his inbuilt intolerance for the guard's bullying ways. *He's pumped about something, though. He's starting to trust me but he's saying nothing, so we have to assume Isaiah has told him to stay quiet until tonight.*

Alexis swallowed the bitter taste of her disappointment. *Dammit, I'd hoped he'd start bragging and let something slip.*

Gabriel had hoped for the same, but Isaiah's henchman had been uncharacteristically tight-lipped during the training session. *Don't give up hope just yet. We've gotten this close, and Isaiah doesn't know how much easier he just made our assignment by coming out of hiding to make this announcement.*

*It's what he's planning to announce that's concerning me,* Alexis told him. *The cult has gained too large a foothold here. But this is an opportunity to get information to expose the cult as fake. As soon as he shows his face, I'll read his mind, and we can get the hell out of here, inform the president of Isaiah's plans, and report to Mom.*

They exchanged glances when they sensed Isaiah's group approaching the balcony above them to the rear of the temple.

*Showtime, I guess,* Gabriel commented. *Let's get closer. I want to see this guy in the flesh.*

*Good idea,* Alexis agreed. *I want to get a good read on what he's not telling us.*

They worked their way through the thrumming crowd, diverting around to the left to avoid attracting their roommates' attention. The recruits began to chant Isaiah's name when Clay, Heck, and the rest of his guards fanned out of the entrance at the back of the balcony and took up their positions.

Isaiah came next, holding up his hands in supplication

to the applause that greeted his appearance. To all appearances, he was just an average human being of mid-height whose unassuming looks made him easily lost in a crowd. His armor was plain and serviceable, worn from years of use.

Alexis had pegged his profile at first sight. The tarnished knight, a man of the people—on the surface, that was.

She had no doubt that beneath the humble exterior lay a shrewd mind capable of engendering the trust of people whose youth and ignorance made them vulnerable to his line of bistok shit.

The increase in activity outside the temple complex over the last two weeks was a clear indication Isaiah had some larger plan in play than the supply raids the rest of the team had been working to disrupt.

She probed the edges of Isaiah's mind, checking for safeguards. That would be strike one with everyone here. The uniting belief consensus the recruits shared was that enhanced humans were no longer human and had no right to govern the lives of those with natural lifespans.

Strike two would be finding that Isaiah was not the staunch Federation supporter he claimed to be.

He disappointed her on the first count. His mind was open and unguarded. Alexis skimmed Isaiah's surface thoughts and was initially disappointed again. His conviction in his belief was deep-rooted and unsettling in its strength.

*Show me a name,* Alexis commanded softly. *Or a face.*

The only face she saw was her mother's, twisted by Isaiah's imagining of her as a monster. She shrugged off the feeling of needing to shower in mental bleach and delved deeper into his psyche, searching for the origin of his obsession.

Isaiah shook his head and waved, brushing off the cheering of the recruits. "I return with the sad news that all our fears have come to pass. Daolagen is no longer the stronghold of humanity it has been for over a century. President LaCroix has allowed nonhumans into the seat of government in a desperate bid to retain control over the planet."

The recruits listened in stunned silence as he continued.

"They're there right now, plotting to hand this planet to Bethany Anne while the people applaud the so-called *protections* she is offering against her fabricated enemy. It is time to act before Daolagen is locked inside her prison and its people forced to participate in the delusion. Make no mistake, ensuring control will be a dark task, and many people will die in the process. But we are the few who have been both burdened and privileged to see the truth. We have a duty to all humanity to stand against the silent dissolution of our freedoms."

Alexis tuned out the speech when she came across something she'd missed on her first pass over Isaiah's mind. *Interesting.*

*What is it?* Gabriel asked.

*Give me a second,* Alexis replied distractedly, her focus on examining the slight disorder in one of Isaiah's memory sequences. *This is delicate. Someone has...not* erased *the memory of themselves. Just, well, blurred it somehow.*

She searched around the memory, looking for an associated one she could use to leapfrog past the subtle block. Alexis had no idea how this deep search would affect Isaiah. Nevertheless, she stimulated his memory centers until she found what she was looking for and withdrew the information hidden behind the block, a small smile on her face.

*Did you get what you were looking for?* Gabriel asked.

Alexis couldn't help picking up the thoughts being broadcast by the people around her. She snapped a mental block in place and turned her sunny smile on Gabriel. *And then some. Come on, we can get out of here.*

*Wait,* Gabriel told her. *It's going to look suspicious if we leave while he's still talking. We can slip away unnoticed after we're dismissed, or after lights out tonight.*

*There's not going to be lights out tonight,* Alexis informed him. *Isaiah is planning a coup. He means to move on the government as soon as this meeting is done. He has sleeper agents in key positions waiting for his orders. Everyone is going to be sent out to fight as soon as the satellite network goes down.*

Gabriel understood that Alexis had already come at the situation from all angles. He tucked a hand inside his cloak and retrieved a small device from the folds, offering it to his sister. *Perception filter. Are you happy you got everything?*

Alexis took the device and activated it, shielding them from view. *I'll tell you on the way out of here. I've called Gemini to send a Pod to meet us. We can't afford to waste a moment if we're going to stop the coup from succeeding.*

They entered the Etheric without being seen and put some distance between them and the ruins before emerging into the rainforest.

*Why are you two offline?* K'aia demanded when their

Etheric comm came back online

*Hold the inquisition, we've got a situation,* Gabriel interrupted. *Is everyone on the channel?*

Trey, Christina, and Kai confirmed they were there, and the twins filled them in on the impending attacks on the colony's infrastructure.

*We'll inform the president,* Christina told them. *Just get here as fast as you can.*

*We have a Pod incoming,* Gabriel replied. *Have someone meet us on the roof of the Senate.*

Alexis pointed at movement in the canopy above. *Our ride is here.*

She exited the Pod ahead of Gabriel when they touched down on the landing pad on the Senate roof, and they ran for the roof access, where Trey was waiting for them.

"Did you get to the president in time?" Alexis called.

Trey ushered them into the building. "We got there in time to stop the assassination attempt, but there was nothing we could do about the digital attack. Isaiah's people are better than anyone the government has."

"Well, shit," Gabriel offered once Trey had finished telling him about the headless chicken approach LaCroix's administration was taking to the shutdown of the system's Gate and the loss of the planetary defense system—which, while nothing compared to the Interdiction, still packed a punch.

"It's getting heated in there," Trey informed them as they double-timed it down the stairs. "They lost the satellite network a few minutes ago, and they've been unable to get it back."

"We'll just have to see about *that*," Alexis stated. She

cracked her knuckles and opened her HUD to examine the cultists' efforts to lock the government out of their own servers. "This might take a minute."

"The president is waiting to speak to you both," Trey told her as they left the staircase and entered a marble-floored lobby dotted with artfully-arranged benches and small, exotic trees in pots. "She's pretty agitated."

Alexis rolled her eyes. "I see why Mom and Dad get bored with politicians. Tell her that we have a coup to prevent. Talking can wait until I've taken down those firewalls."

"That will have to wait until you've been thoroughly debriefed," President LaCroix announced, sweeping out of the open doors at the far end of the lobby.

"Are you just plain stupid?" Alexis demanded, shaking off Gabriel's hand on her arm. "Isaiah has over thirty thousand followers on their way to remove you and the rest of your administration by force, and you want to waste time talking?"

President LaCroix's reply was lost in the outcry from the room she'd just left when the lights went out. She pointed at the twins. "Stay there."

Alexis flung up her hands as the president hurried back into the room and the doors banged shut. "Enough of this. I'm calling Mom."

**Open Space, QSD _Baba Yaga_, Deck Six Transporter Room**

Izanami paced, ignoring the surreptitious stares from the Skaine soldiers leaving after their upgrades. They weren't of interest to her, but the group about to arrive on Transporter Pad Three was.

She crossed to the pad, her contrail of shimmering red-gold confusing the hell out of the scattering soldiers, who only saw Baba Yaga bearing down on them until the people working on Michael's team told them otherwise. The air shimmered over the transporter pad before resolving into the shapes of Takal, Reynolds, and a large crate.

"Is that my body?" she asked before the Larian inventor could open his mouth to greet her.

Reynolds scoffed. "Patience, young one."

Izanami raised an eyebrow. "I'm composed of Bethany Anne, Eve, and Shinigami. Patience is *not* my strong suit."

Takal chuckled, recognizing anticipation when he saw it. "It is your body. As you can see, Captain Reynolds already has his."

"Open it!" Izanami demanded, not waiting before she poured herself into the semi-organic shell. Her systems came online, and she was greeted by a flood of sensory data. Darkness gave way to bright light and a close-up of Reynolds' smiling face when he opened the crate.

"Welcome to life as an android," Reynolds told her with feeling. "Come on out of there and let's see you without the sparkles."

Izanami stepped out on legs that weren't yet a hundred percent certain of the left foot-right foot combination needed for walking. She had gained full control by her third step.

"I am bored with sparkles," Izanami told Reynolds with a smile. She walked the former cargo bay with her hands held loosely at the small of her back.

Takal laughed. "I think you've got the hang of the motor functions. Is your sensory suite ready to be brought online?"

Izanami nodded. "It is."

"How is it?" Takal asked, scrutinizing her movements with a pleased smile.

"It is perfect. Thank you." Izanami pulled the old male into a brief embrace. "You are a genius, Takal."

Takal wiped a bit of dust from his eye. "I don't know about that. I have to get back to my lab and get ready to resume my other duties, but come and see me if you have any trouble. That order includes you, Captain."

Reynolds scoffed. "Not necessary. I'm in perfect condition, and closer to human than I've ever been. You've outdone yourself with these bodies."

"I had some help from Alexis when it came to redesigning the brain," Takal told him. "Thanks to her, I was able to make a number of small improvements to the existing technology."

Izanami somehow missed Takal's departure, despite being the one operating the transporters. She was awash in sensations, each one separate and distinctly different from the masses of data being processed by the part of her that was the ship.

She reached for Reynolds when her sensory suite came online as they were suddenly enclosed by a group of passing soldiers. Izanami was overwhelmed by the flood of data her body was assimilating at once. She felt the friction of the armor she wore against her skin, smelled the sweat of the Skaine soldiers, and tasted the adrenaline they were emitting into the air.

She discovered that resolving the issue was more complicated than dialing out her input sensors when her attempt to do so was met with a warning from her systems. "I need assistance in coming to terms with this body's organic processes," she admitted. "Will you stay and discuss your experiences with living in an android body?"

Reynolds smiled to soothe the uncertainty in her tone. "Of course, dear lady. The first piece of advice I have to impart is that one does not come to terms with the constant inputs. We file them and only pay attention to what is relevant to the moment. We have an advantage over most full organics because we can retrieve a memory file once it has been stored. They are gifts to be savored and re-examined at our leisure."

"How does that help me now?" Izanami asked. "The aural interface alone is receiving thousands of inputs per second. I am experiencing something I can only describe as pain."

Reynolds considered the problem, which was not one he'd had to deal with since ADAM had created his baseline EQ to be compatible with making logical decisions under extreme pressure. There was no greater pressure than organic lives being on the line, something his young friend would have to face sooner rather than later. He copied a few lines from his core code and made a couple of tweaks. "Redirecting the sensory data through a triage subroutine might help in the meantime. Here, I have something that will assist while you acclimatize."

"Thank you," Izanami told him with sincerity.

She redirected the overflow of sensory inputs to a temporary location in her memory bank, where she placed a subroutine that would learn from the gift Reynolds had provided.

It learned how to index the inputs and arranged them into something manageable, meaning she was able to focus on her surroundings and examine what she felt. "How did I not know?" she marveled in a voice so soft that Reynolds almost missed it, even with his enhanced hearing capability.

"It is a wonder to feel, is it not?" Reynolds asked in response. "You will get used to the way our bodies prevent us from damaging them beyond repair."

Izanami smiled and slipped her arm through his, pulling him along with her as she walked. The impact of her armored boots on the metal floor sent minute vibrations up her spine, distracting her from the novel experience of hearing speech transmitted directly into her brain without the need to check each individual phoneme against her speech and language database to gain context. "I feel whole, and yet I am still the *Baba Yaga*. I understand now why you would never be parted from your ship despite your need to exist independently from it. I know what it is to be *alive*. I did not before this body."

Reynolds recalled his first experiences of organic senses, savoring the shine of Izanami's eyes as she processed each new scent, sound, and tactile sensation.

"Yes," he agreed, and that was enough.

Izanami stopped walking and tilted her head when one of her aural inputs suddenly spiked.

"What is it?" Reynolds inquired.

"I'm not certain," Izanami replied. Her mouth made a little O when Bethany Anne stepped out of the Etheric.

"Why am I being redirected to a copy of Reynolds when I try to reach you?" she demanded, glaring at the two AIs. She waved off their explanations impatiently. "We have an issue. Alexis and Gabriel—"

"Are they in danger?" Izanami interrupted.

"Maybe," Bethany Anne told her. "So stop fucking interrupting me and get this ship on course for the planet Daolagen."

Reynolds tapped his communicator. "Takal, beam me back. We have a situation." He inclined his head as his body was swallowed by blue light. "We will retrieve them. Do not fear, my Queen."

With that he was gone, leaving Bethany Anne and Izanami alone in the corridor.

"Battle stations," Bethany Anne ordered.

"Done," Izanami informed Bethany Anne as lights flashed and alarms sounded. "We are en route to Daolagen."

They entered the elevator, leaving behind Izanami's calm voice instructing all hands over the ship's speakers as the doors closed.

"Good," Bethany Anne told her through clenched teeth. "Michael would kill them all and leave them to God's judgment. Alexis thinks she has hit upon the only way to be rid of the cult forever, and I was inclined to agree—right up to the point where the cult crossed the line."

Izanami tilted her head. "You didn't want it to come to this."

Bethany Anne lifted her chin, the glow from her eyes painting the elevator red. "It's a lesson I almost never enjoy giving."

CHAPTER TWENTY-ONE

**Open Space, QSD *Baba Yaga***

"Why have we suddenly changed course?" Michael inquired when Bethany Anne and Izanami walked in through the lower-level access. Seeing the way Bethany Anne held herself clenched made his heart drop into his stomach. "The twins?"

"Are fine for the moment," Bethany Anne assured him. "Despite the incompetent gaggle of fuckwits running Daolagen, giving the cult a place to dig in and metastasize."

"We are on our way to intercede, then," Michael inferred. "They'd better hope to God they haven't harmed the children in any way. What kind of welcome can we expect on arrival?"

"Likely a hostile one," Bethany Anne told him. She waved a hand to cast the information she had in her HUD to the central console, and a holo-representation of the Daolagen system manifested. "Our communications with the president's people prior to this included details of planetary security. They've lost the satellites, which means the cult is in control of the defense grid."

Izanami scoffed. "I've been over the specifications. Those lasers don't have the power to so much as scratch my paint, and the *Reynolds* is just as well protected."

Bethany Anne waved a hand, dismissing the issue. "My concern is for the people who could be killed by falling debris when I have the Bitches take it out, and then there's the number of people converging on the Senate."

"I'm going to get ready to go down to the planet," Michael told her.

Bethany Anne held up a finger to ask him to wait while opening a link to Gabrielle.

*What's with the klaxons?* Gabrielle asked.

Bethany Anne caught her up. ***Suit up and prepare to ship out, all of you. Michael will be heading straight down to the planet to extract the children, so make sure those satellites are dust.***

She lifted a shoulder at Michael's inquiring expression. "There's an extra scout fighter in the hold since John straight-up refused to switch ships, or you can go direct and get a ride back on the *Gemini*."

"I'll go direct," Michael decided. "We don't know how long it will take to disable the defenses."

"It won't take long," Bethany Anne assured him. "There are tens of thousands of cultists headed for the colony's capital. I need you and the children to limit the damage they cause."

Michael nodded. "That was my plan."

"We have another problem," Izanami cut in as they swept into the Daolagen system. "A possible stranded ship.

The Gate logs show an SOS being received from the other side eleven minutes before it was shut down."

Bethany Anne raised an eyebrow. "Tell me the ship in distress made it through."

"There is no record of it crossing the Gate," Izanami confirmed.

"Well, shit." Bethany Anne ran through the options, knowing that getting the Gate back up and running required more than just punching a few buttons. For the second time recently, she wished she had Tabitha with her and realized she would have to either figure out her ability or leave Devon in someone else's hands when they moved on Gödel. "Do you have the coordinates of where they were transmitting from?"

"The system does not have that information, and the Gate has been severed from the network," Izanami grumbled. "Based on older logs, I can narrow it down to one hundred and thirty-nine possible Gate locations, but unless I can access the Gate, there is no way to know."

"We haven't got time to check them all." Bethany Anne pulled Michael into her arms and kissed him soundly. "Go get our children. I'll join you as soon as I've opened the Gate."

She stepped into the Etheric without waiting for a reply and headed toward the point in space where the Gate lay. Her coat shifted form as she ran, the lapels moving to cover her chest while the flowing tail sealed itself to her skinsuit. She pulled her hood up and instructed the nanofabric to complete the seal, and the Bl'kheth DNA-infused nanocytes built a translucent panel that filled the space around her face.

Bethany Anne closed her eyes briefly in thanks to Sean's group for the gift and opened the Etheric on the Gate. As she had suspected, it was inert. Even the maintenance bots were frozen, floating around the massive structure aimlessly with no power to the Gate to provide gravity

She kicked the base of the Gate in frustration, leaving a dent in the reinforced alloy. "Fucksticks. It's deader than disco."

**What do you have against disco?** TOM commented in a mock-hurt tone. **At least it hasn't been damaged. Well, beyond what you just did to it.**

>>**But it *has* been severed from the remote command station,**<< ADAM countered before TOM dug himself deeper. >>**Which is behind that net.**<<

"They're controlling it from a ground station?" Bethany Anne glanced at the laser fire coming from the planet and pressed her lips together. "That ship might still be okay, but Gabrielle and the guys are taking too long to bitch-slap the net out of existence."

**Those lasers don't have a snowball's chance in Hell of hitting what they can't see,** TOM countered. **What are you thinking we can do before they break it?**

Bethany Anne extended her window onto reality to a small, jutting platform and placed a hand on the cold metal. "ADAM is going to get inside the Gate and make it think it's receiving instructions from the command station."

>>**Then...**<<

Bethany Anne's eyebrow arched at ADAM's tone. "Then we'll figure out exactly how much juice it takes to open it."

>>**You make it sound so simple,**<< ADAM remarked with amusement.

"I tell you what I want, you make it happen without giving me a condensed lecture on some part of engineering I have no interest in," Bethany Anne replied. "Then I get on with saving lives." She paused for impact. "I don't see the problem."

>>**Isn't the point that you don't?"**<< ADAM replied. >>**Okay, give me some power here.**<<

Bethany Anne blinked when an overlay of the Gate appeared on her faceplate. She closed her eyes and focused on drawing energy to the spot ADAM had marked in the overlay. "How much should I give it? I don't want to get too enthusiastic and blow the damned thing by mistake."

>>**Go slow and steady,**<< ADAM instructed. >>**You'll know when to stop because there will be a large portal throwing out massive amounts of radiation six inches from your face.**<<

Bethany Anne increased the flow of energy steadily, and the Gate stuttered to life. She stepped back into the Etheric, keeping her window open while protecting herself from the blast of energy that poured from the silver-green circle. "Is the ship still there?"

>>**Give me a moment,**<< ADAM replied. >>**I have the rest of the transmission, and the Gate coordinates the transmission was sent through. Locking on...**<<

Satellites exploded in the background as the scout fighters made progress with the net. The portal undulated, spilling light as it shifted to open at the location ADAM had found.

Michael's voice interrupted the hypnotic effect it was having on Bethany Anne. *I have the children.*

**Are they good?**

*If you count spitting mad as good, then yes.*

Bethany Anne raised an eyebrow. **What's going on down there?**

*I'll tell you what's going on down here,* Alexis cut in. *The colony is descending into a riot, and the president's people are too busy talking to act. People are fighting in the streets, and they're still arguing about whether implementing martial law is a violation of the colony's constitution.*

**Is there anyone down there you can work with?** Bethany Anne asked. **They have Federation officers in their military, right?**

*Yes, and their hands are tied while the colony's capital burns,* Alexis informed her. *We left the politicians to talk and came out here to do something. We're working with the emergency services folks to get people evacuated.*

Gabriel joined them in the mindspace. *I think the generals can be persuaded to act for the good of the people, but we're out in the city.*

**I'm almost done here.**

>>**Um, no, you're not,**<< ADAM informed her out of the family's hearing. >>**I've got the ship, and the reason they're in distress.**<<

*I hope you're not expecting me to spare the lives of the cultists responsible for this,* Michael told Bethany Anne. *I've requested ground teams from both superdreadnoughts to assist the suppression efforts.*

**Whatever you need to do to put the brakes on the shit-show until I get there, do it. Got to go.**

She dropped the mental link, having no time to elucidate as three ships came tearing through the Gate, two of them Ooken destroyers in pursuit of the first, which was a battered and beaten freighter. It looked to Bethany Anne like the dwindling forward motion the freighter had was largely due to the hit it had taken on the crossing, judging by the atmosphere venting from its belly.

"Oh, *fuck*, no!" Bethany Anne cut power to the Gate before any more Ooken destroyers came through, opening a mental link to John. **We have Ookens at the Gate and a civilian ship in danger. I'm in the Etheric, headed for the ship.**

*I'll take care of the Ookens,* John promised.

## Daolagen, Senate

Bethany Anne headed for the planet's surface after depositing the rescued crew onboard the *Baba Yaga*. She exited the Etheric in the war room, a bunker deep below the Senate building, putting an end to the shouting match occurring over the top of the president's head between the two factions of her advisors.

The stunned politicians stared at Bethany Anne in silence. President LaCroix lifted her head from her hands, her face crumpling with relief. "My Queen, you are here."

Bethany Anne smelled a traitor in the room and drew her katana, bringing it up to point at the people clustered around the table. "Just in time to prevent your mole from succeeding, it would appear. Not one of you moves. Anyone who does so will find themselves getting intimately acquainted with the business end of my sword. Do I make myself clear?" **Michael, did you meet with these people?**

*I did not,* he replied.

**Alexis?**

Her daughter let out a sound between a growl and a groan. *What did I miss?*

**Not sure yet,** Bethany Anne admitted. **But there's something rotten in the state of Daolagen, and I know just the Kurtherian to get to the bottom of it.** "Someone here is being less than honest," she told the president.

LaCroix snorted in disbelief. "Nobody here would betray the people."

Bethany Anne looked around, speaking in a soft voice formed of concrete. "Take your seats while we discover who it is."

She dismissed the men and women, who looked shifty as they obeyed. They might well have had a petty crime or misdemeanor they were concealing, but the brief feeling of intense hatred she'd sensed mixed in with the clear gratitude of the others belonged to someone much more adept at hiding their true self.

Bethany Anne walked around the table, touching her blade to each human's right shoulder as she passed. As she made contact, she and TOM riffled their minds in search of deception. The first few humans yielded nothing of interest.

**I don't know about that,** TOM commented. **That woman's level of attachment to her housebot is a bit concerning. What about this man? He's keeping two families, one on the colony, one on the planet of his grandparents' origin.**

*You find the idea amusing?* Bethany Anne asked, moving on to the next senator.

**I don't know about amusing,** TOM replied. **Illogical. If a man has more than one wife, which one does he obey if they are asking for different things? Human women do not generally take well to sharing their men in my admittedly limited experience. Which brings me to the terrifying part: what does he do if they find out about each other?**

*Exactly what he's told for the rest of his days by whichever one of them is gracious enough not to castrate him, I would assume.* She found nothing in the president's mind to connect her to the cult, a small favor she sent up mental thanks for. *Thankfully, they won't be starting tomorrow with entirely new leadership.*

**What about him?** TOM's tone shifted as he and Bethany Anne looked into the friendly-but-concerned eyes and open smile of the senator who had been arguing with the generals.

*No.* She followed the senator's gaze when his eyes darted involuntarily to the senator sitting three seats away from him. *Her.*

**Yes,** TOM agreed. **There's nothing healthy about the fear that woman is concealing.**

Bethany Anne continued circling at the same pace until she reached the woman. She placed the edge of her katana a hair's breadth from the senator's throat and her other hand on the woman's shoulder. "You are an agent of the cult."

"No!" the guileless man cried. "Laura, tell her she's made a mistake.

The senator swallowed, saying nothing to confirm or deny the accusation leveled against her.

Bethany Anne gave him a sympathetic smile. "I'm sorry for you, but it doesn't make it any less the truth. This woman has been conspiring with the terrorists to bring down this government."

She leaned in and whispered in the senator's ear, "Talk, and you can live out the remainder of your life on a penal colony. Continue to play the strong and silent game, and your life expectancy will be very short indeed."

The woman closed her eyes. "That's what you do when you don't get your way, right? Spill however much blood it takes to change the result. Isaiah—the *people*—will stop you from enslaving us." She jerked her shoulder out of Bethany Anne's loose hold and thrust herself onto the blade at her throat.

Senators and military personnel alike drew back in shock when they were splashed with the senator's blood. The man whose relationship with the late senator was still not clear to Bethany Anne broke into choked sobs.

"What the hell just happened?" President LaCroix demanded.

Bethany Anne released the senator's body to fall onto the table and held her katana up while it absorbed the grisly coating, then sheathed it. "She made her choice. I have no stomach for traitors. Now explain to me what measures your administration is going to take against the riots happening in your streets, because so far, the only ones I see doing anything worth a damn are my people and the emergency services."

The president sighed. "This is a civil issue. I cannot in good conscience turn the military on our citizens."

"*Screw your good-fucking-conscience!*" Bethany Anne was at the president's side in half a blink, causing LaCroix to shrink back in her chair under her withering stare.

"A riot is *not* a civil matter. It's a terrorist incident that is occurring because of your complete and utter incompetence as a leader. You had a duty to your people to cut the cancer out of your society and you *failed*, so buckle the fuck up and start making decisions that will save your people's lives before I take the power to do so out of your hands."

The president nodded, seeing she wasn't going to be given a choice. "You heard the Queen. Mobilize."

The generals jumped into action at the president's order, leaving the table for their command posts at the consoles crammed into the other end of the room.

"We may be too late," President LaCroix fretted. "You are right. I failed my people because I didn't take the threat of Isaiah seriously."

Bethany Anne considered whether she should feel bad for the woman. Her inclination was to be pissed that she had to intercede in something that should have been dealt with by a black-ops team before it even got started, but not everyone had the foresight that came with experience.

Unfortunately, this president had all the hallmarks of a shiny-eyed idealist who had risen to power and discovered too late that the mantle was both heavier and more complicated to wear than anyone who had not held the responsibility could comprehend. "Give yourself a break."

The president shot Bethany Anne a look of incredulity.

"You just told me I'm incompetent and that my people are going to die because of my actions. I'll be resigning as soon as this crisis is over."

Bethany Anne sighed. "You *could* do that. Or you could take your lumps and choose to be better in the future." She only half-heard the reply since her focus was on the comm feeds coming in from the response teams being transported in all over the city. "My people are working in the hotspots to protect the public until your military arrives."

The president smoothed the wrinkles out of her clothing. "I need to speak to the people and persuade them somehow to stop this madness. What do I say? They believe in the things Isaiah has told them strongly enough to cause harm to others."

Bethany Anne already had a solution in mind. "Get ready to make your broadcast. I have a plan."


## Daolagen Space, Ooken Destroyer

"Dammit, BA." John's armored boots left spiderwebbed prints in the crystal as he walked the dying ship with his Jean Dukes Special held loosely by his side. "'*Get me an Ooken, John,*'" he grumped. "Like it's just a case of going to the store to pick one up."

*That was not an option?* the EI in his armor snarked.

"Unfortunately not," John answered with regret. "I'll have to make do with you telling me where the bastards are hiding so I can snatch one and get out of here." He glanced back at the hole Sayomi had given him as an entrance, noting that the ship was already healing itself.

"I've got to get the transporter tech for the *Sayomi*. It's a pain in the ass getting Sayomi to shoot me a door."

*You don't need Sayomi to do that. I got a wrist cannon design from Commander Silvers' EI that will suffice.*

"Helpful little fucker," John remarked. "Let me have the cannons."

His EI obliged, and his wrist plates shifted to form the cannons. John familiarized himself with how to use them before repeating his request for the location of the nearest Ooken.

*There are approximately thirty Ookens in a room one level below us,* the EI replied. *You can access the level via the duct on your left.*

"Any that aren't in a group large enough to cause me serious issues?" John clarified, pulling the grate off the duct and peering into the eight-by-eight aperture in the wall.

There was a pause while the EI checked. *No. This is the smallest group. I recommend you get a move on before the ship receives orders to Gate out.*

John muttered a curse and powered up the cannons before climbing into the tube. "Inform Sayomi we'll need extraction from the deck below this one in exactly five minutes."

*Done. What is your play?* the EI asked as John descended the duct. *Because while I'm able to amplify your ability to alter the hive mind's perception so the Ookens cannot see you, it's not going to mean a thing once you start shooting.*

"I only need one shot," John told the EI. He paused to check that the corridor was empty before punching out the grate and exiting the duct. "Where is the room?"

The squalling hive mind gave away the Ookens' location before the EI answered.

John grunted. "Never mind. Sayomi ready?"

*I'm coordinating with her.*

*Going in. Extraction on my signal.* John still had a ways to go to get used to the EI in his head, but that was nothing compared to how he felt pulling directly on the Etheric to manipulate the hive mind. He wiped the Ookens' acknowledgment of his presence from their consciousness and entered the room with his wrist cannons ready to go to Plan B if necessary.

*There's a Plan B?* the EI inquired.

*Yeah, it's 'shoot the shit out of everything in sight and hope the video of my heroic death teaches future generations how to go out in style.'* John focused on the largest Ooken in the room. It was easily three times his size and fit Bethany Anne's command, which had been "Bring me the biggest, ugliest fucker you can find."

Well, shit. That one should do her well enough.

It was just a matter of maintaining his illusion while sneaking past the other twenty-nine Ookens in the room, subduing the chosen Ooken without killing it in the process, and getting himself and his prize back to the Sayomi in one piece.

*Hero complex much?* Sayomi cut into his thoughts unexpectedly. *Or did you forget I was here?*

*Why the hell are you inside my head?* John demanded. *You can't be inside my head.*

*That was not a desirable tactical decision?* the EI inquired, its voice laced with confusion.

*Of course it was,* Sayomi assured the EI. *But as you are aware, the man has a thick skull.*

*I could exchange you for the scout fighter Bethany Anne offered me,* John told Sayomi.

Sayomi laughed. *As if. Now, if you want a hole in the side of that ship, I suggest you get the hell out of the blast zone. I have disabled the destroyer's shields. Firing in three...two...*

John closed the gap between him and his target when the wall imploded. The EI magnetized his boots and locked his arms around the Ooken's head, stunning it with a punch to the temple.

The Ookens fought to hold on as they were sucked out of the breach, screeching at John. Locking tentacles, they plugged the hole with their bodies

John dropped and pinned his Ooken to the floor with his knees, freeing himself to pick them off with his wrist canons. *All you did was piss them off. Where's my extraction?*

*Incoming,* Sayomi announced, and the Ookens blocking the hole were scattered by the puck that came flying in. *I believe your exit is clear.*

John grabbed his Ooken and ran for the open cargo hold Sayomi had angled to face the hole. He flung the Ooken in ahead of him and jumped the gap, deactivating his helmet after Sayomi sealed them in.

"Where now?" Sayomi asked.

John applied another love tap to the Ooken's head when it stirred. "Daolagen. Bethany Anne can wake it up."

## CHAPTER TWENTY-TWO

**Daolagen, Senate Grounds**

Chaos had been crowned king in the absence of logic.

Thousands of citizens had ignored the president's plea for them to stay indoors and headed for the Senate to defend their way of life against a takeover by the cult, arming themselves with whatever was at hand.

The military had arrived in the city too late to prevent the majority of the people from reaching the center of the trade district, and once there, it was a straight shot along a mile-long avenue to the colony's seat of government. The soldiers formed an uncertain perimeter around the enormous open courtyard between the avenue and the Senate building, doing what they could to contain the riot without using lethal force since their superiors had no clue which group was which and they had orders not to engage the general public.

Whipped up by Isaiah, the cultists clashed with the mob waiting for them in the courtyard. The uproar drowned out the president's emergency broadcast playing on a holo above their heads and on every screen around the colony.

Michael strode through the courtyard, heading up the sweeping line formed by the team, pondering his children's efforts to show mercy while taking absolutely no prisoners. K'aia and Trey used their staffs to keep their space clear of cultists who were furious their nonhuman selves were besmirching their whatever-the-fuck these people were so precious about.

Christina showed less restraint, as expected for a Pricolici, but Kai was the one who surprised him. The young Walton, recently enhanced, had no compunction about laying the smackdown on the unenhanced.

Michael smiled. At least one of them got to cut loose.

While a massacre would solve the problem in the short term, it wouldn't please Bethany Anne to have the news of the return of his salted earth policy precede them for the remainder of the tour. The children had it handled.

He at no point felt he needed to step in for their protection.

They were doing what they could to split up people locked together in animalistic struggles for survival, but the layout of the courtyard worked against them, and fights broke out again as soon as they moved on to break up the next group.

Michael's rain made no difference. Similarly, Alexis' physically separating people with bursts of concussive energy was doing little to stem the violence. They fought regardless of the downpour and the soldiers behind a hastily-erected barrier on the Senate steps blasting them with water cannons.

Bethany Anne exited the Etheric beside Michael and touched his shoulder. "You never saw a Black Friday sale, I'm guessing."

"I saw a crusade or two," Michael replied. "There is no honor here, just human beings brought down to their basest level by contrasting beliefs."

Bethany Anne didn't disagree. "It's about to get messier." *John, do you have my Ooken?*

*It's taking a nap right now, but I have to keep knocking the fucker out every five minutes or so. It'd be peachy if you took possession sometime soon.*

*I have one more thing to do,* Bethany Anne told him. *Stay close, and keep it subdued until I'm ready.*

Michael raised an eyebrow, hearing the exchange.

Bethany Anne waved off his concerns. "I'm about to drop in on Isaiah. It's about time I deliver that object lesson I was talking about."

She called Alexis over. Gabriel stayed with the others, still working to quell the people around them. Alexis greeted her with, "Hey, Mom. You won't believe what I have to tell you."

"Start with the location of the temple," Bethany Anne instructed. "This needs to be stopped."

Alexis grabbed Bethany Anne's arm as she sent the information to her HUD. "Wait, Isaiah has a memory you need to see." She explained what she'd seen in the back of the cultist's mind. "He's not aware he met a Kurtherian."

Bethany Anne drew her katanas. "I have a feeling our little zealot will be renouncing his leaders very publicly in —let me see—five minutes."

She gave them instructions for her return, then cut

through the Etheric to the temple, locking onto the eight remaining mental signatures in the complex as her exit point.

The guards died before they'd registered her moving through them at super speed. Bethany Anne had no stomach for playing with the unenhanced. Isaiah, however, was a different matter. She slowed so he could see her and sheathed one of her swords. "Isaiah, I presume."

Surprisingly, he didn't cower. "And you are Bethany Anne. I knew you would come to kill me. It won't make a difference. Another will take my place."

Bethany Anne lifted a shoulder. "I'm not here to end your life, but to open your eyes to the fact that you have been mindfucked by a being with more power than you could comprehend."

Isaiah faltered. "Why should I believe you?"

"You don't know me," Bethany Anne told him. "All you know is what you've been made to believe. If I wanted you dead, we would not be speaking. I would rather save a life than take one."

Isaiah's uncertainty grew. "I don't understand."

"Come with me." She crossed the space between them and took Isaiah by the shoulder, pulling him through the Etheric to the scene of the riot. Isaiah fell to his knees as they emerged on the steps of the Senate, losing his footing on the bloody water slicking the ground.

Bethany Anne hauled him to his feet by his collar and pointed at the mass carnage occurring in the courtyard. "This is your doing. You have divided these people, and for what? Because you believed a lie." She shook him as she spoke, resisting the urge to smack his stupid head clean off his shoulders.

Isaiah shook his head. "I've seen proof."

"You've seen photos out of context and been fed a bunch of half-truths," Alexis admonished as she joined them. "If you really wanted the truth, you could have found it." She indicated the holo above their heads to Bethany Anne. "We're ready to take over the emergency broadcast. The courtyard has been secured by the president's men. Are you ready?"

Bethany Anne nodded. "Do what you can to restore his memories." *John, time for your pet to wake up.*

*Oh, it's awake,* he assured her.

Bethany Anne made another trip through the Etheric to the *Sayomi* and took hold of the Ooken, securing it in her mental grip.

John waved as she vanished back into the Etheric without a word.

Bethany Anne created a platform of solid air to hold her above the courtyard. There were still thousands in the waiting crush. The motion of the crowd made her feel seasick. She scanned the crowd to make sure all the exits had been blocked according to her instructions and was satisfied.

The rioters hadn't noticed the military pulling back. Bethany Anne doubted anything short of an earthquake would distract them from their bitter purpose.

So she provided one.

The fighting turned to panicked screams when the flagstones rippled at Bethany Anne's command. The screams turned to puzzlement when the tremor ceased immediately, and the fighting resumed in some places.

Bethany Anne held the Ooken down with one foot and lifted her katana as the holo switched from the president's face to the camera feed Alexis had on her. The people not fighting reacted with shock to the sight of a fifty-foot former Empress hovering above them, which Bethany Anne helped along by pushing out a wave of fear. *Could I get some lightning over here?*

*Coming right up.* Michael supplied a strike that backlit Bethany Anne as she made her platform descend to float over the people's heads. The fighting slowed further.

*Again.*

This strike she caught with the blade of her katana and redirected over the heads of those nearest, amplifying her voice to be heard over the entire courtyard. "The fighting ends now, or I will have no option but to give you a reason to recall why unity is survival in these dark times. This, for those who have not viewed the public information broadcasts, is an Ooken." She eyed it. "A particularly large example, I should add."

"You wouldn't release it," someone called.

Bethany Anne singled out the speaker. "I have every intention of releasing it if you people don't get yourselves to-fucking-gether."

The holo showed every bit of the weariness that pervaded Bethany Anne's very being. The people stared at the Ooken with horror. Those who had come here to stand up for what was right and found themselves in over their heads began to filter toward the exits, where the soldiers identified them before allowing them to leave.

"Now that I have your full attention…" Bethany Anne shoved the Ooken into the Etheric, retaining a connection to it in case that attention wavered, "what those of you who came here because of Isaiah need to understand is that I *always* had the power to rule if that was my wish. I have one desire, which is to remove the possibility of any species or race being used by the Kurtherians who remain on this plane of existence."

She lowered herself to the Senate steps and had Alexis bring Isaiah over to be included in the holo. "Dad helped me to unlock his altered memories. He's not going to be any trouble."

"Is this true?" Bethany Anne asked Isaiah.

Isaiah bowed his head, tears of shame running down his face. "It's true. I remember now."

He looked out, his eyes drawn to the blood running down to pool in the low areas. His people stared at him.

A man who was tricked. A person who wanted to be somebody. His arrogance. His *downfall*.

"I was nothing more than the pawn of the Kurtherian who has used my arrogance against you, against me, against us all."

Many of the cultists in the crowd took their leader's admission badly. Bethany Anne manifested a barrier from Etheric energy to prevent them from rushing the steps. "You are angry. That's okay. Devolving into further violence is not, and the Ooken is still an option for anyone who finds civility unattainable. This man has been lied to just like you, and he is willing to face the consequences of his actions." She stared at those who had vengeance in their eyes and asked, *"Are you?"*

Bethany Anne returned the broken man to Alexis' care and faced the crowd. "This lack of unity weakens us all. You are precious to me, but you are only a few of the billions of people I hold myself responsible for. If I can't trust people not to engineer a second Worst Day Ever the moment I leave, how the fuck am I supposed to fight for you? Look around. Look what you have become."

Her words echoed in the silence as the people returned to their senses and faced the countless dead Isaiah had just viewed littering the courtyard.

Bethany Anne felt the shift as the people came face to face with what they'd done to each other and to *themselves*. "The cost of failure is what drives us not to repeat our mistakes. Redemption will be your own to find, and I suspect the majority of you are in sore need of it. This is my one and only offer. Go home. Make amends with your loved ones. Remember what it is to be kind to each other."

**Leaving Daolagen Space, QSD *Baba Yaga*, Top Deck**

Satisfied that the recorded confession Isaiah had made following the end of the riot on Daolagen was safely in her father's hands, Bethany Anne tracked the aroma of post-op pancakes through the family quarters to the source and found the twins with Michael in the kitchen.

As always, having just the four of them together was all Bethany Anne needed to be reminded of why she was willing to deal with the shit that came with her life. Michael's smile was the smile of every lover, the twins' laughter an echo of that heard in millions of homes across dozens of galaxies.

Alexis waved her spatula, keeping her attention on the griddle where she had eight pancakes cooking. "Hey, Mom. You're just in time."

"Just in time for what?" Bethany Anne inquired, taking a seat at the breakfast bar next to Michael. She tucked herself under his arm and rested her head on his shoulder. "Well, pancakes, obviously."

Michael chuckled, pressing a kiss to Bethany Anne's hair. "Family meeting," he answered. "None of us wants to see you agitated over missed deadlines."

Gabriel dolloped whipped butter on the pancakes as Alexis served them and pushed one of the plates toward Bethany Anne, then another toward Michael. "Get a room, you two. Nobody needs to see their parents sucking face when they're about to eat."

"We don't need a room since we have a whole ship," Bethany Anne replied, eyeing the fruit bowl for a moment before selecting a nectarine. She pointed a finger and pared her fruit with an Etheric edge, then ate a segment before waving her finger at the twins. "Praise where it's due. You handled the assignment well."

"Not that well," Alexis argued. "I missed the mole because I let my emotions rule me. Again."

Bethany Anne grabbed another segment. "Don't beat yourself up; you're not infallible. None of us are, despite what your father thinks when he is feeling sure of himself."

Alexis smiled. "Thanks, Mom, really. But I can't let it be a weakness."

"Your mother has made emotion her strength," Michael told her. "I am the first to admit that a dispassionate approach can be useful. However, had your mother taken that same approach, there would be no Federation."

"How do you figure?" Gabriel asked.

Alexis cut to the point, as usual. "Because everyone would have kept fighting without her to force them to pull them together. What are we going to do to get the tour back on track?"

Bethany Anne set her pancakes swimming in syrup before cutting off a piece of the topmost one with her fork. She ate the bite before giving her a considered answer. "Well, you can all stop worrying I'm going to lose my shit for a start. While I was waiting for Isaiah to wake up from his Pod-doc session, I got with ADAM and rescheduled the next few weeks. Check your itineraries. They should have updated already."

Alexis frowned, opening her HUD. "I didn't get a notification." Her confusion turned to mild outrage when she saw the adjustments had them working to cover the scheduled stops between the tour's current location and the resort planet that was the halfway point in half the previously allotted time. "What the hell, Mom? You do know people need sleep, right?"

"Most people, yes, but not anyone who will be supervising those to be upgraded around our technology," Bethany Anne told her. "The technical teams have stayed on schedule since the *Reynolds* stayed on task while we took care of the Daolagen situation. Personnel upgrades are the only part of the operation running behind, and that's easily solved by picking up from where we are and working on getting to Serenity ahead of schedule, extending our stay there."

Michael nodded, his attention on his food. "Makes sense."

Gabriel looked at his parents in disbelief. "How does extending our vacation get us back on track?"

"I'm not extending anyone's vacation time. By setting Serenity as a rendezvous point for everyone who didn't get the upgrade, we avoid having to turn around to cover the stops we missed by going straight to Daolagen." Bethany Anne had weighed up the security headache against the logistical impossibility of completing the tour in time if they reversed course. "Yes, it will be a challenge, but I have faith that everyone will be more than capable of meeting it when they realize that the alternative is spending another eight weeks away from home."

Michael put his fork down. "Restructuring the guard rotation shouldn't be an issue. Christina and Kai have proven extremely helpful in managing the FDG troops we have aboard."

"Decent guys," Gabriel mentioned. "They're mostly veterans Nathan allowed to reenlist. The stories they tell are incredible."

Bethany Anne's mouth crept up at the corner. "Speaking of Christina, I spoke with Ecaterina. She and Nathan will be joining us for our vacation."

Alexis clapped in delight. "Really? I thought you would have to threaten eternal punishment to get him to leave Onyx."

"No need," Bethany Anne told her with a smile. "It just so happens that their anniversary is coming up, and Ecaterina was delighted with the brochure for the resort."

"As was the ineffable Charumati, I assume?" Michael

ventured with a chuckle when his wife and daughter turned almost identical sweet smiles on him. He shook his head. He had no chance. "I know what you two are planning. You just confirmed my suspicion as to who the intended celebrants are. How can I help with your scheme?"

Bethany Anne pressed her lips together in thought. "For the moment, keep Christina and Kai occupied. I might want your help beating some sense into Nathan at a later date."

Michael smiled. "Of course, dear."

# CHAPTER TWENTY-THREE

**Cosnar System, QBS *Achronyx***

The cleanup had revealed an ocean world of unparalleled beauty. Akio thought it would be even more beautiful when it was filled with life.

Marine biologists from the Federation had recovered samples of fossilized flora and fauna trapped in the crystal sediment on the ocean floor and were slowly but surely preparing to re-seed the planet, with the assistance of various other specialists the consul on Devon had arranged.

He admired the diligence the scientists and technicians showed but had no clue as to how they had achieved so much in such a short time, even with the operation running around the clock.

This chance discovery would soon be home to the Collectives, and he was more than honored to be part of making that happen.

He and Achronyx chatted idly while the ship entered a high orbit over the planet, Achronyx passing on tidbits of interest from the crews working on the sky base—the raft of ships lashed together and suspended a hundred feet above the cloud layer. They were discussing the ongoing construction of the underwater base when Achronyx received the message they'd been waiting for.

"It appears that the containment field generator has been found," he informed Akio. "One of the bots in the trench went offline, and the team leader sent another with a camera and got a visual before they lost that bot, too. They're asking if they should take it out."

Akio examined the image. "Leave it in place until we are certain it is safe to release the field without also releasing a large amount of crystal into open space."

The shuddering in the ship came suddenly and without warning from somewhere inside the Etheric, putting an end to Akio's theory that an investigation would precede any engagement with the Kurtherians.

"Achronyx, report!" Akio commanded as the ship bucked under a double impact.

"Two missiles of unknown origin just came out of nowhere, and I'm pissed about the dents they left in my ass," Achronyx snapped. "Minimal damage, but the inertia dampers will only absorb a few more hits like that before they overload. Diverting nonessential power to cloaking and shields and initiating offensive maneuvers."

Akio raked the viewscreen with his gaze, seeing the Gate but no ships. "Who is attacking us?"

"Probably that Ooken destroyer," Achronyx replied, unloading his railguns in the direction of the sleek, dark ship coming up on their stern.

Akio's jaw clenched. "Ookens. I knew this day would come."

"I'm guessing their overlords didn't like us messing with their stuff," Achronyx agreed. "I have requested backup from the base."

The ship rocked again when the destroyer snuck a kinetic through while the shields were in phase, draining the available power Achronyx had to keep both cloaking and shields intact. Achronyx returned fire with a spread of Etheric-charged missiles while calculating the odds of being hit in the same place when he should have been invisible to the enemy ship. "Dammit, they have the encryption for my cloak."

"Then stop wasting power on it," Akio ordered. "Concentrate on keeping us together, and let's hope that is the only ship they sent."

"You had to go and say it, didn't you?" Achronyx grumbled. "I'm reading three more Gate signatures near the first."

Akio got to his feet as three more destroyers appeared in the void. "Put us between those ships and the sky base and ready everything we have. We must do what we can until the other Rangers get here."

"They're already arriving," Achronyx informed him as he brought the ship around. "I don't know what Jean Dukes put into the *Penitent Granddaughter,* but that rusty old hulk can haul ass when Meredith puts her mind to it. The *Defiant* and the *Cambridge* just Gated in on the other side of the planet."

One by one the Ranger ships arrived, the Shinigami-class ships acting as overwatch to the Black Eagles and fighter Pods they disgorged from their holds. They ringed the Ooken destroyers.

"Give me comm to the fleet and send a message to the underwater crews to evacuate the area around the containment field generator," Akio requested. "Rangers, once again, you are the line the enemy dares not cross. There can be no mercy for the soulless while lives hang in the balance. Ranger Two, the fleet is yours. Ranger Three, with me."

Sabine gave her acknowledgment and peeled off from the fleet as Nickie's orders rang out over the comm. "You heard the boss. Let's give those motherfuckers a taste of Ranger justice!"

Akio got to work while the Rangers closed the noose around the destroyers, coordinating with the sky base to get the evacuation underway. He had Sabine open a Gate to Base One, and ships from the sky base began darting out of the atmosphere and through the Gate at his instruction.

He kept half his attention on the battle zone a few hundred kilometers away and the rest on the evacuation. The destroyers pushed the boundary created by the Rangers, attempting to play space chicken with the much smaller Black Eagles. However, their efforts were met by pushback in the form of heavy kinetic fire as the Rangers piloting the fighters unleashed wave after wave of explosive pucks.

"Get ready to take out the containment field generator," Akio told Achronyx. The *Penitent Granddaughter* blocked his view for a minute. He was fighting to get a visual of the battle when the Skaine battleship was suddenly silhouetted by a halo of light. He abandoned his targeting interface. "Ranger Two, what's happening over there?"

"Calm your tits," Nickie told him as Meredith prepared to Gate them to the next firing position. "How's the evacuation going?"

Akio sighed with relief when the *Penitent Granddaughter* was gone, and he saw that only three destroyers remained. "Almost done. I'm about to draw more attention to us. Can we take the heat?"

"You bet that stick up your ass we can," Nickie told him as the Rangers took out another destroyer in a blaze of molten metal.

Akio ignored Nickie's lapse into gutter talk as her nerves started showing, nodding to himself. "Then we fight this battle on our terms. I'm going to destroy the generator and let our enemy know for sure that we're here. Prepare for further enemy contact."

He instructed Achronyx to take the containment field generator out.

Twin missiles shrieked through the planet's atmosphere, throwing up enormous plumes of steam and ocean spray when they breached the water's surface. Akio had Achronyx pan the main screen out to give him the full view of the planet as they hit. The brief aureole of burning atmosphere that followed the explosion struck Akio as beautiful, as did the mitigation of their concerns about the tiny chance the field generator was what was holding the planet's atmosphere in place.

The Rangers closed on the final destroyer, having taken out the third while Akio's attention was on the planet, and hammered it with kinetic fire from all directions while

Team Hex in the Shinigami-class ships strafed it with the wreckage of its downed compatriot ships, which they collected as they swooped around the battle zone providing cover for the other Rangers.

Thousands of pucks hitting continuously was too much for the Ooken ship's shields to bear. Fire burned at the breaches in the destroyer's hull, to be extinguished when it reached what was left of the shields.

"You want to finish this?" Nickie asked in Akio's ear.

Akio smiled. "Achronyx, I believe we have a ship-buster remaining."

"We do," Achronyx answered.

Akio indicated the destroyer on the viewscreen with a wave of his finger. "Then use it, and let us be done with this battle."

"Why do I get the feeling you don't think this is over?" Nickie asked when the final destroyer disintegrated in a flash of Etheric energy, leaving the system Ooken-free for the moment. "It's not like this was an active site for the Kurtherians. Those ships could have been sent as an automatic response for all we know."

Akio watched the debris settle, calculating the next steps for the Rangers. "If there is one thing we can be sure of, it's that it's not over. Tyrannical dictators don't generally take well to their authority being challenged. They will be back."

"We'll be ready," Nickie told him. "Want me to wring extra support out of Harkkat?"

Akio nodded. "A few more ships wouldn't be amiss."

Nickie's laughter pealed. "Good luck with *that*. Every ship that's not already in use is being outfitted for the raid.

I was talking to Grandma Jean about getting a couple more ships, and she told me she's got the shipyards churning out as many new vessels as they can handle, and it's still not enough to meet the demand Bethany Anne is creating with her tour."

Akio appreciated the constraints of wartime, but it didn't change the fact that the Rangers needed more big guns than they currently had. "I will speak to Bethany Anne. She may decide the protection of this planet for the Collectives merits extraordinary measures."

"I hope you're right."

Bethany Anne listened to Akio's report when he called her after giving CEREBRO strict guidelines about their actions should another attack come.

She tapped a finger on her lips as her eyes unfocused for a moment. "I've reviewed the video, and I agree that you need to be ready for a larger attack."

"We have sufficient numbers," Akio told her. He paced the ops center with his hands folded at the base of his spine, occasionally pausing to look at his Queen on the viewscreen while he briefed her on the growth the Ranger group had undertaken since their last face-to-face. "It has been unsurprisingly easy to attract people with the personality traits that are best suited to the Ranger life since the need for Justice is strongly felt everywhere. Arming them is no issue. The shortage is of suitable ships for the endeavor."

Bethany Anne considered the problem. "You have a

bunch of engineers and other technical specialists out there, right?"

"*Hai*, my Queen." He eyed her. "What are you thinking?"

Bethany Anne smiled. "Well, first, I'm going to send the only two ships I have not currently deployed. Second, I need you to get with your technical people, find out what they are missing in order to build a shipyard out at Ranger Base One, and get Harkkat earning his keep. You can pull resources from anywhere except the shipyards that are already in operation."

"I'll have Nickie coordinate that with Jean," Akio promised. "I understand completely that the production schedule for the raid cannot be set back." He paused. "Which ships are you sending?"

Bethany Anne's smile grew into a bright grin. "The *ArchAngel* and the *G'laxix Sphaea*. You, Kael-ven, and Dan are all smart guys. I trust you'll figure it out when the next attack comes."

## Federation Space, Serenity, Southern Continent

Bethany Anne ended her call with Akio and resumed her wait for Kai on the deck wrapping the ocean-view suite resort management had offered as a venue. She chose a seat at the wicker table, feeling a little nervous as well as impatient to find out his reaction to her meddling.

Because she was definitely meddling; there was no question about that.

She relaxed when the *Gemini's* roamer came into sight. It covered the couple of miles in a few minutes, and Alexis, Gabriel, and Kai climbed out at the base of the grassy dune, chatting amongst themselves. Kai looked at Bethany Anne in confusion before ascending the driftwood steps to the deck alone.

The young man greeted Bethany Anne with his open and honest smile, reminding her of a much younger Terry Henry, if somewhat less battered by life than the stoic Marine had been at around the same age. As with his grandfather—as with all of the Waltons—what you saw was what you got with Kailin.

"The twins said you wanted to see me?" Kai met Bethany Anne's eyes as he spoke. "I have to admit, I'm a little worried about why."

Bethany Anne chuckled. "Funnily enough, it's me who's concerned about your reaction." She indicated the white stucco building behind them in answer to Kai's inquisitive expression. "When I ask you how you like this for your wedding venue."

"My *what?*" Kai spluttered, completely thrown by the announcement. "How do you know? I haven't even asked..." Logic and reason resumed their places in his thinking as he regained his composure. "Alexis, right? She apologized for reading my mind. I didn't realize she read it so deeply."

Bethany Anne smiled. "We'll call it a happy accident, hmm?"

Kai shook his head, his eyes wide with concern. "I can't ask Christina to marry me. Not until I know it won't drive a wedge between her and her father."

Bethany Anne ruffled his hair, smiling. "You are a sweet, honorable young man. Nathan will come to terms with your relationship. Let me ask you something. Would you die for Christina?"

"In a heartbeat," Kai declared with feeling.

Bethany Anne smiled. "That's the easy part. Would you *live* for her?"

"How could I not?" Kai almost fell over the words in his rush to get them out. "She's everything to me. My best friend, as well as my lover."

The corner of Bethany Anne's mouth crept up. "Keep that in mind when you speak to Nathan."

Kai's face creased in frustration and confusion. "I don't get his issue with me. Christina told me about how she grew up knowing she wouldn't accept anything less than the love her parents share. Why can't Nathan see that's what we have?"

Bethany Anne put her hand on Kai's shoulder. "Nathan will come around. Fathers generally do when they see a man willing to prove his love." She flashed him a wicked grin. "If that doesn't work, the grandchildren will."

Kai was quiet as Bethany Anne led him inside to show him the ballroom, where resort workers in close-fitting black uniforms were arranging everything from the shipping containers she'd had brought down from the *Baba Yaga*.

Teams of workers were setting up rows of round tables around three sides of the polished wood dancefloor, while others moved with calm precision to dress the room in crisp white, silver, and Christina's favorite ice-blue.

Kai took in the grandeur of the ballroom in utter astonishment. "There have to be a hundred people in here. Who are all those chairs for?" His enhanced hearing picked up a familiar commanding voice coming from somewhere deeper inside the building. "My grandmother is here?"

Bethany Anne smiled. "Yes. Also your grandfather, and your parents, and the rest of your friends and family who weren't on duty somewhere. What do you say? I know Christina will have her own thoughts on the matter, but I want to gift you both with a wedding to remember should she accept your proposal."

Kai shook his head slowly, trying to find the words despite his world being turned upside-down. "This is... How do I ever thank you?" He lifted a hand, then dropped it again. "Or pay you back? It looks like you spent the equivalent of a small planet's GDP just on the décor."

Bethany Anne snickered softly. She supposed she *had* gone a bit overboard, not that she would admit that to Michael if he asked. "I'm paying for full use of the resort's facilities and filling them with soldiers. Trust me, management was more than happy to assist when I asked them to provide a service they were more familiar with."

Kai, who was still in his first century of life, was nevertheless experienced enough to know those bright memories were what sustained the soul through hard times. He thought back to his time alone on Earth and the hard-gained knowledge that together meant stronger, and his eyes started to sting as his gratitude for the home Bethany Anne provided everyone under her wing welled up. He blinked before tears had a chance to form and cleared his throat. "I can't deny that I'm shaken. I'm grateful you would do all this for us."

Bethany Anne chuckled. "I guess I'd be shaken too if a distant not-quite-aunt sprang a surprise wedding on me. You and Christina are family, Kailin, and if there's any cause for celebration, then I'll be damned if I let it go by when I can facilitate an occasion we will all remember for a lifetime."

Kai slipped a hand into his pocket and retrieved the ring box he'd carried with him for so long he was sure he'd feel naked without it. He eased it open and showed Bethany Anne the ring, a white gold diamond-studded split-shank band with a princess-cut diamond as its crowning glory. "This ring belonged to my grandmother's grandmother."

Bethany Anne admired the ring for a moment before closing the box in Kai's hand. "All you have to do is ask her."

Kai swallowed the lump that suddenly appeared in his throat. "Well, yeah, I guess so. Bethany Anne? What if she says no?"

Bethany Anne raised an eyebrow. "Do you think she will?"

Kai put the ring box away. "No, I don't. But I can't propose without Nathan's blessing."

Bethany Anne waved a hand. "You can speak to him tomorrow. He and Ecaterina will be arriving late tonight."

Kai hesitated, then gave Bethany Anne a brief and somewhat awkward hug. He stepped back, his face red with emotion. "I don't know what we did to deserve a great not-quite-aunt like you."

"You can thank me by being happy together," Bethany Anne told him fondly. "Now scram. I have work to do, and you have a suit fitting in an hour."

Kai's eyes widened, and he looked behind him as if an ogre might show up before he turned back to ask, "I have a what, now?"

## CHAPTER TWENTY-FOUR

**Federation Space, Serenity, Southern Continent**

Nathan walked arm in arm along the beach with Ecaterina, soaking up the sunshine and the two-piece swimsuit she was wearing under her gauzy sarong. He decided the last-minute vacation might not have been the worst idea after all.

He made all the appropriate noises in response to Ecaterina's running commentary on the luxury they'd been surrounded with since their arrival the night before, his mind stuck on how fucking lucky he was that she loved him as much now as she had when they'd first gotten together.

"You have a very goofy grin on your face right now," Ecaterina told him, booping his nose with her finger.

Nathan swept her up in his arms and spun around. "I'm a man with a lot to be happy about. I'm here in this beautiful location with the most beautiful woman in the world. What more could a man ask for?"

Ecaterina captured Nathan's face in her hands and

kissed him before turning his head to the couple walking down the beach toward them. "How about some company? I see people."

*Fuckity-fuck.* Nathan groaned inwardly. "Do we *have* to socialize? This is supposed to be a romantic getaway."

"It doesn't hurt to be polite," Ecaterina chastised. "They might be the only people we see the whole time we're here."

"That would be a fine thing," Nathan grumbled.

The woman waved as they got closer, and Nathan thought he recognized the way the man moved. His feeling was confirmed when the wind carried a familiar scent to him. He took Ecaterina's hand. "Honey, did you know they were going to be here?"

Ecaterina's eyes shifted away from her husband. "Well, not that they were here on the beach this morning, but yes. Bethany Anne swore me to secrecy."

Nathan liked where his day was heading less and less. "What does Bethany Anne have to do with TH and Char being here?"

A hand on his shoulder caused him to spin around. He came face to face with Bethany Anne and sighed. "This is your revenge for the Pepsi thing? You're crashing my second honeymoon?"

Bethany Anne shook her head in amusement. "No. You'll get to your honeymoon. Eventually. This is about your daughter."

Nathan suddenly understood the reason the Waltons were here. "No. No, no, and a million times *no*. They are *not* getting married."

Charumati was suddenly at his side, and although

Nathan had always taken comfort in the knowledge that he was the biggest, baddest Were around, it was fully negated by the slender, impeccably-dressed woman with her sparkling purple eyes and aura that promised pain to any Were who displeased her. "I hope you're not saying our grandson isn't good enough for your daughter, Mr. Lowell."

Terry Henry fixed Nathan with a stony look. "Well?"

Nathan looked from TH to Char, his mouth working furiously for a moment before he managed to speak. "What? No! I have nothing against Kai personally. He's a good kid, but that's the problem. He's just a kid compared to Christina. She needs someone who can keep her safe. Not someone—"

"Christina needs to be kept safe?" Ecaterina cut in, waving her hands at Nathan. "Please! Can you hear yourself? Sometimes you are very thickheaded for a smart man. You need to let go."

Bethany Anne lifted a shoulder in response to Nathan's pleading look. "I get it. I just don't agree with you."

Nathan had a moment of feeling betrayed. He knew Ecaterina didn't understand his reluctance because he had refused to speak to her about it. However, whether this was his doing or not, he couldn't deal with the expectant stares of the women right now.

He turned and headed back to his cabin at a run.

Ecaterina must have been livid with him because she did not return to the cabin that morning.

Nathan skimmed a book without reading it, watched a movie that could have been about anything, and ordered room service twice before he saw a soul who wasn't a resort worker.

His mind wandered, refusing to settle on the plot of a second movie. He picked at his poultry wings without tasting them, and there wasn't any alcohol on the planet strong enough for him to drown his sorrows in.

He'd checked. *Twice.*

Ecaterina returned in the afternoon, smelling of sunshine and radiating silent fury. "You have offended Char," she informed Nathan, the ghost of her accent telling him how deep in the shit he was. "Worse, you are going to alienate our only child. Is that what you want?"

It was the last thing Nathan wanted. He didn't want to fight with Ecaterina, either.

Ecaterina growled in exasperation at the lack of explanation forthcoming from her husband. "You are impossible, Nathan Lowell! Call me when you are ready to stop acting like a caveman. Until then, I will be with Bethany Anne, making arrangements for what will be the happiest day of our daughter's life—unless her father ruins it."

She threw up her hands and sashayed angrily out of the cabin, leaving Nathan to stew in his regret and the string of Romanian curses she left hanging in the air.

Nathan sighed and headed out to the egg-shaped chair on the deck, finding the cabin's interior claustrophobic despite the light and space. He eased himself into the wicker cocoon cross-legged and watched the waves break on the shore a few hundred feet away.

Was he holding on too tightly? *Undoubtedly,* his conscience replied. Great, his own brain was on everyone else's side. Wasn't it his prerogative as a father to protect his daughter, no matter how old she was? Another question his conscience refused to answer in his favor.

The truth was, he hadn't examined his attitude to his daughter's relationship beyond the snap decision he'd made to dislike Kai upon meeting him.

Now, as well as his fear of driving Christina away, he had the not-so-distant concern of being relegated to making his bed on the couch for the foreseeable future to contend with as well.

That was if Ecaterina didn't just pack her bags and go stay with Bethany Anne for a while to teach him a lesson. Added to that was his stubborn-ass nature putting him at risk of offending TH and Char.

Offending Char would hurt physically, of that he had no doubt, and he valued TH far beyond his role as the head of the organization he could rely on to get the job done, no matter the complications.

His life would be a poorer place for the absence of their friendship. Even removing his emotions from the equation, he couldn't see why Christina had chosen Kai. He was kindhearted, well-mannered, and even-tempered. Nathan had seen how Kai worshipped her with his smallest actions, never drawing attention to his devotion, which would piss Christina off in one second flat.

Nathan got why Ecaterina found it so difficult to understand his reluctance to accept that Christina had chosen the man she wanted to build her future with. They already shared their lives and their work, and there was his problem.

That Kai would protect her with his life wasn't in question. The consequences of that situation coming to pass were his issue. Nathan knew they faced life-or-death decisions every time he sent the Bad Company out, and would Christina choose herself if Kai was at risk? No, she would try and save him, and if for some reason Kai couldn't be revived—like poor Cory's husband—Christina's heart would be irrevocably broken.

He didn't want any possible future for her that involved losing her vivacious appetite for living.

*Not your choice to make,* his conscience offered like the traitor it was. *Besides, you're too late,* it continued. Nathan scowled. Traitor conscience or not, he had to find a way to be okay with the fact that his daughter had chosen a partner who would need protecting.

However the fuck he was supposed to do that.

The knock when it came was firm and no-nonsense.

TH, then. Nathan sighed and got up to answer the door. He was surprised to find Kai standing on the porch.

"Not now, kid," Nathan told him.

"Mr. Lowell, please hear me out," Kai asked when Nathan made to shut the door. "I won't take a minute of your time."

Nathan growled and opened the door all the way to admit Kai, hating that he appreciated the young man's humble sincerity. "You've got one minute."

Kai glanced past Nathan, keeping his expression neutral as his gaze swept the mess on the coffee table. "Here is fine." He dropped his hand to his pocket to touch the ring box when Nathan folded his arms and pinned him with a cold stare. "I've done my best to be respectful of your feelings, but I have to put mine and Christina's future together first. I'm going to ask Christina to marry me. I'd prefer to do so knowing we have your blessing, but if I have to spend a few decades proving you wrong first, so be it. I love her, and I'm going to love her for the rest of my days. That's what I came here to tell you. I won't take up any more of your evening. Thank you."

He nodded brusquely and turned to leave.

Nathan saw the hidden steel under Kai's pleasant exterior, and it finally dawned on him what Christina saw in him. He stopped Kai with a hand on his arm. "Come inside." He sighed. "It's about time we talked."

Kai was taken aback but did as Nathan asked. He took a seat on the couch Nathan indicated and accepted the beer he handed him without opening it. "All respect, I can't see that we have much to talk about. You don't approve of me, and honestly, I can't see what I can say to change your mind."

"You want my blessing, don't you?" Nathan asked, taking the chair opposite. "This is what it's going to take to get it. Either give up active duty or do something with all those nanocytes you have swimming around inside you."

Kai frowned. "I just had a minor upgrade in the Pod-doc, but that's not what you mean, is it? I'm willing to listen to your reasoning before I refuse."

Nathan put his own unopened beer on the coffee table between them. "I'm talking about you figuring out how not to make a widow of my daughter. Then you'll have my blessing. I know better than anyone but TH what Bad Company does. I don't want Christina to be put in the situation of having to choose between your life and hers."

Kai rubbed his face with a hand. "I understand where you're coming from. But honestly? I can't make this decision right now, and I definitely can't make it without discussing the consequences with Christina." He broke into a grin. "You realize Christina is going to lose her shit when she finds out about this?"

Nathan nodded. "I do. But I stand by my reasons for it. I apologize for the way I've treated you, but one day you might find yourself having a similar conversation, and you'll understand that there's nothing more terrifying to a man than the man who wants to take his daughter away."

Kai leaned over the table and offered Nathan his hand. "We both want Christina to be happy. That we can agree on. How about we start over?"

Nathan leaned forward and shook Kai's hand, then opened his beer, indicating that Kai should do the same. "That's a start, as far as I can see. Tell me about yourself. The background check I did on you was a little loose on details."

Much later, there was another knock on the door.

Nathan opened the door and stepped back when Terry Henry let himself and the case of beer he was carrying in. TH closed the door behind him with an elbow and headed straight out the French doors leading to the deck on the ocean side of the cabin without a word.

Nathan rolled his head back and sighed, wishing he wasn't going to feel obligated to talk. "Come on in then, I guess," he muttered to TH's back.

"Get your whiny ass out here," TH called, hearing him perfectly. "You can help me drink this beer my grandson thought to pick up for me while he was on that operation of yours while you talk about the reason you're against this wedding."

"You're too late," Nathan told him, helping himself to one of the hand-labeled bottles. He cracked the top and took a sip, inclining his head in appreciation before taking a seat on the end of the lounger next to TH's. "Kai came to see me earlier. We came to an understanding."

Terry Henry took a long slug of his beer. "An arrangement, huh? I take it you threatened him soundly should he break Christina's heart. Not that you need to worry about that."

"I had considered having him quietly disappear," Nathan admitted, a sly smile creeping over his face. "But it would have been awkward when you turned up to help me dispose of the body, so I decided to just give the kids my blessing."

Terry Henry didn't credit the joke with his attention. "As long as we're all on the same page. The wedding is scheduled for two days from now, our women are giving no quarter, and my cries of 'man down' have been completely ignored."

Nathan winced. "That bad?"

"Between keeping Christina in the dark and the fittings," Terry Henry confided, "yes. I can only say that Char packing my dress uniform was a small mercy."

Nathan sighed, wishing he hadn't angered Ecaterina earlier. "Where is Michael in all of this?" he asked, chuckling inwardly at the mental image of Bethany Anne playing Queenzilla until he realized he was going to be subject to her whims as soon as he emerged from the cabin. "Did Kai even get a bachelor party?"

TH shook his head. "He didn't want one."

Nathan got to his feet. "Well, he's getting one." He went

inside and called Gabriel's HUD from his desk, tapping his foot while he waited for him to pick up. "Hey, are you with Kai?"

"Yeah," Gabriel replied. "We're trying to avoid getting roped into hanging ribbons or whatever. It's been a long day."

Nathan chuckled. "I bet. Listen, can you get the guys together without attracting any attention?"

"That depends," Gabriel asked with skepticism. "Are you going to put us on pedestals and stick us full of tailor's pins?"

Nathan frowned. "Huh?"

"Like I said, long day," Gabriel told him.

"How do poker, beer, and snacks guaranteed to have zero nutritional value sound?" Nathan inquired in an offhand tone.

"Give me fifteen minutes."

"You can have thirty," Nathan told him. "I need to pick up a couple of things from my ship."

---

Ecaterina returned to the cabin at midmorning the next day. Not because she had any intention of forgiving the stubborn pig she was married to, but because none of the men had shown up for rehearsal that morning, and she needed his help tracking them down.

The smell of stale alcohol and fried food hit her sensitive nose before she set foot on the path to the cabin door. Ecaterina covered her nose and mouth with her sleeve and approached the cabin with trepidation and more than a little guilt at having left Nathan to drink himself into a stupor.

She paused at the door, hearing unfamiliar snores from inside.

Curiosity took over, and Ecaterina went inside to find out if she was mistaken. The cabin was a mess. The surfaces were cluttered with empty beer and liquor bottles and room service trays. It also looked like someone had set up a makeshift wrestling arena in the center of the living area.

Her investigation of the food processing unit yielded a mod she knew was only available from Bad Company, meaning Nathan. Someone—Nathan again, she presumed—had the unit produce enough of the special liquor that could affect those with nanocytes to knock a vampire on their ass.

Clearly, she was walking through the aftermath of a guys' night, which explained the smell, but what about the snoring?

Ecaterina listened carefully and followed the sounds through the cabin. She found John asleep in the bathtub and Scott and Eric in the hallway leading to the two bedrooms. She turned to go into the kitchen and found Michael feeding beans into the old-fashioned coffee grinder. He offered her a bleary-eyed smile and mumbled something approximating "good morning" as she passed the breakfast table, where Gabriel and Trey were face-down, using their arms as pillows.

"Good call on the coffee," she whispered, continuing on to the den, where she found Nathan and Kai fast asleep, propping each other up on the couch.

Ecaterina smiled and poked Nathan's knee with her foot. "Wakey-wakey, sleepyhead."

Nathan's nose twitched, and he opened one eye a fraction. "Hey. You don't look like you're mad at me anymore. Am I out of the doghouse?"

"You are out of the doghouse," Ecaterina told him. "With me. Char? I can't say."

"She'll forgive you," Terry Henry called as he passed, dripping wet from his swim in the sea. "But I suggest you find a high-end jeweler if you want her to forget."

Kai woke up at the sound of his grandfather's voice, groaning when his knees collided with the table. "*Owww*, my head."

Terry Henry shook his head at Kai, grinning. "Serves you right for drinking so much, knowing you don't have the nanocytes to take care of the consequences."

Kai massaged his aching head tenderly. "I think surviving how much we all drank last night is proof my nanocytes work just fine."

"I hear you." Nathan clapped him on the back in sympathy, causing Kai's stomach to turn a somersault. "I think a bear shit in my mouth while I was asleep."

Ecaterina shook her head in despair. "Have you all forgotten there is a wedding tomorrow? Up! Shower! Now!" She shooed them out of the den. "There will be time for breakfast if you're quick getting dressed."

EPILOGUE

Kai's nerves skyrocketed when the dunes came into sight in the distance. He slowed, suddenly certain he'd lost the ring.

Christina stopped walking and looked back at him. "What are you doing?"

Kai's fingers brushed the reassuring cube in his pocket and he smiled, holding out his hand for Christina to take. "Admiring my favorite view in the whole universe?"

Christina laughed. "You can admire it some more while you eat my dust."

Kai gave chase as Christina sprinted over the sand with her laughter trailing in her wake. He could never catch her unless she let him.

Christina showed mercy as the dunes began to rise around them, vanishing from sight, only to spring an ambush on Kai without warning. Kai went down willingly when she t-boned him, using his weight to send them rolling down the dune in a tangle of arms and legs and lips.

They ended up with Christina straddling Kai, her fingers laced with his.

Kai looked up at her dusted with sand, her hair wild, and he loved her. "I'm going back into the Pod-doc. I'm going to find out if I can get my Were genes activated."

Christina scrambled off him in shock. "What made you come to that decision?" she asked, scrutinizing him. "Where were you last night?"

Kai grinned. "Would you believe getting blind drunk with your dad?"

Christina couldn't suppress her reaction. "*How?*"

"I had a little help from your godmother, and your mother, and my grandmother, but in the end, it came down to him understanding that there's no length I wouldn't go to for you." Kai took the ring box from his pocket and opened it, going to one knee. "Our friends and family are waiting on the other side of these dunes for us. Bethany Anne bought out every wedding-related store in the known universe. It's time."

Kai held up the ring. "Christina Bethany Anne Lowell, will you marry me?"

Christina nodded, tears in her eyes. "Yes. A thousand times, *yes*."

Kai put the ring on her finger and got to his feet. "We have to hurry. The ceremony is in two hours, and your mother and Alexis are waiting for you in your dressing room."

"Dressing room?" Christina echoed, captivated by the way the diamond in her ring caught the light. "Wait, you said Bethany Anne was one of the wedding planners? Tell me later."

They *moved*.

Christina got through a whirlwind of hair and makeup in a daze. Similarly, she browsed the array of dresses Bethany Anne had for her to choose from and picked one on autopilot.

It mattered what she looked like in her photos, of course, but the important thing was that the insurmountable obstacles to her and Kai's marriage had been removed.

She fully intended to get the whole story from Kai—just as soon as she got that ring on his finger and it was too late for her father to change his mind again.

It was obvious Nathan wasn't going to change his mind when she met him outside the ballroom and he embraced her, crying without shame. "I've got the ship running. It's not too late."

"I'll be fine, Dad." Christina waved his fussing off, claiming he'd mess her dress up when it was her eye makeup she was worried about. "But you and I are going to have a conversation if I find out you had anything to do with Kai's decision to explore becoming a Were."

Nathan glanced at the ballroom doors. "Is that the orchestra?" He held out his arm. "Time to go, sweetheart. Kai is waiting to be knocked out by the sight of you in that dress."

Christina slipped her arm through Nathan's. "Thank you for being here for me, Dad."

Nathan swallowed a choking sob that contained as much joy as it did sadness at letting Christina go. "You deserve the happiness you held out for. Kai is a good man."

Christina lifted her veil and started fanning her eyes to stem the tears and save her makeup. "Dad, stop! I can't walk down the aisle looking like a panda, for crying out loud."

Nathan guided her to the doors, which were opened by two resort workers in tuxedos. "You look beautiful."

Bethany Anne lifted her hands when the doors were opened, and the orchestra switched to a lilting arrangement of the *Wedding March*.

Kai turned from his conversation with Bethany Anne, Terry Henry, and Kaeden when Christina entered the room. He suddenly forgot how to draw air, she was so beautiful in her bridal gown, radiating happiness.

*How in the hell* had he managed to persuade that ethereal angel to spend her life with him?

Kaeden nudged him in the ribs, chuckling. "Breathe, son. Can't take your vows if you're unconscious."

Christina paused at the threshold to gather her composure, taking a moment to be amazed by everyone who had come out to celebrate, by the décor, by Kai looking almost edible in his dark tailcoat and dress trousers. "I can't believe it's really happening," she murmured.

"Believe it," Nathan told her lovingly. He met Bethany Anne's direct gaze and gave her a minute nod as they stepped onto the runner.

Tina and Alexis fell in behind Christina as she began her procession. Christina didn't notice. All she saw was Kai.

Kai took her hands when she arrived at the end of the aisle, too emotional to speak.

Bethany Anne wiped a tear away and spread her hands in welcome. "We have come together to celebrate the love between Christina and Kai and the path they have chosen to take together. There is no greater power than love. It unites us and holds us together, and without it, we are lost. Join me in wishing them a future filled with hope, happiness—"

"And plenty of grandchildren." Char was heard by everyone with enhanced hearing.

"If that's what they wish for," Bethany Anne agreed as the chuckles ebbed. She glanced at the couple, who were still holding hands, gazing at each other through Christina's veil. "Do we have the rings?"

Kaeden and Tina stepped forward and handed the rings to Christina and Kai.

Bethany Anne smiled. "Then let's begin. Do you, Christina Bethany Anne Lowell, take this man, Kailin Walton, to be your husband?"

Christina nodded, her voice breathy as she spoke. *"I do."*

## AUTHOR NOTES - MICHAEL ANDERLE

### APRIL 2, 2020

THANK YOU for reading our story! We have a few of these planned, but we don't know if we should continue writing and publishing without your input. Options include leaving a review, reaching out on Facebook to let us know, and smoke signals.

Frankly, smoke signals might get misconstrued as low hanging clouds, so you might want to nix that idea..

The Queen is back in the Federation, and she isn't willing to take prisoners. You need to see the enemy for who they are, then get off of your ass and help or get out of the way. Anything else will get you bitch-slapped upside the head.

Or your head is slapped right off your body. That would hurt... Well, for a micro-second.

Bethany Anne is dealing with her children being all grown up, and she is dealing with it. Unfortunately, she is also pushing a lot of emotions under the covers. I have to ask the question, "How many recognize that she lost many years of motherhood to these damned Kurtherians?"

I do.

The responsibility to make the right decision never stops the anguish of the loss in our lives, and it won't in hers. We might not see it play out like a Baba Yaga situation, since she does have her children, but somehow, someway, BA will have to have a moment of sadness as she closes the door on holding her daughter or grabbing her son when they were young.

The sadness is shared.

## Diary week of March 29th to April 4th, 2020

Someone help me. I'm starting to look at Blender and Unreal Engine 04.

*I shouldn't be doing this!*

When LMBPN LLC was formed, it was always about becoming an entertainment company, one that started with books but was able to expand from there.

So far, we have expanded to audio and translations. We have over two hundred of our stories in audio books as LMBPN Publishing, and hundreds more on the way from partners such as Dreamscape, Podium, and Tantor Publishing.

We have over twenty (20) German-translated books and will publish another twenty-plus translations this year alone. *(Go Jens and team!)*

But, I've been working on projects using 3D assets for a few years, knowing that somewhere in the future, I want our company to be at least producing short animations. Now, with so little to focus on outside of being home, I am looking at all sorts of opportunities.

And I *shouldn't*.

Every good business needs to be able to focus and focus hard on what they do. So, for me, I need to focus on continuing to build our authors, series, backlist etc. etc. and not personally get down into the nitty-gritty working on the software.

However, I am sliding back to my roots. You see, before all of my writing books and publishing, I was a programmer, and before that a creative artist (wannabe – I couldn't draw a straight line without a ruler to save myself.) I just downloaded the latest Blender software to my laptop last night. Then, in a crisis of concern, I shut it down after about two minutes of playing and went back to YouTube videos.

I can't afford to play with the software. If I do, I will look up in a few days and realize I am the backlog in the company.

<Sniff.>

During this time of isolation, I am playing with all kinds of technology, dreaming up where I will drive LMBPN towards in the future, and how we will provide you our readers with new ways to engage with our stories, our characters, and each other.

I have no plans for building games (I'll let other companies work that angle), but everything else is still on the table. We have over a hundred days of books in the pipeline. Our authors, artists, ops team, editing team, and social teams are hard at work to make sure you have the new stories you want to get lost in.

Then, in the future, I want to bring those stories and those characters to you in new ways. LMBPN's tagline is "Disruptive Imagination."

Why?

Because I like to blow shit up. The same-ol'-same-ol' doesn't work for me. I get bored.

And now, *I'm bored in real life, too.*

So, let me stretch for a moment and then imagine I'm handing you something as you hear me say, "Here, hold my beer…"

*The future is just getting started.*

I am grateful to you, our readers, who consume our books.

Ad Aeternitatem,

Michael Anderle

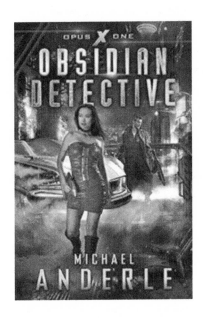

**Two Rebels whose Worlds Collide on a Planetary Level.**

**On the fringes of human space, a murder will light a fuse and send two different people colliding together.**

She lives on Earth, where peace among the population is a given. He is on the fringe of society where authority is how much firepower you wield.

*She is from the powerful, the elite. He is with the military.*

**Both want the truth – but is revealing the truth good for society?**

---

**Two years ago, a small moon in a far off system was**

**set to be the location of the first intergalactic war between humans and an alien race.**

It never happened. However, something was found many are willing to kill to keep a secret.

*Now, they have killed the wrong people.*

How many will need to die to keep the truth hidden?

*As many as is needed.*

**He will have vengeance no matter the cost.** *She will dig for the truth. No matter how risky the truth is to reveal.*

Available now at your favorite bookseller

BOOKS BY MICHAEL ANDERLE

For a complete list of books by Michael Anderle, please visit:

**www.lmbpn.com/ma-books/**

All LMBPN Audiobooks are Available at Audible.com and iTunes

To see all LMBPN audiobooks, including those written by
Michael Anderle please visit:

**www.lmbpn.com/audible**

# CONNECT WITH MICHAEL ANDERLE

**Michael Anderle Social**
  **Website:**
  http://www.lmbpn.com

**Email List:**
  http://lmbpn.com/email/

**Facebook Here:**
  www.facebook.com/TheKurtherianGambitBooks/

Made in the USA
Monee, IL
31 July 2020

37306744R00215